Peter Pan 2:
The Phantom of Neverland

(A Christmas in Neverland)

BASED ON CHARACTERS BY J. M. BARRIE

James Bereece

STORIES TO DIE FOR PUBLISHING

ISBN-13: 979-8-88563-011-5 paperback
ISBN-13: 979-8-88563-021-4 second edition
ISBN-13: 979-8-88563-012-2 hardback
ISBN-13: 979-8-88563-009-2 ebook

Cover design by: Sonya Reid
Printed in the United States of America
United States Copyright Office Number: TX0009202651

*A special thanks to my mom and dad,
my sister Jerica, and my talented friends Sonya,
and Ashlie for all your help and support.*

Table of Contents

PETER PAN 2:
THE PHANTOM
OF NEVERLAND

CHAPTER ONE

An Unexpected Visitor

All children, except one, grow up.

Or so we have heard before. It had been four years since Wendy and her brothers first left on their magical flight to Neverland. Four years to the day. The town was once more blanketed with snow, the lanterns were all aglow in preparation for the setting sun, and all good little boys and girls were at home in their beds, thinking up wonderful things to put on their Christmas lists.

All children, except one, that is.

Peter always seemed to find his way to Kensington Gardens whenever he got bored or lonely. Normally, there was an awfully big adventure lurking around every corner, but for some reason, things had slowed down in Neverland. Poor Peter couldn't even revel in the glory of his previous adventures because, well, he couldn't remember any. He couldn't remember the way he defeated the bloodthirsty pirates of the *Jolly Roger* nor the way the pirates had slaughtered most of the great warriors of the Piccaninny tribe. His mind was a clean slate, and therefore, he couldn't possibly hope to discover why there seemed to be fewer adventures in Neverland.

He supposed he kept coming back to Kensington Gardens because that was where it all started. It was where he first met the fairies, where they taught him to fly, and where they eventually showed him the way to Neverland. It saddened him how little he actually remembered about his first real adventure. It didn't stay in his mind like a memory — he merely knew it as a fact: the sky is blue, swords are sharp, and Peter Pan became Peter Pan in Kensington Gardens.

His bad memory didn't use to bother him, not until he met Wendy. She was frightfully worried he would forget her, and of course, Peter was equally worried he would forget her as well. He had promised to come back for her every year for spring cleaning, and, to his great dismay, he discovered he had missed an entire year.

How could I miss an entire year with Wendy and not even realise it? he would wonder. After that, he remembered a game Wendy used to play to make sure she didn't forget her parents during her stay in Neverland. He had refused to play it then but now plays it regularly to ensure he'll never forget his new mother, Wendy.

Peter found himself playing with the winter pixies of Kensington Gardens. They were enjoying their solstice festival. Winter pixies, as you may already know, are the ones who make it snow. If you should catch them frolicking at one of their seasonal celebrations, you might find them riding on oversized snowflakes, sliding and bounding across slumbering trees and their leafless branches — or quite possibly, ice-dancing under the Serpentine Bridge. But fair warning, these mischievous little sprites can't hold their ale and love to play jokes on mortals nearby, so consider yourself warned.

Peter had always liked to sit outside people's windowsills and listen to stories. It was what first attracted him to the Darlings' nursery. Mrs. Darling always told the most wonderful fairy tales, and he could really use a good tale about now.

By the time he reached that ever-familiar house with the No. 14 on the side, the sun had disappeared from the horizon, and the exceptionally bright moon hung fat in the sky. All of the stars were awake and attentively watching the lonely boy fly up to the windowsill, just as they had done four years ago.

In the former nursery, the boys were all dressed for dinner, bustling about boisterously, excited about something.

"What are you going to ask for, John?" Michael asked eagerly.

"I don't know," John replied, distracted with helping the former Lost Boys decorate Nana's Kennel. The boys thought it would be a nice surprise for the old girl while she was enjoying her day off.

The children all possessed the same Yuletide energy that every child possesses in the latter weeks of December, but, of course, Peter didn't know that. He was simply intrigued by the odd behaviour of his former Lost Boys.

This was only the adopted Darlings' third Christmas, and they liked the holiday a great deal. Toys, games, and plenty of good food to grow fat. What more could any child want? Sadly, some of the boys were at that unfortunate age when they began to lose faith in magic. All of the Lost Boys had nearly forgotten their time in Neverland. They had begun to dismiss it as a dream — and for most of them, this may be the last year they still truly believed in Father Christmas.

"Well, I'm going to ask for a pop-riffle!" Slightly exclaimed.

"I've seen your report card," Nibs interjected. "You're better off asking Father Christmas for a new brain."

"Now, boys," Mrs. Darling called, overhearing them from the other room. The boys quieted down as Mrs. Darling entered the former nursery. "You are all such lovely and intelligent children. I'm sure Father Christmas won't forget any of you." She gave them a hug and a loving kiss on their foreheads and went back to her bedroom.

This struck Peter as rather odd. Slightly had just requested a toy, and then Mrs. Darling mentioned something about a *Father Christmas*. What was a *Father Christmas*, and why was its opinion so important? He inspected further and noticed that all of the children had a piece of paper. They were, peculiarly enough, writing down things they wanted on it and then giving an overall evaluation of their behaviour for the year.

But why?

He supposed it was a strange new game they started playing, but the more he listened, the more he doubted it.

Peter began to get that sinking suspicion that he was missing out on something. Something big!

In another window, George was in the middle of one of his traditional money rants. Peter overheard Mrs. Darling telling her husband that Christmas was a time for children. He, like all fathers, was mentally calculating the Christmas expenses and watching, in great terror, as the pounds began to pile up.

"Let's see," Mr. Darling continued, "with Curly and the Twins . . . and we can't forget Nana and Liza. Oh, and we'll also have your parents staying with us this year, which puts us at . . ." His voice cut short with a weak wheeze. "Good lord, Mary! I think I need to sit down."

"Don't worry, sweetie," Mrs. Darling said, rubbing her husband's back. "We'll get through it." She kissed his forehead. "We always do."

Her words were comforting, but a part of him still wanted to crawl over to Nana's Kennel and take a nap — just as he did four years ago when his children flew away home. Christmastime is never easy on a family's budget, but it's especially perilous for the Darlings. Ever since their children had returned from their fateful flight, they no longer had to provide for three children — they had to provide for nine.

Of course, the Darlings were well-off these days. George had gained fame and notoriety for being the man who lived in a kennel for half a year until his children returned. Confidentially, you can still catch him playing in the kennel when he thinks nobody's watching. He also received praise and adoration from his peers — not to mention a great many promotions — for being the great man who had adopted six motherless children and worked to give them a better life. But having such a large family was still painfully expensive. And even though George was much kinder and humbler than he once was, he was still an accountant at heart, and numbers mattered. Still, he loved those boys and wouldn't want it any other way.

"Remind me," Mr. Darling started. "When will your parents be here?"

"Any minute," she replied.

"In that case," he said, "I think I'll have my Scotch now."

Peter felt a sharp twinge of excitement in the air. It was infectious and started to make him feel indignant. It was unfair that he and his newest Lost Boys were missing out on one of childhood's great adventures . . . Christmas!

In his excitement, Peter accidentally bumped the window but quickly ducked back into the shadows. Mrs. Darling glanced over; she didn't say anything but suddenly got another one of her suspicious feelings.

"Well, at least it's not a Friday," she smirked.

"What, dearest?" George inquired.

"Nothing, George," she replied. "Why don't you get dressed for dinner?"

Some of you would be interested to know that Mr. Darling has taken to wearing a clip-on tie these days. And he never scolds the children for whining about the foul taste of their medicine anymore.

Peter made his way around the house, peeping into every window, looking for the one person he wanted to see more than anybody — Wendy. He glanced into the tiny window in the back-bottom corner, and there she was, dressed in an apron and helping their maid Liza in the kitchen. Wendy found that she enjoyed cooking, and helping Liza prepare the Christmas pudding had become one of her Christmas traditions.

Even though Wendy was taller and blossoming quite rapidly, Peter didn't notice. He never noticed those things. Besides, he was far too preoccupied with finding out the great mystery that was Christmas.

Peter knew that Mrs. Darling had only agreed to let the children join Peter for a two-week journey in the spring. He had little hope in taking Wendy back with him this early — but that didn't preclude him from trying.

Wendy was finishing up when she began to wonder about Nana. They all knew she was a dog, yet she carried herself with such dignity that they often forgot. Of course, it was easy to forget. Nana was such a professional and clearly the best nurse in the neighbourhood. She could still handle her charges even after they multiplied. Now, Wendy had always known that Nana got every Thursday off but only recently had begun to think about it. The thing that baffled her was, what does a Newfoundland dog do on a day off?

She had asked her mother once, who glibly replied, "I suppose she goes shopping or over to the salon. That's what I'd do with my day off." And that was enough. Wendy could easily see Nana pop down to the haberdasher and spend a day trying on hats. However, she couldn't really imagine Nana cavorting with the ladies at the salon.

She liked getting pampered and looking her best, but she despised idle gossip.

"Liza," Wendy started. "What do you suppose Nana does with her day off?"

"As if I knew what a dog does with its spare time," Liza retorted, adding raisins to the pudding. "Truth be told, I hear she likes to catch up on her reading."

"Nana likes to read?"

"Yeah," Liza added. "She has a whole trunk full of romance novels in the basement."

Now, this did surprise Wendy. Not that Nana had a trunk full of novels, but it was a trunk full of *romance* novels. Nana didn't seem like the type. Too proper.

"I suppose that's what she's doing now," Wendy stated.

"Naw," Liza shook her head. "I heard she's got a date."

Wendy's eyes bugged out. "A date?"

"That's what I heard."

"Is it another dog?" Wendy asked curiously.

"I don't know, but apparently he's taking her to that new Italian restaurant," Liza replied with a wink. "Now I have to finish setting up the table."

With those words, Liza was out the door, and Wendy was alone. This was exactly what Peter had been waiting for. Wendy was putting the pudding away when she heard that ever-familiar *crow*. Her eyes lit up, and an enormous smile crept across her face as she exclaimed:

"Peter!"

When she turned around, the window blew open, and he flew into the room. It was all exciting until Peter stopped with a jerk, getting stuck. It was a small window. Wendy tried not to laugh, seeing the comical pout forming on Peter's face, and immediately rushed to him.

"You know, you could have used the door, silly," Wendy mused, assessing the situation. "Are you all right?"

"Of course, I'm all right," Peter snapped. "I just . . . I just need a little push."

Wendy gave a loving smile. She put on her jacket and then went out to help him. Once more, she had to fight the urge to laugh. The sight of the great Peter Pan, with his rear end sticking out of their tiny kitchen window while his legs kicked helplessly in the air, was hilarious.

"What's so funny?" Peter asked, hearing a slight snicker from Wendy.

"Nothing," Wendy replied sweetly. The whole ordeal reminded her of their Home Underground in Neverland.

"Then hurry up and give me a push. This is embarrassing."

Wendy went to oblige, then stopped, trying to decide where was the proper place for a young lady to push. The legs would be ineffective, but it would be improper for a young lady to place her hands on a boy's bottom . . . finally, she discovered the problem.

"Hold still, Peter," she ordered. He hovered perfectly still, and the second she unhooked his belt, he glided elegantly into the room. Wendy carried the sword that had made Peter's hips too big into the house.

When Wendy re-entered the kitchen, Peter was *crowing* and jumping around joyously because of the clever way he had gotten himself unstuck. Wendy smiled, handing him the sword, happy to see that things hadn't changed.

"Oh, I'm so glad to see you, Peter," Wendy said. "But you know I can't go with you. It's not spring yet."

"Wendy, what is Christmas?"

The words caught her off-guard. Was it possible Peter really didn't know?

"Christmas?" Wendy repeated in disbelief. "My goodness. Don't you know?"

The boy shook his head. She thought to herself for a minute. Peter mainly came for them in the spring these days, and Christmas was long gone by then, but wasn't their first adventure in the winter? Of course, it was. She distinctly remembered Liza preparing the Christmas pudding while Nana barked outside. It was their stories that had attracted Peter, and children are told more stories at Christmastime. She remembered it was the story of *Cinderella* that brought him over there when he lost his shadow. But didn't they mention Christmas at all?

Of course not. When Peter arrived, they had completely forgotten about Christmas. They were learning to fly, going to Neverland, seeing mermaids, and fighting pirates. They had no time to remember it was Christmas. And there was the whole memory thing on the island. She remembered how quickly you started to forget things in Neverland, and Peter already had a regrettably bad memory.

Just then, Wendy felt a sharp sting of guilt, thinking about what a rotten Christmas they had left behind for their parents. She hated the fact that they hadn't even cared in the slightest.

"Oh dear," she muttered to herself. "Well, you see, Christmas is a wonderful time of year when families get together and appreciate all that they have. They have parties, play games, tell stories, and go out of their way to show how much they care for one another."

"And what's a *Father Christmas*?"

She stopped, realising that Christmas was complicated. Christmas was something that should be experienced, not described. Just then, she got an idea.

"Peter," she said. "How would you like to stay for supper?"

"Supper?" Peter stammered, feeling uncomfortable at the thought of dining with the Darlings.

"Yes," Wendy replied. "I'm sure mother won't mind."

Peter took a step back to think it over.

"If you want to know about Christmas," she added, "then you need the proper atmosphere to experience it."

CHAPTER TWO

An Awkward Dinner

Mrs. Darling was adding the finishing touches to her evening gown — just as she had done before every special occasion. As she sat at her vanity, she thought about how time changes. It seemed like only yesterday Wendy was just a little girl, waiting to see her mother dress up in elegant gowns — and secretly imagining she was playing dress-up. But now it was Mrs. Darling's turn to wait to see how beautiful her daughter looked in lovely gowns — and secretly wishing Wendy was only seven again.

Poor Mrs. Darling. Sometimes it's hard to be a mother at Christmas. Especially when you start to notice that one of your children has nearly grown up and you begin to realise that those warm December evenings as a family were getting numbered. She glanced back at her husband — who was going through their cheque-book and adding up the compound interest rates into their final Christmas expenses — and let out a sigh of relief to see that some things would never change.

She gave herself one last look in the mirror when Wendy entered the room.

"Uh, mother? Father?" Wendy called, poking her head through the door.

"Yes, dearest?" Mrs. Darling replied, turning to greet her.

"How would you feel if I invited someone to dinner?"

"Someone to dinner?" Mrs. Darling repeated. Was Wendy already bringing home a suitor to meet the family? She supposed her daughter was at that age where many girls get engaged, but Wendy was still so much a child at heart. Besides, Wendy would have mentioned it. Wouldn't she?

"I suppose it should be all right," Mrs. Darling agreed cautiously.

"Oh, good!" Wendy exclaimed. "I told him you wouldn't mind."

"Him?" Mr. Darling interrupted, turning from his counting desk. George, like all fathers, never seemed to notice his daughter age after twelve. Then one day, they are rudely awakened by the presence of some nervous-looking, acne-laden young man. "So, this is a he?"

"Yes," Wendy replied. "You see, he's never had a Christmas before, and I thought maybe we could give him a little taste of it tonight."

"Never had a Christmas?" Mrs. Darling asked, feeling that suspicious inkling return.

"Must be one of those Jewish chaps?" George deduced. "Well, it's a good thing we didn't go with ham tonight. Very well, tell Liza to set an extra plate for dinner."

"Wait a moment, Wendy," her mother called, getting up from her vanity. She walked to Wendy in the doorway. "Do I know this boy?"

"Uh, sort of," Wendy replied.

"And does this boy happen to fly and fight pirates?" Mary pressed on.

"Uh," Wendy giggled, embarrassed. "Maybe."

Mrs. Darling opened the door the rest of the way, and there stood Peter Pan, who merely smiled and gave an awkward wave. Once again, she noticed the boy still had all his First-Teeth. He hadn't even grown a millimetre in four years. She had remembered seeing Wendy and Peter standing at the same height once upon a time, but now, Wendy was considerably taller.

"I thought I heard somebody listening outside our window," Mrs. Darling smirked with a sly smile.

"What's this ragamuffin doing here?" Mr. Darling bellowed, standing up.

Peter hissed.

"He's come to have Christmas dinner with us," Wendy replied.

"I think that's a wonderful idea," Mrs. Darling chimed. "So often Wendy and Michael go with him, but we never once had him over here."

"But dearest," George beckoned, hoping to talk sense into his overzealous wife. "Your parents will be here any moment. And you know how they are."

"Well, he does need a bath," Mrs. Darling agreed.

"A bath?" Peter sneered, coiling back.

"But I suppose one of the boys' suits should fit him quite nicely," Mrs. Darling continued, trying to size him up.

"Suits?!" Peter exclaimed.

"No offence to your darling leaves," Mrs. Darling apologised. "It's just that we all dress up when company arrives."

"But Mary," George pleaded again. "It's not just his appearance or even his manners. If he's going to stay, he has to promise not to fly, crow, or gully your father."

"Sir," Peter said, bowing with an elegance that surprised even Wendy. "I swear on my honour not to fly or cross blades with any of your guests."

"That settles it!" Mrs. Darling declared.

"Easy for him to say," George muttered. "He hasn't met them yet." He took a large gulp of his scotch. "Very well, alert Liza and the children. And prepare a bath."

Wendy and her mother sprang into action, leaving Peter and Mr. Darling alone. They stood there awkwardly, staring at one another, struggling to think of something to say.

"You . . ." Mr. Darling began, ". . . really never had a Christmas?"

Peter shook his head.

"Never decorated a tree? Never hung up a stocking? Never sung Christmas Carol?"

Peter's intrigue made him temporarily forget himself enough to take a step closer to Mr. Darling. "What's it like?"

"It's. . . uh . . ." George stammered, trying to find the words. "It's wonderful."

"Tell me everything," Peter begged with a wide-eyed innocence that overcame Mr. Darling.

George pitied the boy but also felt an empathetic energy that made him reflect fondly on his own childhood. "Christmas is more of a feeling," he replied. "A very wonderful feeling. Warm and cosy, like snuggling up with a loved one by a warm crackling fire on a cool winter's night. Christmas is wonder and enchantment for children everywhere. A time when magic seems real, even to grown-ups. It's a time for spoiling children with cakes and pies and pudding . . . and presents."

"Presents?" Peter exclaimed.

"Yes," George said with a smile. "Toys and games."

"What kind?"

"Well, if you promise to behave at dinner," George bartered, "I'll take you down to the shop windows, and you can see for yourself."

Peter smiled, feeling the excitement rush through him. At that moment, he decided that this George fellow wasn't such a terrible man after all . . . for a grown-up at least. Peter started to ask more questions when Mrs. Darling and Wendy returned.

"Your bath is ready," Mrs. Darling announced.

Peter looked up at Mr. Darling. "Do I have to?"

"I'm afraid so," George replied. "And when you're done, we'll show you everything."

Pan nodded and followed Wendy to the lavatory. She opened the door and gestured to the bathtub, but he just stood there.

"Don't tell me the great Peter Pan is afraid of a little soap and water," Wendy teased.

"I'm not afraid of anything," Peter snapped. "Besides, I go swimming with the mermaids all the time."

"Oh, so it's the soap that makes you nervous," Wendy smirked in an undeniably flirtatious manner.

Peter gave a wry smile, then, in a near mocking manner, swaggered over to the bathtub and rested his arm on its rim.

Mrs. Darling came in with some nice clothes. "These used to be John's," she said, setting them on the chair in the corner. "They should fit you nicely, I think." She smiled, and Peter couldn't help but smile back. "If you should require any assistance, just give a holler, and George will rush right over to give you a hand."

With those words, Wendy and Mary took their leave. They shut the door behind them, giving Peter his privacy. Peter scoffed at the notion that he may need help from an adult, then turned to face the tub.

"So, we meet again," he glowered as if greeting some long-lost foe.

Wendy listened outside the door for a moment, and when she was about to leave, she heard Peter clamour: "By Jove, the water is warm!"

Wendy giggled, then went into the nursery, where the boys were excited and chattering about the prospect of having Peter Pan over for dinner. Once more, the former

Lost Boys had nearly forgotten their time in Neverland and only thought of it as a dream. However, they made a sincere effort to remember and believe. It was a great struggle, but a part of them will always know their captain was real.

"Ah, yes, Peter Pan," Slightly boasted. "An excellent chap. I remember the way he used to fly and wave his hook around. I even saved his life a few times."

"Uh, Slightly." Wendy chuckled. In the four years she'd known him, he never stopped being full of fairy droppings. "Peter never had a hook. And you might have saved his life before I was a part of the story, but I seem to remember you nearly costing him his life due to your water weight and tampering with your tree."

"I think I remember Peter," Tootles said bashfully in the corner. "I think I remember him fighting with Captain Hook. And . . . I think I remember being tricked into shooting you with an arrow, Wendy."

"Poor Tootles," Wendy cooed, giving him a comforting hug when she saw the guilt resonate back into his face. He clearly remembered the most out of the former Lost Boys, but she supposed that was due to his sweetness and his guilt. Secretly, she was hoping for a sign that one of the boys had remembered something from their time in Neverland. But a part of her hoped Tootles could have forgotten that particular incident to relieve him of his unconscious burden.

She supposed it would all come back to them once they saw their old chief again, but there was no way of knowing.

She was delighted to find that her brother John still remembered most of their adventures. Secretly, he wished he could remember more about the mermaids. He was reading a book by Hans Christian Anderson about one who fell in love with a human and wished he could see them again.

Wendy supposed the reason that she and her brothers were able to remember as much as they did was because they had only spent about six months away from home. Fortunately, whatever magic that island possessed to distort people's memory hadn't had a chance to fully set in. However, she did remember struggling to retain simple details about their life in England by the end of their first great adventure.

She began to explain Peter's Christmas curiosity one last time when they heard a *knock* downstairs. All in the house were conscious of the *banging* at the front door.

From across the hall, George Darling turned to his wife. "It's them."

The Darlings sprang into action as Liza answered the front door and announced Mary's parents. "The Crustisons have arrived."

Mrs. Darling went to the children and told them to go down and greet their grandparents while she checked on Peter.

"Peter," she called with a gentle rap on the door. "How's it coming in there?"

"Almost done," answered Peter's muffled reply. A moment later, the door opened, and there he stood. Peter had a shirt inside out and backwards, an evening jacket for pants, and a pair of trousers draped around him like a sash. "Well?"

She tried not to laugh, realising that he'd probably never worn formal attire before. "Let me give you a hand there."

"No, no," George replied, coming up behind her. "I got it." He started fixing the shirt. "After all, they are *your* parents."

Mary nodded and grinned. George was right; besides, she would be much better at explaining their special guest than her husband. So, she headed downstairs once more, leaving George and Peter alone.

"Never mind the in-laws," George advised.

"How should I act?" Peter asked.

"For the most part, I believe children should be permitted to act like children at Christmas," Mr. Darling replied gingerly. "And it's a time for adults to act a little less grown-up."

Peter smiled.

"Basically," George elaborated, "I'm telling you to be yourself, just, uh . . . no flying, no fighting, and no disrespecting your . . ." He looked at Peter. "No being rude to grown-ups, even when the older ones are rude to you."

"That last bit doesn't seem all that fair," Peter complained.

"Tell me about it."

Downstairs, the children entertained their grandparents in the parlour. It was the usual gay greeting. They would start by giving them a hug, and then the grandparents would mention how much they had grown, to which the children would ask if the grandparents had brought them anything, and so forth. Then the Crustisons would hear all about what was new in their grandchildren's life — all the while taking mental notes for gentle criticism for their daughter and son-in-law. Then they would greet their daughter Mary, mention how beautiful she looked, and compliment her on the fine job she's done with the boys.

Confidentially, they weren't too keen on their choice to adopt six lowly urchins at first. They were so low-bred and common, but of course, their obvious lack of education and refinement eventually won over the uppity Crustisons. They were the perfect example of childlike innocence, and they were always sincere: Nibs, so handsome and charming; Slightly, with his adorably flawed anecdotes; Tootles and his general sweetness and humility; Curly's high energy and mischief; and the adorable way the Twins finished each other's sentences. But the biggest thing that impressed the adoptive grandparents and the Darlings was how well they did what they were told. Of course, Wendy knew this was all due to their years of servitude to a boy they all admired — a boy who could fly. It was their willingness to take orders that allowed the Darlings to shape them into fine young gentlemen in less than four years. Sure, their report cards still left something to be desired, but considering how far behind they had started, there was nothing to be ashamed of.

Mary was explaining about their special guest and his Yuletide ignorance to her parents when George entered the room and gave a formal introduction to their guest.

"Ladies and gentlemen," George addressed, "I give you, Master Peter."

With those words, Peter walked out of the shadows and made his way into the parlour. Wendy felt her heart stop momentarily; she had never seen Peter in anything but his skeleton leaves, even at the Fairy's Ball. Wendy never imagined how elegant and debonair he could look when he was cleaned up and dressed in one of John's old suits. She imagined the kind of music the orchestra must have played when Cinderella entered the ball.

Suddenly, that feeling of hope stirred up inside her once more. That feeling she had been trying to suppress for all those years. That notion that maybe one day he would stay, grow up, and finally be with her. He looked so handsome with his hair combed back, revealing his shimmering countenance. Of course, he had an uncomfortable and awkward look in his eyes, but to Wendy, that made him all the more precious.

For a fleeting moment, Wendy was ashamed she had let herself get so much older than Peter, but if she could have her Christmas wish, she wouldn't let that stop her.

"My, how handsome you look," Mrs. Darling complimented.

"He sure does," Wendy uttered louder than she had intended.

"This is kind of uncomfortable," Peter whispered to Mr. Darling. "Is that normal?"

"Yes," George replied. "But one tends to get used to it."

"Peter, I'd like you to meet my parents, the Crustisons," Mrs. Darling introduced.

"Pleased to meet you," Mary's father greeted with an extension of his hand.

"Pleased to meet you too," Peter said, feeling sickened by the words. For Peter, it was never a pleasure to make the acquaintance of an adult. Still, he had to admit, the atmosphere in the house was strangely enticing.

"Peter," George hinted, nodding toward Mr. Crustison's open hand. "I do believe he wishes to shake your hand."

"Oh!" Peter exclaimed in realisation. "He wishes to see if I'm unarmed." Peter smiled, then happily shook the old man's hand. "The Piccaninny Tribe has a similar custom."

The boys giggled while George, Mary, and Wendy looked over at the grandparents to see how that little response went over with them.

"My . . ." Mr. Crustison said, "what an interesting lad you got there."

"Quite," George replied.

"Should we adjourn to the dining room?" Mrs. Darling suggested.

The group nodded and started heading over.

"What does adjourn mean?" Peter inquired.

"It means to take a break or depart," Mary replied. "I'm sort of telling everyone it's time for dinner."

"It's dinner time?" Peter asked.

She nodded.

"Why didn't you say so?" Peter bent his head back and let out an ear-splitting *crow*, which startled everyone except his former Lost Boys, who instinctively sprang up and bounded into the dining room.

"What the devil was that?" Mrs. Crustison demanded.

"I was just calling everyone to dinner," Peter declared.

Wendy started to giggle again until she felt the prudent jab of her mother's elbow.

"Quite," George replied again. That was when he noticed the newest Darlings behaving uncharacteristically wild. They were running and jumping and pushing each other out of the way to get the best spots at the dinner table.

"Boys! Boys! Boys!" George shouted, trying to break them up.

The boys stopped and looked around, embarrassed, unable to understand what had just happened.

"Sorry, father," Tootles apologised. "I don't know what came over us."

"Honestly, children," Mr. Crustison admonished, "that display was simply deplorable."

"I've got it from here, Chester," George interceded, annoyed by his lack of candour.

"We're sorry," Nibs added. "We would never do anything to embarrass our family. Would you, Curly?"

"No, never," Curly replied. "Would you, Slightly?"

"No, never," Slightly agreed. "Would you, Twin?"

"No, never," the First Twin replied. "Would . . . ?"

"It's all right, children," George interrupted. "Gosh, I haven't heard you guys do that since . . ." He stopped dead in his sentence, then turned back to Peter. "Oh, dear."

It had never occurred to any of them how Peter's presence might affect the boys; after all, he had been their captain for many untold years. It only stood to reason that old habits would die hard, and the second Peter *crowed*, it triggered something inside them.

"Let's forget the whole endeavour," George proposed. "And sit down to a nice dinner."

The group entered the large dining room and took their places at the table. Peter took the seat he was most accustomed to and sat at the head of the table. Being accustomed to precisely the same spot, George sat down, unaware it was occupied until he heard a *yawp*! He shot back up!

"Oh, sorry!" George apologised, then realised where Peter was sitting. "Uh, Peter. I do believe you're in the wrong seat."

"No, I don't think so," Peter disagreed.

"Well, the rules of etiquette clearly dictates that the seat at the head of the table is reserved for the head of the household," George rebuked.

"Isn't that what I am?" Peter asked.

George merely smiled, then looked over to his family, giving a clumsy chuckle. "Isn't that adorable? He's here five minutes and is already trying to usurp me."

"Peter," Mrs. Darling intervened, "the head of the household is typically the person who owns the house and provides for the family."

"Well, that's a silly rule," Peter replied. "Shouldn't the seat belong to the greatest warrior?"

"Well, father is sort of the chief of this house," Wendy explained. "The seat for the bravest warrior is right over here." She smiled, tapping the seat next to her. "Unless," she taunted, "you don't think you're the bravest warrior."

Peter stood honourably and walked over to the chair next to Wendy. "I declare the position of the greatest warrior!" Peter proclaimed. "Let any who challenge step forward!"

"Oh, just take the damn seat!" Mr. Crustison snapped.

Peter sat down arrogantly, and Wendy and the rest of the children had to fight back their laughter.

"Don't encourage him, boys," Mrs. Crustison hissed.

"Honestly, George," Mr. Crustison criticised, "no wonder no one respects you. You can't even get an ill-mannered whelp to listen to you."

"What did you call me?" Peter snarled, thrusting his dinner knife in Mr. Crustison's direction.

"Peter!" Wendy snapped, placing her hand on his shoulder. "Remember your promise."

"After he insulted the greatest warrior?!" Peter cried.

"Not to mention the chief," George grumbled.

"And the chief!" Peter agreed. "That insolence would have gotten this old codfish horsewhipped and scalped back home. Does the chief wish me to bestow this punishment?"

Mr. Darling smiled, thinking it over.

"George!" Mary cried.

"Oh, all right," George conceded, then turned to Peter. "Let's spare the old codfish for now."

Peter nodded, setting the knife down, and Mr. Crustison gasped in disbelief.

"Why are you humouring this beastly child?" Mr. Crustison roared. "In my day, when a child acted up, he felt the back of my cane!"

"I'd like to see you try it!" Peter glowered, grasping the dinner knife once more.

Mr. Crustison stood up and approached Peter with his cane raised. "I'm going to teach this arrogant whelp some manners!"

"*Father!*" Mary cried.

Peter hissed, jumping on the table and readying his knife in a battle stance.

"*SIT DOWN!!*" George bellowed, leaping up from his chair. "Both of you! Now let's get this straight. We are to sit and have a quiet dinner. There will be no floggings, no scalping, and no arguing in my house! Is that understood?"

They nodded hesitantly.

"Now, put down your weapons and shake hands," George ordered. "The Big Chief has spoken."

The two looked at each other with distrust, then finally managed to reach out their hands and shake. Mrs. Darling looked on, relieved. She hated seeing her family fight. She wanted to be respectful to her parents, but she was ashamed of her father's snarky attitude toward her husband and a little disheartened by how quickly everything escalated between him and Peter.

"Very good," George declared. "Now, Liza has worked very hard to prepare this meal. We will sit and enjoy it civilly. No insults. And the only topic that shall be discussed at the dinner table shall be Christmas related. Now, we will show our young guest what a caring family Christmas is like. Anyone who has a problem with these rules should leave."

The Crustisons sat silently, thinking it over.

"That sounds fair," Mrs. Crustison said.

"And Chester," George confided, "I know he's just a boy. However, from what I've heard, I wouldn't lay a finger on him. You might not get it back."

Mr. Crustison glanced at the strange boy, pondering George's warning.

"Let's say grace," Mrs. Darling suggested, desperate to move on.

Peter was utterly baffled by the Darlings' custom of saying grace. Even Wendy had neglected to enforce that rule during their Neverland meals, but he sat there and obliged. To Peter, that little custom was a lot like the natives back home, who would make an offering to their gods and the spirits of their ancestors. The only difference was there was no fire, drums, or group chanting.

It didn't take long for Peter to forget the incident with Wendy's grandfather. He was lost in the excitement of the food and dessert. He had never seen anything like it before. Each silver platter contained another food item that tantalised the senses. This was undoubtedly a grand banquette worthy of the King of the Fairies. It was a banquette worthy of a great warrior such as Peter Pan.

When they pulled back the large silver platter revealing the turkey, Peter walked over and offered to carve it. He flicked the carving knife into the air, then caught it and spun it around his wrist, wielding it like a skilled swordsman. At that moment, Mr. Crustison finally understood George's warning. George merely smiled and allowed the little warrior to carve up the bird. The group stared and marvelled at Peter's dexterity. They couldn't believe how perfect and exact his cuts were, especially considering how fast and arrogant his handwork was. There was a whirlwind of steel, then perfect slices of meat flew onto everybody's plate.

The children were in awe, and the grown-ups were simply stunned.

"By Jove!" Chester uttered. "Wherever did you learn that?"

Peter started to answer, then George interrupted. "You probably don't want to know."

Once more, Peter was lost in the excitement of the evening. The food was remarkable! So were the desserts! Sugar-plums, cakes, mincemeat pies, and the Christmas pudding! He had never tasted anything like them before. It was sublime! And everyone was talking about Christmas, and it was even more amazing than he had expected. By the end, even the Crustisons weren't wholly immune to Peter's charm.

CHAPTER THREE

The Streets of London

It had grown dark, but the effervescent moon and the ever-watchful stars helped light up the night, making the freshly fallen snow gleam with a magical beauty. The lanterns glowed, illuminating the streets, which were filled with the laughter and joy of children and grown-ups alike. The shops and street vendors called to their potential customers with the inviting aroma of roasted chestnuts, warm apple cider, and the scent of holly and poinsettias. Carriages rode by with sleigh bells *jingling* joyously to enrich the season, and motor cars decorated their grills with festive wreaths. Everyone enjoyed the excitement and splendour of the winter's blessings.

The Darlings had enjoyed a truly unforgettable dinner, which began their Christmas adventure with Peter. Now they walked along the cobblestone roads of London with the evening fresh in their minds.

They had sung Christmas carols and played games such as Charades, Yes and No, and a delightfully messy game involving a bowl of Christmas pudding and a cherry

39

— which, of course, was Peter's favourite. It was a race. You had to be the first person to push the cherry up from the bottom of their sloping pudding using only your nose. The cherry kept slipping and sliding and getting their faces covered in pudding. Everyone was laughing, even Mrs. Darling, who was playing Christmas accompaniments on the piano. And of course, the evening wouldn't have been complete without Mr. Darling being talked into an exhibition round, where the children could watch and laugh as poor George's face wriggled around in the pudding, getting messier and messier.

Now the children were peeping into store windows and gazing at all of the incredible toys. They gawked and salivated as they announced their favourite toys and Yuletide wishes from good old Father Christmas. A toy train for Tootles, a toy drum for Nibs, a pop-rifle for Slightly, a tin soldier for Curly, and a carousel for the Twins.

"Which one's your favourite, Peter?" George asked.

"I like all of them," Peter whispered reverently. "I've never seen anything like these before."

"Really?" Mrs. Darling asked.

"Yeah. Back home, the only toys we have are the ones we whittle ourselves," Peter explained. "I suppose I would be happy with anything." Peter took a second look, then clarified, "Well, maybe not the toy swords or bows and arrows." He turned back, facing them. "I already have the real things back home."

The Crustisons gave their daughter another quizzical glance, which Mary simply smiled and shrugged off.

They made their way down the street when they heard a strange sound coming from the distance. There were glowing lights down the road. The closer they got, the more they recognised that the noise they heard was singing.

"I do say. Are those Carollers?" Mr. Crustison wondered.

"I believe they are," George answered with a smile. "Look, Peter. Carollers."

Peter ran over to get a good look.

"Isn't it a little early for Carollers?" Mrs. Crustison criticised.

"Yes," Wendy agreed with a smile. "But when Peter's around, anything's possible."

Peter watched the merry band of travellers laugh and sing as they held their candles reverently. "What are Carollers?" Peter asked.

"Remember those songs we taught you?" Mary hinted.

Peter nodded.

"Well," Mary continued, "Carollers go around singing Christmas carols from house to house, bringing tidings of goodwill and cheer. And then, the Master and Mistress of the house will traditionally reward their humble guests with treats, drinks, and sometimes a few coins."

"Really?" Peter murmured. "Why?"

"Because it's kind to remember your neighbours and the less fortunate during the holidays," Mary replied. "They travel out in the cold, offering good luck and blessings to the household, with wishes of love, prosperity, and a Happy New Year. The least one can do is show a little hospitality and cheer."

"Besides," Mrs. Crustison inserted. "It's frightfully bad luck not to offer them something."

"I should like to try it," Peter declared.

George was silent for a moment. There was so much they needed to do that night. Suddenly, he realised it wasn't a request. Peter had already wandered off to join the chorus, and following close behind were the former Lost Boys. George shook his head. Only yesterday, the boys would have waited patiently and pleaded for their father's permission. Obviously, Peter was in charge that night, and George did not like that. Not one bit.

They caught up to the Carollers, who had extra candles and invited them to join their band. George accepted but told the children it was only for a couple of houses. Of course, they got so caught up in the joy and merriment of the season that they ended up going to a half dozen houses before calling it quits. There were songs, jovial companionship, and homes with mince pies, ribbon candy, and fine liquor. There was such good cheer that no one seemed to mind that it was over a week early for this sort of activity.

Peter, I'll have you know, had no ear for music. But that didn't stop him from screeching his tone-deaf little heart out — with wrong lyrics, of course. Wendy would just giggle, finding him cuter and cuter by the minute.

At the parlour entrance of one of the homes, Peter was puzzled to see something that appeared to be growing over the doorway where George and Mary stood.

"Do these people know they have fungus growing above this door?" Peter asked.

Wendy laughed, seeing the festive decoration hanging above her parents. "It looks like father and mother are standing under the mistletoe," she chimed.

The group laughed and made *whooping* noises.

"That's called mistletoe," Wendy explained, walking Peter over so he could get a better look. "People hang it up every year, and if a lady and a gentleman find themselves standing under it, the man has to give the woman a kiss."

"Oh," Peter said, reaching into his pocket. He clutched the thimble, which Wendy had once called a 'kiss,' and smiled.

George wrapped his arms around his wife and gave her a big old snog while the group erupted with an approving cheer.

"Wait a minute," Peter demanded. "I thought you said that was a thimble."

Wendy just gave a guilty giggle, feeling her cheeks turn bright red. She remembered that four years ago, she had offered Peter a kiss but chickened out and gave him a thimble instead. She eventually wanted a *real* kiss, and instead of admitting her embarrassment, she had kissed him and told him it was called a thimble.

"Well, I was mistaken," she replied with an awkward smile — embarrassed to see her family watching. "That's a kiss."

"Then what's this?" Peter asked, holding up the thimble.

Coyly, she shuffled her feet and replied: "A thimble."

She was deeply touched to see he had kept her 'kiss' all those years and treasured it enough to take it with him wherever he went. She regretted she didn't have Peter's 'kiss' anymore. The button that had saved her life had shattered when Tootles shot her down with his arrow, but she still wished she would have kept it.

"Oy!" Slightly called. "Mother and father aren't the only ones under the mistletoe."

The group laughed as Wendy and Peter realised where they were standing.

"Now you have to give her a kiss, Peter," Nibs added with the raise of an eyebrow.

Peter turned and looked into Wendy's bewitching blue eyes as the crowd clamoured for a kiss.

"Kiss her! Kiss her! Kiss her!" the group chanted at the befuddled youth.

"I'm a little confused," Peter whispered.

Wendy just grabbed him and pulled him in close. "Just be quiet and thimble me already." The group gave an approving *cheer* as the awkward youths shared their first Christmas kiss.

It was all so much fun, but alas, George had to finally put a stop to it, knowing that Peter's Christmas would not be complete without a tree. So, he hailed a cab and paid the driver to take them to the woods. The coachman was compliant but still advised against the Darlings' wishes for a Christmas Tree.

It was customary to wait until the 24th of December to put up a Christmas Tree. However, the Darlings decided to put one up early, determined to give Peter the complete Christmas experience. It was over a week early, and they were well aware that it was said to be bad luck to put up the tree early — just as it was unlucky to take it down after the 5th of January — but they decided it was worth the risk.

The coach took them to the outskirts of the wilderness. They found a nice-sized hill, so they let the children take turns riding the toboggan they had brought to help transport the tree. They had snowball fights and made snow angels, and finally, George made up a new game called *Find-the-Perfect-Christmas-Tree*. The group walked along row after row of fir trees, but none of them felt right.

Peter struggled to maintain Mr. Darling's no-fly rules. Flying had become such a part of his identity that he required gentle reminders from Wendy and the rest of the Darlings. He knew how much easier it would have been to soar around and find a tree worthy of Wendy's Christmas. And even more tempting still was the fact that George had turned tree-finding into a game, and Peter liked to win.

"Honestly, father," John complained. "Why don't you just buy a tree at the market?"

"Because," George explained, "there are no trees at the market. And there won't be any trees for sale until next week."

"Maybe we shouldn't do this?" Mr. Crustison advised. "I heard the Applebottoms put up a Christmas Tree early last year, and their house caught on fire."

"Edward Applebottom starts fires every year," George scoffed. "He always puts too many candles on the tree. Besides, we'll take this one down when Peter leaves and get another one next week. I'm sure the fates won't begrudge us a *Peter Tree*."

"You know," John said. "I heard that in America, some rich folks have started using electric lights on their trees, like the ones at the Savoy."

"Pixie lights in homes?" George smirked. "It'll never catch on."

Peter turned to Wendy. "The Savoy has pixies in their trees?"

She giggled. "No, Peter. Pixie lights are just what people call electric lights on strings. Theatres use them decoratively."

They continued their search, and Mr. Crustison went over to George.

"So, when is he leaving?" Mr. Crustison inquired.

"Mr. Applebottom?" George asked.

"No. Peter."

"Oh," George replied. "Probably tomorrow. I doubt Peter could last that long here."

"Have you thought about how you're going to handle Father Christmas?" Mr. Crustison asked.

"I'm working up to that," George replied. "I'll probably explain the basics and then read that poem: *A Visit From St. Nick.*"

His father-in-law gave him a stern stare.

"Yes, I know it was written by an American," George acknowledged. "But we'll try not to hold it against him."

They were about to give up and take one of the big trees and cut the tip off when they heard Peter *crow*. The group rushed over and beheld the most breathtaking tree they had ever seen. It wasn't too big to fit into the parlour, and yet, it wasn't too small to cover all of the potential presents. It shimmered radiantly by the moonlight and stood proud and erect with an inviting warmth that only the truly great Christmas Trees possess.

The group smiled and embraced one another, feeling a fate that dispelled all of their superstitious concerns. This was meant to be.

George chopped it down, and the boys helped it onto the toboggan. It was the perfect touch to what Peter declared a truly magical evening.

CHAPTER FOUR

Learning About Father Christmas

"Now there's a Christmas Tree," Mr. Crustison professed.

The whole family gathered together. They had decorated the tree with candles and tinsel and now were admiring the beauty of their labours. It had been an especially cold night, even with the children all bundled up. But now, they enjoyed the glow of the tree with warm apple cider filling their bellies and a log *crackling* in the fireplace.

The children sat on the Persian rug in front of the hearth and tried to explain Christmas' final mystery to Peter, Father Christmas.

"Where do we begin?" George said, taking another sip of cider.

None of the family could remember the last time they had so much fun. Despite Peter's arrogance, his youth and his innocence were invigorating. It made George and Mary remember when their children were little and full of excitement and wonder.

"Father Christmas lives in a palace up North," George began. "And once a year, on Christmas, he comes down and travels around the world, bringing gifts to good little boys and girls everywhere. But if you're a spoiled, nasty child, you get nothing but a cold hard lump of coal."

"Why?" Peter asked.

"To reward children who are nice and do what they're told," Mary explained. "It isn't always easy for a child to play nice with their siblings or behave in school, and Father Christmas believes it is important to reward those who at least make an effort."

"Then why give coal?" Peter wondered.

"Well, only the most ghastly children ever get coal," George clarified. "The ones who are mean, selfish, and go out of their way to make other people miserable. Coal is cold, black, and unmovable, just like these children's hearts. It's supposed to make them realise what they are becoming, in the hopes that it isn't too late for these children to change their ways."

"Like Scrooge?" Nibs asked.

"Yes," Mr. Darling affirmed. "Just like Scrooge."

Wendy had been reading the boys *A Christmas Carol*, which was about a man named Ebenezer Scrooge, who was wicked enough to need ghosts to intervene.

"Of course," Mrs. Darling assured. "Such children are rare. And so far, none of my children have been naughty enough to merit coal."

"Or ghosts, for that matter," Michael added.

"How does this Father Christmas know if you've been good or bad?" Peter asked.

"He sees everything we do," Wendy replied.

"He has a list," John added, "with everybody's name on it, and he's constantly checking it with the help of his elves to make sure everyone is judged fairly."

"Elves?" Peter asked. He had heard of such creatures but had never met any. There were fairies, mermaids, gnomes, trolls, and various other mythical creatures in Neverland, including the occasional witch, but as far as elves were concerned, there were none.

"They live in Father Christmas' Workshop up North," Michael replied with an enthusiasm only a child could muster. "They are small and childlike, with pointed ears, and help make toys for children all over the world."

Peter had heard that elves were industrious creatures. He even recalled a story Wendy had told him about a poor overworked Shoemaker who needed a miracle. One night, these little men, with their skilled hands, had made enough marvellous new footwear to save the poor Cobbler and his shop.

"It's the elves' magic," Wendy continued, "that make all those wonderful gifts for all the boys and girls around the world. It also makes them fit into one sack."

"Tell him about the reindeer," Curly requested. "That's my favourite part."

"Oh, yes," Wendy mused. "I was just getting to that. On Christmas night, Father Christmas flies around the world delivering presents in a sleigh pulled by magical flying reindeer."

"Flying *rain*-deer?" Peter repeated. He was puzzled. Peter hadn't ever seen a rain-deer, much less a flying one. He gathered they must look like regular deer, only black and grey with a thick cloud-like fur. "Do they call them rain-deer because they make it rain?"

"Oh goodness, no," Wendy and the rest of the Darlings laughed.

"Or perhaps it's because they shoot lightning from their antlers?" Peter tried again.

"I believe they're called reindeer," George theorised, "because that particular sort of deer can be *reined* in." He pantomimed bringing in the reins of a sleigh.

"Is that true?" John asked his grandfather.

"No," Mr. Crustison replied. "But your father's on a roll."

"So, these reindeer," Peter clarified, "fly all over the world, making it possible for Father Christmas to deliver gifts to children everywhere."

"Precisely," George smiled.

"Then why hasn't he ever come to Neverland?" Peter asked.

At that moment, they were at a loss for words. It was a legitimate question and had to be answered carefully.

"Perhaps you've been naughty," Mr. Crustison suggested.

"Grandfather!" Wendy admonished.

"I'm just saying," Mr. Crustison grumbled.

Mrs. Darling had told her parents that Peter had a vivid imagination and that Neverland was what he called his orphanage.

Wendy turned to Peter. "You've got to understand that Neverland isn't exactly an easy place to find. Father Christmas may not know it exists."

Peter got a woeful expression that affected everyone in the room.

"I know!" Michael exclaimed. "We can write him a letter!"

"A letter?" Peter repeated, feeling the glimmer of hope return.

"Yes," Wendy agreed. "A letter, telling him about you and the Lost Boys and how you never had a Christmas."

"The Lost Boys?" Mr. Crustison inquired.

"It's what the orphans call themselves," Mary explained.

Mr. Crustison thought to himself a moment. "What a peculiar term."

Mary could tell that this conversation may be a tad beyond her parents' understanding, so she suggested they go freshen up for bed. As soon as they were out of the room, John grabbed a piece of paper from his father's ledger and started writing Father Christmas the story of Neverland. He scribbled with a fierce intensity until he got to the address. He froze, thinking about the odd directions they had been given in the past.

"Do you think Father Christmas can find Neverland just by saying, 'Second to the right and straight on till morning?' " John asked.

"Why not?" Peter replied, unable to grasp the question.

"Well, it's not exactly a normal address," John explained. "There's no latitude or longitude. You don't even know what ocean or continent it's near." Peter thought about it. "Also, you say the second to the right; I've always assumed you meant the second *star* to the right. Am I correct?"

"Precisely," Peter affirmed.

"But which one's the second star? Which one's the first, for that matter?"

"And is it still the second star in the North Pole?" Michael added.

Wendy had commented on Neverland's queer address when she had first met Peter, but Peter didn't understand. Now that he was hearing it again, which was like hearing it for the first time, the notion of Neverland possessing an unusual address made more sense.

"I'm sure he can find it," Mary assured. "As long as he knows it exists, I'm sure he can figure it out."

"Uh . . . Mary," George muttered under his breath. "I think you have forgotten something about the situation." He walked over to Peter. "Look, Peter. There's no way of knowing if Father Christmas will find your home. Why don't we write a letter telling him to bring the presents here, and you can pick them up and bring them back to your Lost Boys."

"That's a brilliant idea, father!" Wendy exclaimed, giving him a big kiss on the cheek. "Peter can go home and bring back the boys, and then we can have one big Christmas here."

"Yes," George nodded, temporarily misunderstanding her interpretation. *"Wait! WHAT?!"*

"If we bring the new Lost Boys here, we can . . ."

"No, no, no," George protested. "We have a full enough load as it is. I was merely suggesting that Father Christmas leave the presents here and have Peter bring them home with him when he leaves."

"But then my boys wouldn't get to experience a real Christmas," Peter implored. "They would merely be getting toys."

"Yes, well . . ." George stammered, falling short of a good argument.

"Didn't you tell me every child deserves a good Christmas?" Peter asked, attempting to manipulate the proud Mr. Darling.

"Well, yes," George mumbled, feeling himself lose control of the situation.

"And shouldn't children have a mother to read them Christmas stories, bake biscuits, and teach them games?" Peter continued.

"Yes, I suppose," George admitted.

"That settles it!" Peter declared. "Wendy will come and help bring Christmas to Neverland! She can teach the Lost Boys all about the Holiday Season and help us prepare for Father Christmas' arrival."

"I agreed to no such thing," George retorted. "Christmas is a time to be with family. I can't have Wendy gallivanting off to some faraway land at Christmastime."

"It would only be for a couple of days, father," Wendy promised. "And I'll be back before Christmas Eve."

"But, but . . ." George was at a loss for words. "Mary!"

"I suppose if they are back by Christmas Eve, it should be all right," Mrs. Darling permitted.

"But . . ." George whimpered.

"Don't worry, father," Wendy assured. "We have the travel time down to a day and a half, thanks to that shortcut the fairies showed us last time." She remembered the first time she followed Peter to Neverland; the trip seemed to take weeks. She and her brothers even learned how to sleep on their backs while riding the winds. It was a way to keep travelling without plummeting to their death.

The kids continued to stare at the apprehensive Mr. Darling.

"Oh, very well!" George submitted. "She can go, but with two stipulations."

"Anything," Peter agreed.

"You must promise that she arrives here no later than supper time on Christmas Eve."

"As good as done," Peter promised.

"And Nana will go along to chaperone," George informed.

"Nana?!" Wendy and Peter cried in unison.

"Yes," George insisted.

"Why not Michael or John?" Wendy asked.

"Because I know how you all get when you're away," George replied. "A week can turn into a month if you're not careful. And you being here on Christmas is too important to risk."

"Well, if Nana's going," Michael declared, "then I'm going."

"Me too!" John joined in.

"Really?" Wendy asked, surprised by John's newfound dedication to Neverland. He had never shown any interest in returning before — he had always been too analytical to believe in their first adventure. He remembered it, but his mind was too grown-up for him to believe it was real — he merely dismissed it as childish nonsense. Wendy supposed Peter's presence sparked this childlike resurgence in her brother.

"But you haven't gone with us in four years," Wendy added.

"Yes," John said, trying to skirt the issue. "And I should like to see it again."

"But you've forgotten how to fly," Wendy reminded.

Horror struck John's face. He had forgotten how to fly. John rushed to Peter's side. "You can teach me again . . . can't you?"

"I suppose," Peter pondered. "Unless you're too old to fly."

"I'm younger than Wendy!"

"Not in your mind," Peter replied. "Or your heart."

"Just tell me what to do."

"Finish writing that letter; then we'll talk." Peter grinned.

John frantically worked on the letter to Father Christmas, explaining the situation and the magical circumstances of Neverland. He wrote about Peter, the Lost Boys, and all the other miraculous forms of life on the island. He listed the new Lost Boys' names: Surely, Pipkin, Jojo, Dribbles, Patches, and Larry. And at the bottom of the letter, he wrote a sincere plea to give these poor motherless children their first Christmas.

When John was finished composing the letter, he sealed it up in an envelope and labelled it: *Father Christmas' Workshop, North Pole*.

CHAPTER FIVE

Flying Lessons

"Now what?" Peter asked.

Wendy and John led Peter to the fireplace and gave him the honour of casting the letter into the fire. They explained how it was customary in England to burn letters to Father Christmas in the fireplace, where they would be magically transported to his Workshop, reassembled and read.

Downstairs, the front door burst open, and in pranced Nana, who felt lighter than air. She had a whirlwind of an evening — the music, the dancing, the laughter! She was so giddy and jovial that she felt like a puppy again. Sure, she had gotten older — her joints ached, her paws were arthritic, cataracts clouded her vision, and her hearing wasn't what it used to be — but none of it mattered. She was happy, invigorated by an evening without all the stress and responsibility that comes with maturity.

She took a deep breath, remembering how Toby had kissed her under the mistletoe and began to feel herself blush beneath her fur. Suddenly, she got a whiff of something in the air. Something familiar but not something welcomed. She remembered that Mrs. Darling's parents were staying with them through Boxing Day, but there was another scent. Instinctively, she felt the *rumble* of a *growl* emanate from her chest. Her ears perked up as she made her way up the staircase to check in on her charges. She could hear George and Mary talking in the parlour while the Crustisons unpacked in the guest room upstairs. That was when she heard a thunderous racket coming from the nursery! It was followed by a strangely familiar voice — a voice she found alarming!

"You think of a wonderful thought," Peter stated. "Remember?"

"Yes," John said, closing his eyes and flapping his arms. "I'm thinking as hard as I can."

"No, no, no," Peter said. "You're trying too hard. You just have to be happy and believe."

"Okay," John declared. "I shall believe."

John closed his eyes and dove off a rather large bookcase when Nana entered the nursery, aghast at the horrific sight.

"WHAT IS GOING ON HERE?" Nana's barks demanded, seeing John crash to the ground.

All of the Newfoundland Dog's charges froze and grumbled simultaneously, unable to find the words to explain their erratic behaviour to their nervous nurse.

Wendy was about to explain when Nana caught sight of Peter, the troublemaker of yesteryear. She remembered how he had seduced her charges into running away and taking up with some rather unsavoury characters.

Her *barks* were clear and demanding as if saying: "WHAT'S THIS RAPSCALLION DOING HERE? IT'S NOT SPRING YET!"

Peter hissed, and his shadow coiled back, recognising the beast that had torn it away from its master once upon a time.

"It's okay, Nana," Wendy soothed, stroking her fur reassuringly. "Mother and father invited him."

Nana could imagine the Mistress allowing such an ill-advised invitation, but not the Master. Wendy explained the situation and told her about their plan to take a quick trip to Neverland and encouraged her to go and straighten it out with their parents. Of course, Wendy neglected to inform Nana that she was expected to accompany them to the land of danger and enchantment. She decided to leave that *honour* to her parents.

As soon as Nana was off to validate their story, they went back to teaching John to fly. They needed to figure out what they were missing soon because Nana was apt to be a particularly unreceptive pupil.

"Peter," Wendy interrupted. "What about the pixie dust?"

She was right. Peter was typically covered in pixie dust and could have easily shaken some off onto John and Nana, but he had had a bath. Peter thought about it for a long time.

"My old clothes!" Peter deduced. "They must have some dust on it."

"Uh," Wendy muttered. "I washed them."

"You what?!"

"Mother wanted to throw them out and give you some new clothes," Wendy explained. "I talked her out of it, but she insisted we at least wash your leaves before returning them." She sighed. "I wish Tinker Bell was still here."

Wendy had told many stories about Tinker Bell, and Peter wished he could remember her, but he just couldn't. He began to wonder, what if Wendy should perish? Would he be able to remember her? He wanted very much to remember his special mother but doubted he would. It was one of the drawbacks of an eternal childhood; life-altering events that make us mature weren't allowed to stick. They must be forgotten to maintain the carefree frivolity of youth.

Peter thought about the dilemma at hand, then suddenly: "My satchel! You didn't wash that, did you?"

Wendy shook her head enthusiastically and dashed off to retrieve it. Peter had lived among the fairies for so long that there was bound to be some residual dust in there. Wendy came back, and, sure enough, he shook out a light sprinkling of fairy dust over John. John closed his eyes, thinking about meeting a mermaid like the one in his book, and when he opened them again, he was levitating off the floor.

"Oh, joy!" John cried, floating above his family. "I really can fly! I knew it all along!"

There had been a time when he had stopped believing it was possible. He simply couldn't believe that he and his siblings had ever defied the laws of aerodynamics, but there he was . . . flying! He supposed it was the spirit of Christmas that allowed the child inside to come forth and achieve this magnanimous miracle by believing.

Wendy, Michael, and Peter joined their clumsy compatriot in the air. It had been a long time since John was able to fly, so his skills left a lot to be desired. They soared around the room, turning and twirling and bounding off the walls. It didn't take long for John to get the hang of it, especially with Wendy and Michael's tips, and soon they were out the door and flying down the hall and back again.

They could hear Nana going ballistic down the hall. "WHAT?!!" her *yelps* demanded.

The kids figured that their parents had just broken the news to Nana. There was a light argument, but Nana was a dog with an unassailable sense of duty. She will always do right by her charges and employers, so it wasn't long before she accepted the Darling's request and made her way back to the nursery.

She was reticent about flying and insisted that they take a train or boat instead, but ultimately it was impossible. Eventually, she allowed Peter to sprinkle some of that strange-smelling powder over her. She was so prudent and grown-up that Peter doubted they would ever get her off the ground. After a few false starts at a happy thought, Wendy stepped in with a few manipulative moves of her own. She had Nana close her eyes and asked about her date with Toby. Nana tried to skirt the issue, declaring it an inappropriate subject of discussion, but there was an undeniable girlish glee about her. That was when Wendy noticed that Nana's tail was wagging.

"Excuse us, gentlemen," Wendy decreed, ushering the boys out of the room. "This is girl talk, so out you go."

When she closed the door, Wendy persisted and got Nana to tell her everything. Well, Wendy didn't fully understand it because she didn't speak dog; however, Nana was wagging her tail fiercely as she *barked* about the dinner and dancing. Once more, she began to feel like a puppy again. Unfortunately, Nana failed to rise into the air. Wendy knew she needed to do something more drastic.

"Did he kiss you?" Wendy whispered.

Nana began to blush once more, thinking about that beautiful moment under the mistletoe when he brought her close and—

At that moment, Wendy stepped back, grinning as Nana lifted off the ground.

"Hold that thought, Nana!" Wendy called.

Nana let out a loud *yip*, seeing the floor pull away from her paws. She, like most dogs, was terribly afraid of heights and began to panic.

Wendy flew up to calm her and teach her some basics. Her first instruction, of course, was not to look down. She told Nana to concentrate on going straight and reaching the adjacent bookcase. It was a comical sight, seeing Nana desperately trying to dog-paddle in the air as if she were swimming. Dogs weren't very knowledgeable about smooth swan-like strokes and movements. Wendy knew it wouldn't be easy, but at least Nana was airborne.

Wendy called in Peter and the boys, and they began to work with Nana. Even if they couldn't make her flying passable, the fact that she could float would enable them to pull and guide her to Neverland with very little difficulty.

Meanwhile, the elder Darlings had rejoined the Crustisons for a little nightcap after breaking the news to Nana. Mary and her mother sipped tea in the kitchen while George and Mr. Crustison smoked cigars and drank a fine imported Cognac in the study. They were discussing current events when they heard a strange rumbling in the halls. Being knowledgeable enough to ignore the noise, George pretended not to hear the clatter.

"Now I'm certain I heard that," Mr. Crustison stated, opening the parlour door.

There was a moment of silence as George joined his father-in-law in the vacant hallway.

"See?" George declared. "It was just your imagination."

Suddenly, as if in response to George's comment, a dog came zooming overhead with an out-of-control *thud* against the wall. It was followed closely by a young woman and three boys whizzing past with a greater control in their flight. They struggled to help the near-catatonic canine around the corner.

When they were gone, George and Mr. Crustison were left standing in the hall, quietly registering what they had just witnessed.

"Did you see that?" Mr. Crustison asked, his eyes fixated on the empty hallway.

"See what?" George remarked, displaying a false sincerity that would have made a member of Parliament proud.

Mr. Crustison glanced down at his drink, bewildered. "Good Cognac."

Peter and Wendy finally felt they had gotten a handle on Nana — who floated with her paws covering her eyes so that she didn't have to see what was happening.

"All right," Peter called as they returned to the nursery. "Off to Neverland!"

With those words, the window blew open. Michael and John flew out the nursery window, just as they had done four years ago. They were followed by Wendy and Peter, who had a hold of Nana and guided her through the crisp December sky. Despite her complete mortification, Nana still insisted the children button up so they wouldn't catch cold.

There never was such a sight as three boys, a young woman, and a terrified Newfoundland Dog flying across the Tower of London by the light of the full moon.

CHAPTER SIX
A Peculiar Letter

Wavering through the cloud-covered night, a special December wind blew through the Darlings' fireplace. The flames fluttered mystically as the gentle updraft flowed through the chimney flue. It wasn't the sort of occurrence that would have alarmed anyone if they were to see it. It was subtle and quite common among old fireplaces, but this was a special wind, and being swept up through this particular smokestack were the remnants of a very peculiar letter.

The smoke and soot wafted up high into the sky alongside the particles of other children's letters. They rode a strong southerly gale that blew them to a very unusual address in the north. The powerful gusts sent them hurtling far and fast, over frozen hills and streams, valleys and oceans — constantly increasing in speed until finally reaching their destination.

By then, the gusts had slowed to a mellow breeze, carrying its contents carefully over a barren, snow-covered terrain. It flowed into a small chasm in the ice, which was so well hidden you could walk past it and never know it was there. The wind swooped through the deep, winding ice-chute before channelling out into a beautiful dale, which was insulated by an enormous igloo-like dome.

The land was lush and green, and there was a gentle stream running along a Mill on the outskirts of what looked like a quaint storybook village lost in time. The determined draft continued to soar above small handcrafted homes and Workshops and, finally, over a large wooden palace that bore an unusual chimney, which sucked the gust down its flue.

The various ash fragments landed on letter-shaped trays at the base of an enormous hearth. The trays were filled with a white sticky substance, which started bubbling in the fire alongside other letter-shaped trays. The liquid swirled the soot into position, causing it to re-expand. When the newly formed paper hardened, the trays popped out along a well-crafted conveyor belt and down to a cooling chute.

The whole process took mere moments before the reconstructed letters were whisked off to the mailroom, where a particularly stressed-out looking elf named Colby fumbled through the mounds of last-minute letters. Though elves possess an unusually chipper demeanour and a love for work, it still didn't preclude them from feeling the sting of being overworked.

Colby's job was to separate the letters by region, according to the flight route. This proved to be a rather difficult task, considering how many different days and aliases the Boss undertook. The Boss had already delivered gifts to countries such as Hungary and Slovenia, not to mention various Germanic regions which celebrate their Christmas around the 5th or 6th of December. But of course, they still had to sift through other Germanic regions that celebrated Christmas from the 24th to the 25th — just as there were other Slovak regions, including Russia, who celebrated Christmas on New Year's. It seemed like every region had a different name and persona for his master.

As the head of the mailroom, he was not allowed to make mistakes. Low hangs the head of the elf who sends a present on the 31st when it was due on the 5th.

Like every other department, the mailroom took on extra workers at the beginning of December to cover all the deliveries on the 24th and 25th. Even at that, everything had to be packed in accordance with international and regional time zones; otherwise, the whole expeditious undertaking would unravel and fall apart.

Toys and packaging were not Colby's concern, just the order the letters went out. He would look at the address and send it along the proper chute. There were many toy-making facilities — even the gifts children wanted tended to be regional. Of course, the packing department also had people double-checking the order the gifts were organised in the gift room before take-off.

Though Colby was stressed, he wasn't worried. Everything was moving along at its usual frantic yet still highly manageable pace. But then, something happened. Something that had never happened before. He had received a letter that he was about to dismiss as merely an England-bound chute until he read it.

There was a band of children living on an island they had no records of. It was no trouble to add the new children to the North Pole's index — children were being added and removed every day. But the discovery of a previously unknown island was downright shocking. The Workshop had prided itself on having the most accurate maps in existence. They even had islands and regions still undiscovered by man. At first, he thought it was a joke. The very notion that there could be an inhabited tract of land missing from their charts was unthinkable.

Of course, it was no joke. Jokes don't make it to the North Pole. Only sincere letters, coming from the innocence of a child's heart, could summon up the magic it takes to transport them to the North Pole.

But still, Colby thought, *children have been known to make mistakes.*

He told his team to proceed without him while he got to the bottom of this Neverland business. He took the letter to the heads of several departments, who were all baffled by its contents. The director of the Naughty-&-Nice Division found no records on these "Lost" children. They tried to track them magically, but it didn't work. They supposed it was because they didn't know about Christmas, and therefore, didn't believe in Father Christmas yet. But still, that never stopped them before, so what was Neverland?

The letter made its way to Barnaby, the Grand High Elf, who ultimately decided to take it up with the Boss in person. Father Christmas was very busy this time of year, so the elves did their best not to bother him unless it was absolutely necessary. Not that they were afraid of him, mind you. On the contrary, they had such a love and respect for the old man that they tried to relieve him of any unexpected burden that should arise. Also, it was often difficult to locate the Big Guy this time of year. He was so in demand by everybody that it was difficult to pinpoint where he was at any given moment.

The Boss was currently in the stables tending to the reindeer when Barnaby came in and handed him the letter. Father Christmas was a little confused but merrily took it. He opened it up, adjusted his spectacles, and quietly read it to himself.

He was silent for a moment or two. He knew that Wendy, Michael, and John Darling missed Christmas four years ago, but there were no records of where they had gone or what they did when they got there. But when they returned, they brought home six orphans who also seemed to have appeared out of thin air. It was perplexing.

This was going to require special attention, so he assembled a team of elves and went to the mystic Watching-Pools. As Father Christmas entered the underground cavern, each lantern sparked to life, filling the tunnel with light in anticipation of his presence. He turned the corner, and the cavern widened out, revealing the pools. The water was clear and glowed with a light blue hue that positively radiated pure magic. He walked up to the water and touched the tip of his staff to the clear blue liquid. As the ripples began to subside, he called out: "Show me Wendy, John, and Michael Darling."

Slowly, a thick black cloud flowed beneath the water's surface, revealing a cloud of darkness with white specks. It became clear those specks were the gentle flurry of snowfall. Images began to form as the rooftops of London appeared below five free-floating figures. As the images cleared, there was a silent shock of disbelief amongst Father Christmas and his elves. With as many unbelievable things Father Christmas had seen throughout the centuries, the sight of a young woman and three boys flying and guiding a petrified Newfoundland Dog over a British landscape was still a first.

"Lakky!" Father Christmas called, still observing the image.

"Yes, sir?" the plump, officious-looking elf replied.

"Prepare my sleigh," Father Christmas said with a smile. There was a certain twinkle in his eye that itched for excitement. "And get Stanley and Tweedle from Tracking-&-Mapping down here immediately. We need to add a new location to our charts."

"Right away, sir," Lakky replied.

Lakky always did what he was told, but he had to admit that he didn't care much for Stanley and Tweedle. They were disrespectful, lazy, and the biggest troublemakers in the Pole. But, to his great dismay, it seemed like most of the other workers preferred them to the resourceful and obedient Lakky. They were a part of the younger, more innovative generation which combined magic with technology. Stanley had his inventive designs and concepts, and Tweedle had his special mechanical (as well as magical) engineering skills, which made it all possible. They had made themselves invaluable to the organisation and took advantage of it.

Stanley and Tweedle also had a wicked sense of humour and liked to play tricks on everybody. Now, Lakky enjoyed a jolly jape as much as the next elf, but sometimes they went too far. Why only last year, when Wiggildy took the sleigh out for the traditional test-flight for the Boss, Tweedle had replaced all of the flying reindeer with regular reindeer. When the team dashed up the ramp, they plummeted off the end, crashing to the snowbank below instead of taking flight.

Then this year, when poor Wiggildy took the sleigh out, they double-checked the reindeer but forgot to double-check the bolt connecting them to the sleigh. So when he pulled on the reins, the reindeer took off, and poor Wiggildy flew out of his seat, desperately clinging to the leather straps as his body flailed helplessly behind the airborne reindeer.

They also made a name for themselves down at the pub for being able to belch *Jingle Bells* while standing on their heads and for making up funny words to other Christmas songs.

Lakky wasn't at all surprised to find Tweedle chatting up one of the female co-workers instead of fixing whatever it was he was supposed to fix.

"Tweedle," Lakky called. "The Boss wants to see you and Stanley immediately."

"We didn't do it," Tweedle responded instinctively.

"Don't worry. You're not in trouble," Lakky informed. "At least not this time. Now, where's Stanley?"

Tweedle thought about it for a moment.

Stanley was where he always was that time of day, down at the Schoolhouse. They had gotten a new teacher, a Miss Bellringer, and everyone adored her. Many elflings and faculty members alike had fallen for the pretty pedagogue. She was beautiful and kind, with flowing blonde hair — she was everything you would imagine a fairy tale princess to be and more. And every day, when her class went out for recess, Stanley would stop by and bring her flowers or chocolates, and then they would talk under the big oak tree.

Tweedle didn't particularly approve of the charming schoolmarm, though he had to admit, she was wonderful in every way. He felt she was something of a bad influence on the young Stanley. Before meeting her, Stanley wasn't disinclined to sing a saucy song or tell a torrid tale, but now, he was too preoccupied with behaving like a *gentleman* to enjoy any of life's rakish delights. He wouldn't even participate in standard pranks! Then there was his hygiene. He started combing his hair and brushing his teeth every day — *where would the madness end?* Still, Tweedle had to admit that if he were in Stanley's pointy-shoes, he'd act the same way.

"Good day Miss Bellringer," Stanley greeted.

"You're starting to sound like one of my students," she replied. "Please, call me Holly."

"Okay Miss Bellringer . . . er . . . Holly," he stammered.

She giggled. She thought Stanley was so cute when he got nervous.

"Uh, Holly," Stanley continued, trying to maintain eye contact instead of averting his gaze down to his shoes. He found it rather difficult because of how powerful and overwhelming her piercing blue eyes were.

"I was wondering," he grumbled, trying to clear his throat, "if you would like to . . . maybe . . . have dinner with me tonight?"

"Of course I would."

His heart fluttered as he saw her smile widen, revealing the dimples on her cheeks.

"We can have a picnic in the snow," he suggested. "I'll bring some hot chocolate and a turkey, and we can watch the sunset together."

"It sounds magical," she replied.

"Stanley!" Lakky called, walking up to him. He looked over at Holly, wondering what she could have possibly seen in his wayward friend. "My apologies Miss Bellringer, but I'm afraid Stanley is needed over at the head office right now."

"That's all right," she replied. "Recess is almost over, and I need to call the elflings back to class any moment now." She turned to leave, then glanced back at Stanley. "And I'll see *you* tonight." She winked and walked off.

Both men were silent until she was out of sight.

"Okay, I'm sorry I took a long lunch break," Stanley apologised.

"I'm not here about that," Lakky assured. "Although you are over an hour late. The Boss needs to see you and Tweedle about an island immediately."

"An island?"

"Neverland." Lakky nodded. "It's not on any charts."

"That's impossible."

Stanley was perplexed. They had a magical surveyor that used electromagnetic radio waves to map out every square centimetre of land on the planet, so how could that be? They knew about the American Continent ages before the Vikings. So how could they have a problem with an island?

Stanley was first alarmed when they entered the Watching-Pools and saw the Boss had manifested into his chubby persona with the red suit. Father Christmas was typically a strong man with chiselled features, wearing a green fur coat with a hood. He only went out as the jolly fat man in red while visiting the Americas or the children of Europe who firmly believed in the Clement Moore poem. So where was he going, and what did he want with him and Tweedle?

Stanley saw Tweedle in the corner, fiddling with a map and their portable tracking device. Suddenly, he got a bad feeling about this whole thing.

"What's going on?" Stanley asked, walking over to his partner.

"Evidently, we're tracking some kids and a dog who are flying to an island that doesn't exist."

It took Stanley a moment to register what was just said. Nothing his friend had just uttered had made any sense whatsoever. Tweedle just pointed to the Watching-Pools across the way, leaving Stanley in a dumbstruck awe when he saw the images in the Pool.

"Ah, Stanley," Father Christmas greeted, merrily observing the young elf's attire. "Hmm, I hope you plan on bringing a coat. It's awfully chilly up there."

"Up wher . . . ?" he had started to say when he saw the reindeer. "Oh, sir. You can't be serious."

"I'm very serious."

"But . . . I'm afraid of heights," Stanley pleaded. "Besides, we're tracking them right now. We'll be able to provide the correct coordinates once they arrive."

"I don't think so," Father Christmas disagreed. "This island has evaded detection for centuries. I suspect we will lose their signal long before we can find it."

"What about the Watching-Pools?" Stanley asked. "I admit my tracking system is still primitive, but the Watching-Pools are old magic. Surely it could show us their journey."

"I suspect the island is a lot like this place," Father Christmas said with a wink. "Not entirely made up by the physical. A realm that hides in the shadows between dreams and reality. I'm sure its presence will be unreadable." He turned and pulled a thick coat out of his magical sack. "Here, have a new parka."

Stanley tried to stammer an excuse as Father Christmas helped him get the parka on but couldn't think of one.

"Come on," Father Christmas encouraged enthusiastically. "There hasn't been a major discovery like this in over a thousand years. Who knows what we'll find out there? It should be an awfully big adventure!"

Stanley forced a smile. "Great."

"Besides, I've never had to follow anyone before," Father Christmas said, unable to contain his excitement. He let out his loud, trademark laugh. "This should be a lot of fun!"

There was no arguing with the Boss. Father Christmas was excited, and he always knew what was best. He just hoped they would be back in time for his date with Holly. Little did they realise what fate had in store for them, nor the dangers which lay ahead.

With the final provisions loaded on the sleigh, and the reindeer in place, Father Christmas gave a call to his team, and they were off! The game was officially afoot!

CHAPTER SEVEN

The Phantom of Neverland

There was a phantom in Neverland. A vicious predator, roving the lands by night and butchering all who crossed its path. It feasted upon toads, reptiles, rabbits, deer, and any other unfortunate creature it happened across. Very few had seen it and lived, but those who had described it as a strange, twisted hermit with a hook and a cutlass. Some of the natives, such as the Piccaninnies, believed it was the ghost of Captain James Hook, back from the dead and punishing the world for his demise.

Bones littered the trails, along with many ominous signs warning weary travellers to ***Beware the Phantom!***

Many Lost Boys had met their end wandering alone in one of the spectre's old haunts. There were only a few places on the island the Lost Boys weren't allowed to go after sunset, and the shores of *Kid's Creek* was one of them. Peter still couldn't remember Jas Hook had existed, but he quickly learned that the creek was a dangerous place to tread.

There was a rabbit resting quietly on a rock. Its ears folded back placidly as it bent down to lap up the cool water from the creek below. It crooked its head and closed its eyes as the hook shot out of the darkness, piercing the terrified critter through the neck. It was dragged into the concealing shadows. There was a loud *snap*, and then all was silent.

"Ah, dinner," a gruff but elegant voice grumbled. It walked back to its hidden cave with the small carcass dangling limply from its hook.

It was delighted. It hadn't had roasted rabbit in quite some time and felt it would be a pleasant change from fish. The *late* captain took his favourite chair and began to skin his supper, wondering how he ended up in his infernal exile. He kept a fire burning in a niche in a rock wall. There was a natural opening leading up to a hole at the top of the cliff, which served as a covert chimney. He finished skinning the rabbit, put it on the spit, and waited for it to cook.

He decided to save the pelt. It had gotten unexpectedly cold, and he needed new mitts. He set it up to tan as he contemplated life as a hermit. He didn't mind the loner aspect of it — how else was he guaranteed to have intelligent company? Still, he hated the sense he was living the life of a coward. Deep down, he knew what he was really hiding from was the bitter shame and embarrassment of defeat. Still, he couldn't shake that feeling of cowardice, afraid to face the CHILD who bested him and his crew. An arrogant little boy who had vexed him for lord knew how long.

There was a gentle water flow trickling down the right-hand side of the cave. It pooled up in his solid gold shaving-basin. He washed the blood off, splashed his haggard face, and began to wonder where it all went wrong.

He replayed the whole thing in his mind. That terrible moment when Peter kicked him into the jaws of that ravenous crocodile. Hook may have revelled in the knowledge that Peter had shown bad form but still cringed, remembering the way the creature's teeth pierced his flesh as it dragged him below the depths.

It is a common misconception that a crocodile will eat its victims whole. Save for the occasional fish or toad, crocodiles usually clamp their teeth onto their larger prey, crushing them as it drags them underwater. Next, they would thrash around violently to disorient and knock out their victim, drowning it for easier consumption.

Hook had dropped his cutlass when the crocodile fell upon him — not so much from the pain, but from the sense of his worst fears being realised — but he still had his hook. He always had his hook! Another proof that the hook was far superior to a hand. When the beast went into its death-roll, Hook let it fly. He started stabbing and clawing at the leviathan with a strength and fury, unlike anything it had ever encountered before. It had loosened its grip when Hook began hacking at its eyes. Even the most ravenous reptile will release its prey when an iron claw gouges its eye out.

Hook managed to break free and swam for his life, ignoring the pain of his fractured ribs. When he came ashore, he noticed the crocodile's left eyeball stuck to the blade. He looked at his wounds, then back to the water, and, in a fit of rage, yanked off the bloody orb and ate it raw. It tasted foul, bitter and salty as it crunched in his mouth — a truly grotesque texture, hard and slimy — but he felt victorious.

"You ate my hand!" he shouted. "And I ate your eye!"

In his own demented logic, he supposed it made them even. An eye for an eye, as the saying went. But still, the clock had wound down, and now there was nothing to alert him to its presence, but he supposed if it were to come back for revenge, he always had his trusty hook.

He was almost surprised it hadn't come for him yet. It had been four years, and tales of the one-eyed killer crocodile of Neverland were beginning to spread. He supposed, much like himself, it was just biding its time — picking up the shattered remains of its wounded pride and waiting for the opportune moment to *strike!*

Everyone thought Hook was dead, and Hook was content with that. He wanted the world to remember him as a strong, bloodthirsty captain, going out in a blaze of glory and good form instead of the pathetic old codfish he had become.

Confidentially, he *loved* the rumours about his ghost. How legendary! Captain James Hook: the man so terrible he continued to torment the living long after his death. It inspired him to decorate the trails with skeletons and warning signs. It was something he learned from

Captain Flint. Bones made good trail markers, but they were even better for warding off unwanted visitors.

Sadly, the one person Hook truly wanted to believe that he was a murderous apparition didn't even know he existed! It was the greatest insult of all!

"How could Peter forget me?!" Hook would holler. They had been each other's nemeses ever since he had landed on the island. It had been towards the beginning of the 18th century, just before his former captain, the legendary pirate Blackbeard, had fallen in the Colonies. Hook had stumbled across an uncharted cluster of islands after his ship, the *Jolly Roger,* had found itself lost in a strange purple fog. They had initially entered the mist to evade the Spanish Armada, but the fog had lingered for days. The ship was jostled by an unsteady tide, pulling them as if with a purpose, and when it all cleared, they saw the island.

Hook had found a lush undiscovered island that would be a great place to make port — especially when he needed to lie low. It was a magical paradise. There were creatures there he had only heard about in fairy tales — not to mention many hidden coves that would be great for stowing treasure. But where were they?

He drew a map using their last known location as a reference. He tried to study the stars, but there were constellations in the sky that he couldn't find on any charts. Then, using the Polaris as a constant, he retraced it to its position just before they entered the fog. It took him months of scrutiny, but he believed he had discovered their route. Unfortunately, there was a certain margin of error due to the unknown star systems and the magical nature of the land. But once he mastered it, he began to come and go as he pleased.

He would go off, plunder, then come back. He had many marvellous escapades. He would drink with Flint, play cards with Kidd, and duel with Barbecue — very few people know it, but our dear Hook was the man responsible for Silver's wooden leg. It was a grand old time. He also began to notice the lack of ageing among himself and his crew. All of his old chums back on the mainland started to wrinkle and grey, but the crew of the *Jolly Roger* stayed the same. The island was a veritable Fountain-of-Youth. It was as close to Heaven as a pirate could ever achieve.

But of course, there was the boy. He was the leader of a tribe of deplorable children. An arrogant whelp who went by the name of Peter. A boy who possessed the remarkable ability of flight. Hook didn't think much of them at first. Just some undisciplined youths, playing around and causing mischief. Still, what more could you expect from boys without adult supervision?

But then they started playing tricks on his crew. Imagine that, children with no fear or respect for pirates? Outrageous! They would laugh and jeer at the drunken buccaneers, then try to lure them into fights. It had taken several years for the hatred to bile up before it all erupted.

But life went on. Hook and the natives had a few delightfully bloody skirmishes. They would occasionally administer savage beatings to the Lost Boys they caught tampering with the ship — a good old-fashioned flogging, the kind Hook remembered from his youthful days at Eton.

Everything was as it should be. The cut-throats would come and go, pillaging the seven seas, before returning to their little island paradise.

They had come back from a particularly disastrous run-in with the Royal Navy when Peter challenged the overwrought captain to a duel. Jas, who had tolerated more than enough of the boy's cocky mischief, accepted. He had to admit, he never intended to kill the little wretch; he just wanted to humble him a bit. He planned to disarm the lad, smack him around a bit, and then conclude his lesson in humility with a savage birching until he begged for mercy.

That's what he learned from his boyhood days at Eton. Fridays were flogging days. If any child had made an egregious school infraction, they were brought before the Headmaster to be whipped. Hook recalled being held on the birching block with his underpants around his ankles and receiving several harsh lashes from the Headmaster in front of the class. It taught him discipline and good form. If there ever was a child in need of a good birching, it was this one.

Peter drew first, brandishing a small but deceptively sharp blade. Hook scoffed at the challenger; after all, he was renowned as one of the finest blades in all of Europe — and that was before becoming a scourge of the seven seas. But he had to admit; he was greatly impressed by the boy's formality. Peter started with the traditional salute, then transitioned into the perfect *en-garde* stance. Hook nodded, drew his sword, saluted the boy back and shifted into position.

Peter advanced with a simple exploratory lunge. Hook deflected it with a simple yet powerful *beat*. He had expected the blade to slip out of the boy's hand, but Peter effortlessly rolled his wrist and advanced with another quick thrust. Hook deflected it with a *bind* and replied:

"Very good, lad. Maybe there's a future for you aboard my ship someday."

"Yeah, as captain," Peter quipped with that irksome arrogance.

One of Hook's crew made the mistake of laughing, so Hook turned to his Bo'sun: "Smee."

Smee pulled out his pistol and shot the giggling imbecile dead.

"Thank you, Smee. That'll be all."

Peter *crowed* with an *appel*, and turned his *Balestra* into a full-fledged attack!

Hook *parried* rapidly, impressed by the strength and swordsmanship of a boy so young. He immediately shifted into a *riposte*, lunging forward. There was a flash of steel, and everyone was in awe. The pirates had never imagined Peter would be such a worthy adversary, and the Lost Boys had felt the same way about Hook.

Hook had assumed he would be easy to overtake, but Peter proved to be a surprisingly formidable foe. They had stumbled across a slain native in the woods, but it had never occurred to them that one of these children may have sent him off to the Happy Hunting Ground.

Regardless, this was but a *child*. So, he put forth a greater effort, driving Peter back and tripping him on a boulder. Hook laughed, stomping forward as Peter did a backwards-somersault, leaping up into flight.

Hook was furious. Peter flew around: twirling, cutting, slicing, thrusting, and buzzing around like a horsefly from Hell.

"That's *not fair!*" Hook roared, deflecting the deadly blows. "*Bad form! Come back down here and fight fair, you ruddy little cur!*"

The battle ensued, and Hook had finally thought he had him. He had knocked Peter out of the sky and pinned his hand with the heel of his leather boot. He kicked the boy in the ribs again and again before letting him have one across the face.

"I give you the great Peter Pan," he jeered to the throng of his crew's derisive laughter. "Very menacing, isn't he?" He brought the tip of his cutlass to the boy's throat. "What shall we do with this scurvy naive?"

There was a caterwaul of grisly suggestions, but, to Hook's surprise, Peter didn't cry or beg for mercy; he just laid there valiantly. This show of good form and honour was almost enough to dissuade the ruthless captain. However, he was still determined to humiliate the boy, even if it meant torture.

Hook looked into Peter's strong eyes and smiled. "Fetch me the cat!" He gestured to the Lost Boys. "And I want those filthy little urchins to watch."

The boys began to laugh. Hook stepped away, flabbergasted.

"*What's so funny?!*" Hook demanded.

They gestured to the ground behind him, and when he turned around . . . Peter was gone. What happened next was still one of the most heartbreaking events of Hook's life. It was as if time itself had slowed down. As he turned, he saw Peter slash at his head. The sword appeared to be moving at a horrifically slow pace, and there was nothing he could do to stop it. He tried to block the blow, but his right arm flowed up in that same tragically slow perspective. His arm managed to raise fast enough to block his neck but not quite fast enough to block it with steel.

He was struck with the sudden sensation of heat as the warm liquid poured down his wrist. When he gazed down, anger and dread flowed through his soul, seeing the stump that once held his hand. He was mortified and physically sick at the sight of his unnatural yellow blood gushing down his forearm. Though he had stated many times that he did not miss his hand, the first glance was still a soul-shattering nightmare come to life.

He didn't hesitate; he drew his pistol and fired at the detestable child, hitting him in the shoulder.

"*Well, don't just stand there, you swine!*" Hook screamed. "*Shoot him!*"

His men sprang into action, firing their pistols at the elusive Pan.

Peter effortlessly dodged the cut-throats' determined rounds, suffering through the pain in his shoulder. While they scrambled to reload their shot, he did something that angered Hook more than anything else. Something he couldn't believe. That malicious little sprite picked up his severed hand and flew it out to open waters, where a hungry saltwater crocodile was swimming.

"Here, girl," he called. "Want a snack?"

The massive crocodile leapt in the air and snapped it up, savouring the sweet juices of Hook's succulent flesh. Peter laughed and *crowed* as the crocodile licked its teeth and headed to shore.

Jas couldn't move, watching the enormous reptile approach the land. It was evident it was coming for the petrified captain, who managed to flee as it crawled onto the beach. The beast scurried after him and had been chasing him ever since. As Hook ran for his life, the only sounds he could hear were the beating of his heart and the boy's contemptible laughter. At that moment, Hook vowed to silence Peter's laughter forever.

Looking back on the whole ordeal, he felt he was sort of asking for it. He had sailed under the name Hook for ages — ever since he gutted a Quartermaster with a fish hook in his youth. It became his calling card, even while serving as Blackbeard's Bo'sun. He started leaving the bodies of his more esteemed victims dangling from fish hooks.

He had heard the Buddhists speak of Karma but had never imagined how inescapable it could be. He just wondered what Karma had in store for Peter.

That event was just the first of many glorious adventures they had shared. So how could he be forgotten so easily?

Easy. Peter had a terrible memory. Why else couldn't he remember that confounded pixie Tinker Bell?

The one who foiled his plan to poison Peter. She had drunk poison for him, and Hook had brought him to the brink of death on several occasions, but Peter's mind had moved on.

Of course, Peter had other foes. Hook had seen his vile replacements, but they didn't last long. None of them had the stamina nor the ruthless drive to pose any real threat. They were all gone now.

Sometimes he wondered if he should end it all. He would lay in his makeshift cot and stare up at the strange stalactite formations hanging overhead and wonder how old he must have been by then. Though he didn't look it, he was positively ancient. But that was the power of Neverland. One minute you land on an island, and the next thing you know, it's been nearly two centuries, and everyone you used to know is dead.

Why shouldn't he think of ending it all? He should have died of old age a long time ago, so why continue?

He would mull it over in his mind, and his concentration would casually drift to Shakespeare. Feeling depression's icy embrace, he would grip his pistol, wander through his cavernous squalor, and recite his favourite soliloquy from the immortal Bard's *Hamlet*.

"To die, to sleep —
to sleep — perchance to dream: ay, there's the rub,
for in that sleep of death what dream may come
when we have shuffled off this mortal coil,
must give us pause. There's the respect
that makes calamity of so long life."

The words seemed to resonate more and more with Hook as time went on. He continued to quote and shout with all the woe and melancholy of a man, half-crazed and ready to die. He didn't break his concentration until the final breath of his last verse:

> *"—Nymph, in thy orisons*
> *be all my sins remembered."*

He would bring back the hammer of his pistol, and then, feeling the itch for the pull of the trigger, Hook would state with quiet dignity:

"Hamlet was prepared to die."

Then he would watch, with a growing fascination, the green moss struggling to grow on the harsh rock surface and remember:

"But not before having his revenge!"

Vengeance had kept him going, but the fight appeared to be out of him. All of his enemies back in civilisation were dead. No one in their right minds would ever believe the Legendary Captain Hook was still alive — much less young. He might as well take his vast fortune, leave Pan to his insipid existence, and enjoy retirement.

Maybe he would take a wife. Heck, he hadn't even seen a real woman who was over three inches tall in ages. He was a tragically lonely man, but with his tremendous wealth, he was sure to find a beautiful young woman to wed.

He didn't have much in that particular cave, but there were other caches. Oh, he had caches all over these islands. He had plenty of rum and cigars stored away, not to mention all of the precious booty he had plundered over the centuries. Yes, he certainly would be a phenomenally wealthy man if he could return to civilisation and bring it with him. Peter had even dispatched of his crew, so now he wouldn't have to. Of course, Hook would have preferred to use them to get all the treasure on board before disposing of them; but the end result would have been the same.

Of course, there was no ship anymore. That contemptible boy had sailed away with it, and when he returned, he returned alone. It pained him to think about what had become of his precious *Jolly Roger.*

All that remained of his former crew was Starkey and Smee. Lord knows what happened to Smee, but his first mate Starkey was now an Indian wet nurse. It was a shame. He probably would have kept those two alive.

C'est la vie.

He walked to the cave's entrance, gazing up at the night sky. There was a change in the wind; he could feel it. There was a strangely unforeboding drift in the clouds. Neverland was typically a hostile environment, rendered more hostile upon Peter's arrival. However, there was something gentle in the air. Something happy. Something that didn't stir up anger and violence in all things. Peter was returning and wanted things to be nice and cheerful on the island.

There was a gentle snowfall — big fluffy flakes wafted down serenely. It was the kind of snow little James used to pray for on Christmas morning.

Why did he suddenly think about Christmas? He hadn't thought about it since he was a boy. At that moment, he realised something was about to happen in Neverland that had never happened before.

The glimmer of hope began to surface as he felt the mirth in the trees. Maybe he would find a way to get off the island and go back to England after all. And perhaps he would still be able to get his revenge in the process. He decided to dust off his old tricks, eat his rabbit, and spy on Peter's crew once more.

CHAPTER EIGHT

Finding Neverland

"Wendy, tell us a story," Peter requested.

They had been flying for hours. Usually, Peter would be off, playing little games and having many adventures throughout their trip, but he had agreed to take responsibility for carting Nana along. He was honour-bound to be by her side — no matter how bored or restless he got. Still, Peter never complained. That wasn't Pan's way. But that certainly didn't stop him from looking for any distraction he could.

Wendy thought about it for a moment. She had many Christmas stories to tell but was hoping to save them for the Lost Boys. Of course, she was willing to tell a story more than once, but which one? She felt *A Christmas Carol* by Charles Dickens was a little long, so she finally settled on the Clement Moore poem *A Visit From St. Nicholas*.

She called to Michael and John, who were playing a particularly dangerous game where they tried to out-daredevil one another. Luckily for Nana, they were flying through some particularly murky fog — not that she was doing a lot of looking around — otherwise, she would have seen what they were doing and had a heart attack. They flew up as high as their lungs and body temperature would allow and then let themselves plummet. They tried to see who could come closest to hitting the ground before chickening out and flying back up.

The flight was much colder than John had remembered — it had also snowed the first time they journeyed to Neverland, only he didn't feel the cold as much back then. He wished he could soar above the cloud line and out of the elements but knew it got colder and harder to breathe the higher they went. The snow whipped at their faces harshly, but they didn't mind. Children who can fly don't feel the cold as much. And most of the clouds were high up, so John only bumped into one low-flying cloud, which was much better than his first time out.

"JOHN! MICHAEL!"

They could hear Wendy up ahead. The fog was growing fatter, shrouding John and Michael's vision. They could barely see one another now. They decided to stick together so they wouldn't get lost. They flew side by side, holding hands and trying to navigate their way back to Wendy. John was getting nervous because there was no sight of her. They were surrounded by a hazy darkness, leaving them directionless and alone.

"WENDY!" John cried, realising the only chance they had at rejoining their group was by sound alone. He continued to yell to Wendy, desperately trying to follow each other's voices. Just when they thought all hope was lost, they bumped into each other — quite literally, Peter struggled to maintain his hold of Nana.

"There you are," Wendy admonished. "From now on, we stick together in the fog."

Nana barked in affirmation.

"All right, now quiet down," Peter ordered. "Wendy's going to read us a story."

Wendy cleared her throat, then began by explaining that St. Nicholas was what the Americans called Father Christmas.

> " *'Twas the night before Christmas,*
> *when all through the house,*
> *not a creature was stirring,*
> *not even a mouse.*
> *The stockings were hung*
> *by the chimney with care*
> *in hopes that St. Nicholas*
> *soon would be there . . ."*

Meanwhile, hurtling through the sky — far above the children and the cloud line — a little red sleigh gained on the trail of Wendy and Peter.

Stanley and Tweedle were by no means used to the trip and were not particularly enjoying it. Though they were travelling at an alarming rate, it was still nothing compared to the velocity Father Christmas and his coursers were accustomed to. The Boss struggled to keep from passing their marks, so the trip was exciting for him despite having to fly so slow.

The frozen elves, on the other hand, did not see it as flying slow. They whizzed through the air at speeds much more rapid than they were comfortable with. Stanley had to admit, he was always curious what the Boss' December ride was like, but he never imagined how harsh and unforgiving it was — especially for those who weren't used to it. It was bitterly cold, even in their parkas, and the wind lashed at their tender faces with a growing fury the faster they flew. And then there was the altitude. There was a risk of blacking out and vomiting from the lack of oxygen and the drastic change in the air pressure, but Father Christmas had created a special mask for the boys, using the basic principles of deep-sea diving suits — except the oxygen line was magically generated.

Of course, Father Christmas didn't need a breathing apparatus. He didn't really feel the cold either. He was used to his trips and was mostly made up of belief and goodwill, so he rarely noticed the elements.

Stanley and Tweedle counted their blessings. At least they were above the clouds, so they weren't getting rained or snowed on. At the moment, they were over a particularly nasty-looking nimbus cloud. It was black and brewing up a particularly treacherous-looking storm. As Stanley stared below, he thought less about the appalling conditions the poor children and the petrified Newfoundland dog were travelling through and more about the picnic he was apt to miss with Miss Bellringer . . . *er* . . . Holly.

He didn't have time to tell her about his latest assignment because they were immediately ushered off to the sleigh. He had asked Lakky and Wiggildy to tell Holly he wasn't going to make it, but there was something in their eyes that told him not to count on it. Something that said Stanley was overdue for a good prank. And in a way, they were right. They had been the central targets for more than their fair share of shenanigans, but this was love.

Once more, he sighed, then gave a grateful grumble that they didn't have to travel through that black storm cloud below.

"Uh-oh," Tweedle muttered. "The signal's getting weak."

"We're about to lose them," Father Christmas exclaimed. "Time to get into visual range."

"Oh no!" Stanley cringed, knowing what that meant.

They braced themselves as they dropped below the cloud line. There was no sign of the children. Of course, it was hard to see anything through that foreboding fog — especially when you're being pelted with hail and thick ice-cold lashes of rain. But Father Christmas' eyes were sharp and spotted the children instantly. They turned through a rock formation up ahead and out of sight. At that moment, the signal on Tweedle's tracking device vanished.

Father Christmas raced after them. He wasn't about to lose them now that they were in sight.

The closer they got, the more they began to see the large rock formations jutting out of the ocean floor. They were heading through a treacherous reef with enormous cliffs surrounding it. Father Christmas darted around them, carefully manoeuvring through the terrain while trying to sense the magic that cloaked the children's location. The waves crashed against the jagged rocks below. The harsh winds rattled the small craft, causing the terrified elves to grip their seats tightly, afraid of being thrown to their deaths.

Finally, he saw it. It was a glint at first, but the closer they got, the more prominent it became. There were many caves along the reef, but only one had a radiant purple hue gleaming out of it. It was one of the caves in the cliff formations, protruding above sea level.

"There!" Father Christmas declared, pointing at the cave. "They went in there."

"Are you sure?" Stanley asked.

Father Christmas nodded. "I'm positive."

Father Christmas guided his team inside the cavern with the luminescent violet glow. The reindeer only managed to get a few steps in before discovering a straight drop. Father Christmas brought his team to a halt and observed the chasm below.

"How deep do you think it is?" Tweedle wondered, peering into the seemingly bottomless abyss.

Whatever this place was, it made their instruments stop working.

"Deep," Father Christmas suspected.

The group continued to stare, hoping to see any sign of a bottom, but there was no end in sight — even with the odd light illuminating the cave.

"We don't really have to go down there, do we?" Stanley asked nervously.

Father Christmas flashed a mischievous smile and then gave the command. Stanley closed his eyes as the reindeer leapt into the void. They flew quite a way before the cavern curved around and up into a strange swirling tunnel. The hard rock chambers surrounding them were vibrant shades of blues, purples, greens, and reds. At first sight, it appeared to be endless, but the second they flew through it, the thick rock walls contracted like an accordion as their speed spontaneously increased. A whirlwind of colour twisted, billowing past them faster than their eyes could handle. In a blink of an eye, the rock walls curved up, and they were out the other side.

"That was it?" Tweedle said. "That didn't seem very far."

"Uh, Tweedle," Stanley stammered, pointing up.

It was now daylight, and the sky was clear and cloudless. They also found themselves over an entirely different sea. When the elves looked at their instruments, they were stunned at where the coordinates told them they were.

"This can't be right," Tweedle muttered.

"What?" Father Christmas inquired.

"Look at where it says we are." Tweedle handed the device to Father Christmas, who merely smiled.

"What's so hard to believe about that?"

"We did that in less than five seconds, and the deer were moving slow," Tweedle explained.

"How's that possible?" Stanley asked.

"It's a magical shortcut," Father Christmas replied. "The world is full of them. They're terribly hard to find but terribly useful if you're lucky enough to come across one. It's sort of how I get around the continents." He smiled. "Looks like I've got a new one to add to my list."

"We have the Darlings signal back," Tweedle announced, showing Father Christmas the tracking device. "Are we in Neverland?"

"Not if you have their signal," the jolly old man replied. "They did mention a shortcut."

"Before we catch up," Stanley requested with a burp, "I think I need to take a minute to throw up."

Less than two kilometres away, Wendy and Peter had finished helping Nana with precisely the same problem. Dogs have notoriously weak stomachs, and the shortcut was just too much for the poor girl — eyes closed or not. John, on the other hand, was positively floored by the swirling cave. Peter hadn't found the shortcut until after their first adventure, so there was no way John could have prepared for it.

"How much further?" John asked.

"Not much longer now," Peter replied.

"Really?" John was surprised. Wendy had said the shortcut made the flight quicker, but he didn't exactly believe it. As he started regaining his memory, flashbacks of the days turning into weeks — and months — flowed back into his mind, so this was a pleasant surprise.

To pass the time, they played a guessing game until Peter guided them up to the familiar cloud. They could tell Neverland was near when they breached the cloud line. The altitude got much kinder the closer they got to Neverland.

"They're going up," Stanley called, watching his tracker.

"Good," Father Christmas replied. "We're getting close."

He pulled up on the reins, guiding the reindeer up above the clouds once more. He wasn't about to lose them.

The first thing they noticed was how much calmer things seemed there.

"I think you can take those off now," Father Christmas informed, gesturing to the elves' headgear.

Tweedle went first and was surprised by how clear the air was: he could breathe perfectly, he didn't get light-headed, and his ears didn't even pop. "Whoa!"

Stanley cautiously went next, and when he took his off, he noticed that even the air smelled sweeter, like fresh-baked biscuits.

"Uh-oh," Tweedle mumbled. "The signal is starting to act funny."

"Then we have no time," Father Christmas declared, whipping at the reins and commanding the reindeer to speed up. "We're about to break through."

They gained on the Darlings, and Father Christmas was able to see the children dive right as their signal went dead. He brought the reindeer to a halt, hovering still in the air, when he saw something remarkable. Every strand of light permeating from the sun's rays had formed millions of golden arrows, pointing out the island through a thin cloud. He noticed the light flicker, only for a moment, as if the sun itself was giving him a sly wink.

The small band stared in awe.

"I think we've found it," Father Christmas declared.

"Do you think we can find it again?" Tweedle asked.

"I think so," Stanley decreed, studying their findings.

"You'll never find Neverland with that," Father Christmas said with a shake of his head. "Oh, you may get lucky half the time, but this is a place that has to look for you; otherwise, you may miss it." The old man gave a gentle smile, knowing how much they weren't going to like his next decision. "Which is why we have to go down and let it get to know us a bit before we can leave."

"You can't be serious." Stanley whimpered, thinking of Holly.

"You mean, down there with all of the beasts and pirates and witches and lord knows what else?" Tweedle added, feeling his bones tremble beneath his skin.

"Yes," Father Christmas replied. "Down there with the fairies, mermaids and a group of orphans who have never even seen a toy."

Father Christmas was a master of filling the elves with guilt, especially when it came to children. The elves relented with frustrated shrugs.

"All right," Tweedle sighed.

"Let's just get this over with," Stanley agreed.

"I love your Christmas Spirit," the Boss quipped sarcastically. "Now, hold on tight. It may be a bumpy ride."

He called to his reindeer, and they burst into action. Stanley took a breath, and by the time he could exhale, he found himself in Neverland.

CHAPTER NINE
A Rude Welcome

There it was! Neverland! Every valley, every glen, every stream, every peak, every cove, every beach, every forest and every creek. There they sat, covered in a shimmering frost.

It was a marvellous sight to behold, though Neverland wasn't exactly how John had remembered it. Things have a way of appearing different when you revisit your childhood. The dimensions shrink for a start, and sometimes colours don't seem to be as bright or radiant. But unlike most memories, the wonder and enchantment of Neverland grew richer and even more extraordinary with age.

As they soared across, they saw Neverland glitter with sheets of fallen snow. The fairies flitted about decorating the forest, filling the land with their festive glow. Holly, poinsettias, and firs sprouted up in anticipation. The whole island looked like an enchanted winter palace, as warm and inviting as a freshly shook snow globe.

Joy filled the air in a way that it never had before. A warm, overpowering reverence had overtaken the land. Even the wind seemed to rustle by with a soothing, melodious whisper, singing to them. It beckoned them to *come*, to *stay*, to *play* forever.

Even Father Christmas and his awestruck elves could hear and feel Neverland's warm embrace. They could tell that it was a place brimming with a life and a will of its own. And though it chose to be inviting and serene, Father Christmas could still sense its darker edges.

The inhabitants pranced along with a newfound joy, love, and humour, though many of them — take the mermaids, for example — were confused by generosity in general. It was also fascinating to watch the mermaids struggle with trying to manoeuvre around the half-frozen lagoon. Neverland was typically a warm climate, and the lagoon had never frozen over — even in winter.

John watched as the mermaids played and groomed themselves in good cheer and grace, despite slipping and sliding and flapping on the ice.

The natives broke bread with their enemies. Ferocious, man-eating bears snuggled up with their cubs, lost in hibernation's sweet slumber. Wendy could see her wolf, whose paw had completely healed, play with her pups.

John almost cried, seeing all those old memories he had nearly forgotten. They flew past the tree which held their Home Underground. Peter had long since moved up in the trees, in the land of the pixies, and John was anxious to see it.

They continued to soar over the Piccaninny's land. The wigwams looked like Christmas lawn ornaments in the snow. The natives watched, bewildered by the fairies decorating their homes and the land with colourful trinkets and baubles.

And finally, deep into the mountainous thicket, hidden by a mist, they came to the Valley of the Fairies. The treetops were full of fairy nests, and the valley glittered with fairy dust. The fairies danced and played and zigzagged along the frozen waterfalls surrounding them — and some of the more youthful sprites sledded down the waterfalls and across the frozen streams below. Other pixies were ice-skating.

Wendy and Michael were puzzled. Even though fairies were typically white, mauve, or the occasional blue, their fairy-light all glowed the same firefly-like tint; but today, they shined in many vibrant colours. There were blues, greens, reds and yellows. They danced about in a beguiling, almost hypnotic display of elegance and colour — leaving behind trailers of multi-coloured pixie dust sparkling in the breeze.

They asked Peter about it, who glibly replied: "Fairies always change the colour of their fairy-light at Christmas." Of course, it didn't occur to him that they had never celebrated a Christmas before, but Wendy knew not to press.

Nana had been too petrified to open her eyes at their current elevation, but with a myriad of new sounds and smells, she took a peek in spite of herself. For the moment, she was far too stunned and wonder-struck to be frightened. It was far more beautiful and unbelievable than anything she could have ever dreamt.

Of course, her bedazzled daze ended abruptly when she saw where the Boy intended them to stay.

Deep into the heart of fairy country, out in the centre of the frozen waterfall enclosure, was what appeared to be a primitive tree-house village. Never-trees towered up as tall as redwoods and held tiny wooden homes on their highest branches. There were simple yet sturdy railings and walkways that encircled the tree, connecting the inhabited branches. Each Lost Boy had his own tree and fashioned interconnecting zip-lines and swingable vines providing access to each other's quarters.

It hardly seemed safe to the practical Newfoundland dog. However, with roving beasts and enemies at every turn, it was an impenetrably safe home indeed. It was well hidden, guarded by fairy magic, and impossible to reach without the gift of flight. And none was safer than the Wendy House.

It looked just the way John had remembered, right down to his old top hat standing in as the chimney. It was nestled on the branch of the fairies' most sacred tree. Its seed was forged from the magic of the first baby's laugh that caused the beginning of fairies. It floated high in the sky, standing as a beacon, reminding us how much power a single child's laughter can have on the world.

It had grown massive with age and proved to be the birthing grounds for countless generations of pixies throughout the ages. Thousands of fairies are born every year — mainly in the Spring — and Wendy always enjoyed playing with the fairy children whenever she stayed over. She had never seen her house in the winter before and thought it looked lovely.

The tree floated thirty metres in the air, hovering over the iced-over water below. The tree received nourishment even though it wasn't connected to its roots — which were buried deep in the earth somewhere. Wendy saw the waterfalls that surrounded it had formed intricate ice sculptures, making her feel like a delicate princess in a crystal palace. And flying by her side was her prince.

Little did they know, they were being watched — and not just by Father Christmas.

"Well, how 'bout that?" Hook muttered to himself atop Never-Peak. He adjusted his most powerful telescope, baffled by the addition of a flying canine. "So that's where Peter and those dirty Lost Boys have been hiding."

It was a magnificent sight, but it made him wonder why he had never seen it before. Hook had scoured the grounds of Neverland with his telescope countless times but had never caught so much as a glimpse of their Home in the Trees. Fortune was smiling on him, he supposed. Whatever it was he was planning to do, Neverland had just given him its blessing.

He hadn't been to *The Watch* in years and decided to take inventory. There wasn't much booty. It served mostly as an arsenal: swords, gunpowder, rifles, pistols, and traps of every shape and size. He even came across his other Long Tom. It was the biggest, most destructive cannon he had ever owned. He had stolen it from a Spanish

Command Ship known as *Martillo de Dios*, which roughly translates to *God's Hammer*.

Now Hook had four other secret outposts, with four other cannons, on the North, South, East, and West coasts — in case the island was ever discovered. But he stowed *The Hammer* in the highest peak, in the centre of the island. He put it on a pivot, knowing full well that it was powerful enough to devastate ships in all directions. After a while, it was clear that the island would never be discovered, so eventually, he forgot about it.

He liked being reacquainted with his destructive old friend. He mused to himself about giving himself a present for Christmas. He'd find out where Peter slept, and on the night of Christmas Eve, he'd aim *The Hammer* at Peter's house and send him back to Tinker Bell.

He chuckled at the thought, then noticed something odd. He stopped and re-positioned the telescope up, even higher in the sky. "What the devil?"

When his eyes beheld it, he could hardly believe what they saw. It was the most ludicrous sight he had ever seen. It appeared he was not the only person watching Peter and the others at that moment. There was a little red sleigh being pulled by — he quickly counted — eight deer-like creatures who could fly. And in the sleigh were two small men with pointed ears, who assisted a rotund, elderly gentleman in a red fur coat with white trim.

My word, Hook pondered, *could that possibly be Peter's new adversary?*

Hook was a child at the end of the 17th century, so his memory of Father Christmas was entirely different from the man in his telescope. His Father Christmas wasn't fat, he didn't wear red, he didn't have white hair, and he didn't have any reindeer. So, he had no way of knowing what he was looking at.

In the end, Hook didn't care much about this stranger's identity. As he peered up at these strange men, he only had one thing on his mind.

"They have a flying sleigh!" Hook exclaimed.

Perhaps he had just found his means off of the island. But he needed to know more. He desperately wished he could make out what they were saying but supposed it didn't matter. Hook continued to study the craft while keeping a careful eye on Peter and his crew.

"Well, isn't that a sight?" Father Christmas gasped with a childlike twinkle in his eyes. "I've never seen a fairy before."

Neither had the speechless elves, and yet there were thousands of them frolicking in the snow-covered valley. Legend has it, elves and fairies were formed from the same first baby's laugh but developed differently over time. The elves had no records of fairies' existence, so fairies were merely dismissed as fantasy — perhaps some exaggerated depiction of some extinct insect. Tweedle watched with a reverent humility, and Stanley wished he could share this romantic sight with Holly.

Father Christmas desperately wished to pop down and say hullo, but it was very much against the rules. He mulled it over — this was, after all, not a normal circumstance. Ultimately, he decided to stick with protocol and avoid interaction — but that didn't stop him from taking a closer look.

He brought the sleigh lower and explored the terrain. When he felt reasonably satisfied, he decided he wanted to get a good look at the children in question. Father Christmas was a master of stealth. His ability to be right next to his targets without being detected would have astounded a Ninja Master.

The new Lost Boys had gathered around Wendy's tree, excited to greet their captain and seasonal mother once more. John ingratiated himself with Pan's new crew while Nana struggled to keep from having convulsions, brought on by the overwhelming nature of the last couple of days — and the overly enthusiastic attention given to her by six orphans who had never seen a dog before. Her etiquette struggled to suppress her urge to bite.

Father Christmas gave a sympathetic chuckle and noted to bring the sweet old Newfoundland Dog something special for Christmas this year. He liked the faces of the boys in front of him. They were so innocent and energetic. It saddened him to know that what they needed most, he couldn't give them. He would love to answer the Christmas Wish of every orphan in the world and bring them a family. But direct interaction with mortals was strictly forbidden, and some things were simply out of his control.

These boys, however, didn't even know to want a family. They were a tight-knit band who merely sought to have fun. It would be quite some time before they would realise a family's worth. They may have been stubborn children, a tad rambunctious even, but they certainly weren't bad children. And he was determined to give them a Christmas they would never forget.

As Father Christmas watched Peter, he realised Peter would require further observation before he could adequately assess his character. He seemed good, but there were an awful lot of naughty traits in there.

Of course, Father Christmas adored Wendy. He loved watching her with the boys. Her maternal instincts were impeccable. If one of the boys had a boo-boo, she'd clean it, wrap it, and kiss it better. Right now, she was telling them all about Christmas. After going through it with Peter, she had mastered the art of filling the boys with knowledge and excitement. Their little heads lit up in anticipation. They couldn't wait for all of the fun things they were going to do, but nothing had touched their imaginations quite like Father Christmas himself.

They began to get nervous when she mentioned the Naughty-&-Nice List. They all could think of things they'd done that could be construed as naughty.

"I didn't know we're supposed to be good *all* the time," Patches whimpered.

"Me either," Jojo added.

"No one said there'd be toys," Pipkin chimed in.

"Well," Wendy said with such a devilishly sombre tone, she had to fight to keep a straight face, "you better start behaving because Father Christmas is always watching."

Little did she realise how true that statement was.

"But what about all the bad stuff we've done?" Dribbles asked.

"Yeah?" asked Surely, who told his share of tall tales.

"Well, I'm sure Father Christmas can forgive all that," Wendy replied. "If you promise to be good from now on."

The boys all cried out with an emphatic: "Yes! Yes! Yes!"

"But first," she declared, halting the eager boys, "you need to tidy up and decorate the Tree Houses."

The boys sprang into action.

Father Christmas laughed once more. When they were done, Peter requested Wendy to re-read *A Visit from Saint Nicholas* for the Lost Boys.

Father Christmas rather liked that poem. It captivated the imagination in a way that other stories didn't. Oh sure, he loved Charles Dickens' subtle nod with the Ghost of Christmas Present. In many ways, it was the most accurate depiction of him at that point in time. But Father Christmas' strength and role in the holiday grew over time, with each generation adding to his story and spreading his legend across the globe.

The poem captured the children's hearts and gave him strength. It had given him a more pleasant, somewhat comical appearance. He didn't much care for that "*belly, like a bowl full of jelly*" bit, but having an appearance that brings joy to children was good for his heart. He rather liked the addition of reindeer as well. He was due for a global unification. It was awfully tiring to manifest himself in hundreds of different forms every year in order to become what each culture expected of him.

He was going to miss some depictions, but he knew he needed to get used to it. Over the next thirty years or so, the Americans were going to change Christmas forever, and soon, the fat man in red was going to take a much more significant role in the world.

Father Christmas simply smiled and watched, astonished by Wendy's amorous nature. He also admired her imagination and all of the festive activities she had created for the boys.

He wasn't the only person admiring Wendy.

As Hook gazed through his telescope, he couldn't help but notice how much older and mature Wendy had gotten.

She was no longer a girl . . . she was a woman!

A beautiful woman whose face lit up when she smiled — the kind of woman Jas could see himself settling down with. She had refused to be his mother four years ago; perhaps he would have better luck taking her as a wife.

He learned early on in his life that if you wanted something, you had to take it!

He thought about what a wonderful mother she would make for his future children. And any child of Captain James Hook was entitled to the best. With her good looks and charm, and his excellent form and fortune, Little Jas could rule the world. He suspected he would make a wonderful father — as loving and doting as his dear old aunt.

Yes! That's what he'd do. He'd shanghai Wendy and whisk her away when he took his leave of Neverland.

He knew she'd fight him at first, but she'd learn to love him in time. But first, he needed that sleigh.

He was satisfied with his plan until he noticed something happening. Something that would ruin all his schemes in a matter of minutes. That little fat man appeared to be leaving.

"Well," declared Father Christmas, "I think we've learned enough."

This was great news for Stanley, who felt that he desperately needed to mend his rift with Miss Bellringer.

As the reindeer started to turn around and slowly rise into the sky, a sea of panic flooded through the captain.

"This can't be!" Hook shrieked. "I thought I had more time." He slammed his fist down in frustration. It landed on the smooth cast-iron shaft of *The Hammer*, and he grinned with one last hope.

The Hammer was a behemoth of a gun, and Hook was afraid of obliterating the sleigh and the deer, but he had no choice. He found a cannonball in the arsenal for his smallest cannon and wrapped it repeatedly in a thick cloth.

Though the sleigh had gotten farther and farther away, he still took his time to position his shot . . . he only had one chance!

He found his angle and held the flame inches away from *The Hammer*. He watched through the telescope and counted down according to his calculations. He could see one of the elves turn to the man in red.

"Are you sure the land has gotten to know us enough yet?" Tweedle asked. "You did say Neverland needed to know you to find it."

Father Christmas thought about it and replied: "If Neverland hasn't cleared us yet, it'll let us know in its own subtle way."

With those words, the sky rang out with a deafening *roar!* Neverland itself seemed to rumble, and within seconds, Father Christmas and his elves were thrown out of the ruptured sleigh.

"Gotcha!" Hook hissed.

Stanley, Tweedle, and Father Christmas plummeted through the air, ripping holes through clouds, hurtling faster and faster to the earth.

Peter, the fairies, the natives, the mermaids, and every other inhabitant on the island turned in shock and alarm — unable to make out the strange figures falling from the sky.

The elves *shrieked,* knowing they were about to be splattered over the earth below. The reindeer tangled up and crashed, trying to flee in all directions. The deer appeared to be all right. The figures, on the other hand, were far less graceful on their descent.

All in all, Hook was rather pleased with himself.

CHAPTER TEN

Cannibal Cove

He woke up in a daze. He didn't know where he was, and the events which had led him there were something of a blur. The only things he was aware of — aside from the throbbing pain in his skull — were the pounding of the drums and the acrid scent of death.

As Father Christmas' mind cleared, he became painfully aware his hands and feet were bound to a large wooden slab. His body ached, his mind was fogged, and, for the first time in centuries, he was afraid. He always had a certain omniscience and not knowing what this place had in store for him was nerve-racking.

Slowly, he began to remember his expedition to a strange new world. He was checking in on some orphans and was about to leave when he remembered hearing a loud *CRASH!*

Did I get struck by lightning? Father Christmas wondered.

He didn't think so. Lightning and Father Christmas had an understanding. Next, he remembered falling, then nothing.

He was not alone. He could feel a group of strange eyes leering at him from the darkness. He decided to leave his eyes shut, not wanting whatever was watching him to realise he was awake. He managed a subtle peek, hoping to find some sign of his poor little elves, but there was no trace of them.

Just a heap of rotting skulls and a boiling cauldron.

He prayed that the boys were all right. He hoped they landed somewhere safe and far, far away from that awful-smelling place.

His heart pounded in his chest as the violent beating of the drums grew louder and faster. The voices of his faceless captors grunted and exhaled in time with the drums as if summoning some pagan god of death to feed. Overhead, the birds scattered, fleeing in all directions, sensing the impending danger.

He tried to free himself with magic, but surviving the fall weakened him and took too much of his strength.

He could smell the fire growing in the distance as the chanting increased. Time was running out, and he prayed his powers would return before it was too late.

Behind him, a pair of natives communicated in a bizarre series of grunts, clicks and words. He tuned his ear, trying to determine if he could recognise the language — after all, Father Christmas was the foremost linguist who had ever lived. He spoke a ready wit in every tongue known to man; however, this particular dialect was still foreign to him. He tried going through various aboriginal tribes from around the world, and some of their words were similar but made no sense when put together.

Father Christmas would have loved to tinker around with it until he finally cracked the language barrier on his own, but he could tell he didn't have long — not that he thought negotiations would help. So, he closed his eyes, hoping he had enough strength to communicate.

He concentrated for a moment. Magic requires a great deal of inner strength and patience. After a moment, he was able to make something out — a word here, a fragmented sentence there — and finally, the foreign words began to unscramble themselves in his mind. He understood everything perfectly and, once again, began to worry about the safety of his elves.

Meanwhile, somewhere far away, a reasonably rattled Tweedle was worrying the same thing about his Boss. Over near the edge of the snowbank, a near-catatonic Stanley was curled up and rocking gently. He was only vaguely aware of what had transpired — and even less aware of the fact he had soiled himself during the fall.

He had the faintest recollection of being struck by a powerful force and then the sensation of the wind on his face as he hurtled faster and faster toward the earth. He lost sight of the big guy early on, but Tweedle was screaming nearby. And as the ground raced up to meet them, he saw Tweedle spontaneously shoot back up into the sky. Stanley wanted to glance up, but his focus was on the large boulder jutting out of the snow directly below him. Right at the moment of impact, he closed his eyes and felt a pair of hands grip his shoulders and yank him upward. The last thing he remembered before blacking out was the sensation of being jostled and the way his foot lightly grazed against the rough, cold stone surface below.

Tweedle talked to one of the boys they had been observing earlier. Evidently, they had seen them fall and managed to fly out and rescue them in time. Peter saved Tweedle, and Stanley was rescued by the tall one with glasses, whom they all referred to as John. They explained how they were able to find and save them when Wendy and the others finally caught up to see what happened.

The elves were unbelievably lucky that Peter and John got to them in time, considering how far away they were. To be honest, Peter only went after them in the first place because he thought Stanley and Tweedle were children. Perhaps some new Lost Boys had gotten into some serious trouble.

It was Wendy who had spotted them. She cried at Peter to save the children, but now, after closer inspection, it was clear that these two were grown-ups.

They had wise, highly intelligent eyes, pointy ears, and an unusual shimmer about their skin. They wore funny clothes and pointy hats. Sure, they were the size of children, but they definitely weren't children. Wendy thought it was fortunate they thought they were kids; otherwise, Peter wouldn't have bothered trying to rescue them.

"Pleased to meet you," Wendy greeted. "I'm Wendy, this is Peter, and these are my brothers, John and Michael."

"Pleased to meet you," Stanley replied with a wave. "I'm Stanley, and this is my friend Tweedle."

Nana approached them cautiously, looking them over and sniffing them discreetly. They had a funny smell, unlike anything she had ever smelled before, and she liked it! She circled them, sniffing more intrusively.

"Hey, be a good girl," Stanley said, patting her head and trying to guide her nose away from his nether regions. "Careful where you're sticking that thing."

Then Nana did something the elves didn't expect. She backed up and *yowled* an apology. She didn't behave like a dog very often, but she always got embarrassed whenever she caught herself acting like one. It was just their scent. Dogs can tell a lot about somcone, or something, by smelling them — and certain unfortunate areas of the body tell more. She didn't mean to be impertinent, but her curiosity and the overwhelming attraction to their scent overcame her. Mostly, she wanted to know what they were, and Wendy understood that perfectly.

Wendy stood there silently, trying to find a polite way of asking what was on everyone's minds. She decided the direct approach was the best.

"I hope you don't mind me asking," Wendy started, "but what are you, exactly?"

"Elves," Tweedle replied, understanding the question perfectly.

"Elves?" the group repeated in pure fascination. They had never seen an elf before — elves weren't known to exist on the island. This was a monumental discovery.

"I didn't know there were elves living on the island," Wendy stated.

"We don't," Tweedle replied. "We're sort of visiting."

"Visiting?" John repeated.

"Look, that's not important right now," Tweedle said. "Did anyone see what happened to our Boss?"

The group looked around.

"The large man that was falling with you?" Peter asked.

"Yes!" Stanley said. "Did anybody happen to rescue him?"

"I'm afraid not," Peter replied. He was the only one to spot him, but it was very brief. "He plummeted near the coves."

"Did you happen to see where he landed?" Stanley pleaded.

"Yes, but it hardly matters," Peter replied. "Nothing could have survived a fall like that."

"Our Boss could," Tweedle disagreed.

"Even if he did survive the fall," Peter said, pointing to the west, "he fell into Cannibal Cove. Nobody lasts long there."

"Cannibal Cove?" Tweedle gasped. He didn't like the sound of it.

"Yes," Peter answered. "The most wretched and dangerous hole on the island. He'll be roasted alive and have his flesh peeled off the bone before becoming the main course at one of their barbaric banquets."

They glanced over to the thickets, seeing the heavy clouds of smoke rising in the distance. Suddenly, they began to hear the thunderous roar of drums.

"What is it?" Stanley asked.

"Sounds like they're preparing a sacrifice," Peter declared.

"*A sacrifice?!*" the elves cried.

"He's as good as dead," Peter stated.

"They can't eat the Boss!" Stanley stood up and exclaimed. "You have to help him."

"There's no point," Jojo explained. "It's too dangerous, and even if he's not dead, he'll be dead before we could get there."

"And even if we could," Peter inserted, "it's too dangerous to risk for a grown-up."

"He's no ordinary grown-up!" Tweedle retorted.

"There's over sixty of them," Pipkin elaborated. "Armed with spears and poison-tipped darts. And if they have their way, they would slaughter all of us, boil our bones, and wear our ears around their necks on a chain."

Wendy stood up, pondering the peculiarity of having two elves being blown out of the sky, when she and Nana heard a noise. They followed it, wandering deeper into the woods. They heard it again, the *rustling* of branches, the *cracking* of limbs, and something else.

Nana crouched low to the ground in an aggressive, predatorial fashion — ready to do what was necessary to protect her charges. She let out a low, uncertain growl. Then they heard the noise again, and Nana *barked*. Suddenly, Wendy understood what the other sound was; it was the *tinkling* of bells. Nana barked at a tree, and when she glanced up, she discovered the reindeer tangled up in the branches.

"Peter!" Wendy gasped with a sudden realisation. "They're going to eat Father Christmas!"

CHAPTER ELEVEN
A Special Stew

The drums raged on, growing louder . . . and faster! The time to feast was at hand!

The chief stood outside of his tent, peering across the icy terrain. It was bitterly cold, which spelt disaster for his people. The unseasonable winter had killed the crops, and that could mean only one thing . . . the gods were angry! The snow came with the arrival of the flying red sleigh. They all heard the rumbling in the heavens as the gods smote the sleigh, casting the creature in red to the earth.

They prepared the sacrificial altar, increased the fire and beckoned to their gods with the pounding of the drums. The ritual was about to begin! They would sacrifice the creature to appease their gods. They would cast its head into the fire as a burnt offering and consume the rest. With any luck, the famine would end, and the snow would stop while the intruders' flesh digested in their bellies.

Time was running out, and Father Christmas knew it. He began to tremble, hearing the horrid things the natives were planning. He had never seen anything quite like the cannibals before. Their peculiar pigment gave their skin a slippery, faded, teal colour. They had squat, broad, muscular frames with long, greasy black hair. The bone piercings and filed-down teeth gave them a goblin-like quality, but these weren't monsters . . . they were people!

"Let's cut out his heart and roast it on the fire," one of the cannibals cried.

"Skin him and sear his meat on a spit!" another added.

"Gouge out his eyes and boil them in a soup with his bones," another suggested.

The more he heard the cannibals' grisly suggestions, the harder it got to hear over the beating of his heart.

"Kill him now," the tall, robust native with a bone through his eyebrow suggested to the squat cook. "I have a headache and no patience for screams."

"Don't be ridiculous," the cook scoffed. "The greater the pain, the greater the flavour. Just consider the screams a blessing."

He was a master. He could keep a victim alive, extracting cut after agonising cut for hours before allowing his prey to finally succumb.

"Could we at least cut his tongue out first?" the tall one asked.

The cook got a wicked smile on his face. "Well . . . I do likes to eat it raw."

The cook licked his lips and approached Father Christmas with a sharp, rusty cleaver. Father Christmas shuddered. He needed to do something . . . something fast!

"Excuse me," Father Christmas called, startling the islander who approached him with the jagged knife. The cannibals were surprised to hear their native tongue spoken by an outsider. "But somehow, I don't think goat's stomach is a good blend for the stew."

The cannibals were stricken in their confusion.

"Personally," Father Christmas continued, "I think vegetables would be more appropriate. Asparagus, perhaps, would be much better suited to Fat-Man stew."

The group looked around and muttered amongst each other, exchanging sentiments of surprise over the oddly cooperative main course.

"Vegetables?" the cook started with an exploratory step forward.

"Yes," Father Christmas insisted. "Chopped carrots, onions, potatoes; essentially anything would be better to bring out the true essence of . . . well . . . me."

The cannibals just stood there blinking in a dumbfounded daze.

"Uhh," the tall one interjected, "you mean . . . you actually *want* to be eaten?"

"Not if you're going to spoil my meat with goat guts or any other sort of slop you're planning on putting in it."

"What?"

"Well, I suppose nobody really wants to be eaten when you get right down to it." Father Christmas elaborated. "However, being that I don't exactly have a say in the matter, I suppose the least I can do is try to be the best repast possible."

"Huh?"

"Think about it," Father Christmas added. "Who wants to die just to have the people that ate them say: 'He was all right, but I've had better?' " He squinted his nose distastefully. "So, I'd prefer it if you don't spoil me by boiling me in a pot, thank you very much."

Just then, the chief barged over, demanding to know what the hold-up was, when he discovered — much to his surprise — the creature in red was not only still alive, he was talking to the preparers in a very cordial manner.

"What's all this?!" the chief confounded. "Why haven't you started?"

"It doesn't want to be boiled," the cook stammered.

"Of course not!" the chief bellowed. "Nothing wants to be boiled alive!"

"It's not that!" Father Christmas chided. "Boiling is just a waste of perfectly good meat."

The chief was at a loss for words and turned to the cook. "What does that mean?"

"It thinks it could taste better," the cook replied.

The chief was beside himself. "It thinks it could taste better?"

"That's what it said."

"And what's wrong boiling?" the chief sneered.

"You don't boil fine cuts of meat," Father Christmas admonished. "The flavour drains out of it, and all you're left with is soggy, flavourless meat. I refuse to be used merely for broth. Choose something else."

This utterly perplexed the cannibals. They stood around, scratching their heads and contemplating their supper's suggestion — not wholly understanding his cooperation, let alone its sense of confectionery pride.

"Well," the squat cook implored, "what do you suggest?"

Father Christmas gave them many ghastly suggestions — each more tantalising than the last. He could feel the magic start to flow in his veins again, but it still wasn't quite enough yet. All he could do was continue to buy time until it could fully return.

He told them about revolutionary cooking supplies and techniques and exotic seasonings from lands they couldn't possibly fathom. The cannibals hung on Father Christmas' every word. Their eyes widened like children opening their gifts on Christmas morning. Their tummies rumbled, and they began to salivate.

And like that . . . it began to happen!

Father Christmas could feel it!

"This is all very interesting," the cook snorted, suddenly getting irritated with being teased by things they couldn't possibly obtain. He took a step closer and leaned in face to face with Father Christmas. He stood, staring eye to eye — their noses were touching. Father Christmas could smell the acrid musk of his breath and body odour.

The cook raised his large, rusty, self-made blade, touching the tip to Father Christmas' throat. "But where are we supposed to get any of that?"

Father Christmas just laughed and looked up at the cannibalistic cook. There was a spritely glint in his eye. "In my bag."

The cannibals all turned toward the limp, empty sack that hung from the wooden post.

"The what?!" the cook grunted.

"My sack."

The cook and the chief turned and pointed at it in disbelief.

"Yep. That's the one." Father Christmas nodded with a self-satisfied smile.

Rage filled the cannibal's eyes. The cook turned, storming to the sack, yanking it down.

"*This sack is empty!!*" he bellowed, throwing it to the ground and stomping on it.

"It most certainly is not," Father Christmas retorted.

This angered the cook further!

"Look inside," Father Christmas insisted.

The tribe looked at each other sheepishly. The bag was clearly empty, but the intruder's certainty confused them.

"You want me to look inside an empty sack?" the cook muttered.

"Not you," Father Christmas clarified. "Him."

He pointed to a small boy crouching behind a boulder. The chief was angry because he realised the prying child was his son.

"The boy?" the chief asked.

"Yes."

"That boy is my son."

"He'll be perfectly safe. Trust me."

The chief mulled it over for a long while, but curiosity ultimately bested his judgment.

"All right," the chief declared. "But if you're wrong . . ."

"If I'm wrong, what?" Father Christmas smirked. "What are you going to do? Decide not to eat and kill me?"

The cook shook his head disdainfully. Cautiously, the chief called to his son. The boy trembled, inspecting the sack, but there didn't appear to be anything sinister or out of the ordinary about it — just empty fabric lying on the ground.

The boy didn't see anything wrong with it and reached his hand into the sack. At first, it seemed like there was nothing, then suddenly . . . he felt something! The tribe watched the boy's wonder-struck face as he dragged out an unbelievably large grill!

"There's no way that was there before!" the cook gasped, looking at the empty bag lying on the ground.

"There's more," Father Christmas added.

This boggled the boy, who glanced down at the completely deflated sack. To everyone's amazement, he reached back in and withdrew fruits, vegetables, and jars of spices and preserves — it was a culinary cavalcade!

"It's witchcraft!" a cannibal cried.

The group stepped back, muttering amongst themselves in fear.

"How does it work?" the chief implored.

Father Christmas smiled. "It's what I do. Back home, we build and collect all the things that people desire.

That bag allows me to access my entire inventory instantly, so I can give good girls and boys everywhere anything they want — within reason, of course."

"Anything?" the cannibals gasped.

"If they're good."

"What do you mean . . . *if* they're good?"

Father Christmas called to one of the more youthful cannibals. "Come here, little girl."

The girl looked up at her mother, who clutched her daughter in a tight, protective grip. They glanced at the chief, who nodded and barked at the mother to let the child go to the stranger.

Nervously, the little girl with a bone in her nose went over to greet Father Christmas.

"Hullo there," Father Christmas addressed. "My, you're such a big girl. What's your name?"

She glanced insecurely at her mother; however, she found herself drawn to this odd stranger in red for some reason. A warmth overcame her, and she felt happy. She liked this jolly old man, and for some reason, she felt safe.

Finally, she replied: "G'takz."

"Well, that's a lovely name," the outsider said. "They call me Father Christmas. Have you been a good girl?"

She was confused. What did this creature mean by a good girl? She shook her head, expressing her complete lack of comprehension.

"Do you listen to your mom and dad and help them when they ask? Are you nice to your brothers and the other children?"

"I guess," she replied.

"Well, I suppose that would qualify as being good," Father Christmas said with a smile. "Do you know what a toy is?"

The little girl shook her head. The word was unknown to her.

"That's all right," Father Christmas chuckled. "I think I have something in there you'll enjoy just fine."

The little girl stared at the sack. She was excited but was more than a little leery about sticking her hand inside. What if she reached in and something sinister grabbed her arm and wouldn't let go?

She looked up at the doting old man and smiled because she trusted him. She couldn't explain why; she just did. So, she reached her hand in and quickly discovered an object. It had a strange smooth texture unlike anything she had ever felt before, and connected to it was something that felt like hair. Slowly, she pulled out the most beautiful doll she had ever seen. As a matter of fact, it was the only doll she had ever seen.

There were very few playthings for the children of the tribe, but what they did have was either made out of wood, bone, hollowed-out gourds, or potato-like wads of fabric. They didn't even resemble anything. There were no details or mobility to their trinkets, but this doll looked like a little girl with beautiful hair and eyes. It had moveable and poseable joints made out of something called plastic.

Joy filled the child's face and warmed Father Christmas' heart. He loved making people happy, even if they were trying to cut him up and eat him.

"You mean, I can just make whatever I want appear?" the chief implored.

"No," Father Christmas said. "Only things that have already been made, either physically or magically, by me and my elves. But only I have unlimited access to it."

Technically, children on his Nice List have some access, but Father Christmas wasn't about to divulge this fact to his captors.

The chief stood there pondering. Witnessing such spectacular magic proved to be tempting for the chief. With the intruder alive, he had access to an untold wealth of treasure, and yet, this stranger *must* die to appease the gods.

"Would you mind," Father Christmas requested, "if I were to give out a few more gifts to the children of the tribe?"

The chief thought long and hard. He didn't think it would be a problem, but he didn't entirely trust it. The creature in red needed to die. But he noticed the youth gathering around, wide-eyed for their turn.

"All right, but this doesn't change anything," the chief declared. "You will still be sacrificed and be feasted upon by the members of my tribe."

"Fair enough," Father Christmas replied with a compliant nod.

The children came one by one. The creature with the magical sack wasn't half as scary as the villagers had made him out to be. He even seemed jolly and sweet. The wide-eyed innocents of the tribe gathered close to get a better look. Father Christmas would invite them closer, and the children would think: *Is there, perhaps, something in the sack for me?* Then one would come forward and be greeted.

"Hullo there, and what's your name?"

"Tzsha. Who are you?"

"I'm Father Christmas," he replied with his infectious laugh. "Tell me Tzsha, have you been a good girl?"

"Uh, I think so."

They'd have a short but very wonderful conversation about her life and interests, and then he'd have her reach into the sack and pull out something extraordinary that was always perfect for each child — even if the child didn't know they wanted it.

Finally, it came time for the elders to come forward to take their turn. The chief walked over. He didn't commence with social niceties. He just went straight to the sack and laughed. "Ha, I wonder what this magic has for me!"

The chief reached inside the bag, and his hand fumbled around frantically. "It's empty!"

"Not quite," Father Christmas stated blankly. "I believe you'll find a little something at the bottom. In one of the corners, perhaps."

He reached in again, thrashing his hand about wildly to find the bottom, and he *did* find something there. It was small and hard. He pulled out what appeared to be a black stone.

"A rock?!" the chief exclaimed.

"I believe you will find that it is a piece of coal."

The chief looked back at his people, then threw the bag to someone else, who reached in and fumbled around before coming up with another piece of coal.

The chief was angry and nodded for somebody else to give it a try, and . . . another coal! The chief stormed over and tore the sack out of the cannibal's hand, throwing it in front of Father Christmas.

"*What sorcery is this?!*" the chief demanded, holding up the piece of coal.

"It's what I do," Father Christmas replied. "I reward those who deserve it the most. The wicked people of the world always seem to thrive at the expense of others and have no regard for other people's lives. Sometimes we forget the rewards of virtue are more important than the rewards of power. I remind the virtuous that there is still love in the world and that goodness hasn't gone unnoticed. Or unappreciated."

"Then why a rock?"

"You were found naughty."

"Naughty?!"

"You hurt people," Father Christmas explained. "You do it for pleasure and power. You also eat them with no empathy. You view human lives as something to use and exploit."

"But the children."

"The children of the tribe are innocent. They don't know or understand any better." Father Christmas explained. "Also, they don't participate in these rituals until later. No. Right now, their hearts are sweet and pure;

but that will change. Soon their hearts will be as black and hard as that stone in your hand. Just like yours."

"I will use it to sear the flesh from your bones!" the chief snorted, drawing his axe.

He approached Father Christmas, and the children cried out in protest.

"Remove them and burn their toys!" the chief ordered, snatching a tin soldier out of a little boy's hands and casting it into the fire below the giant cauldron. "They have been bewitched by his magic!"

"But the magic sack!" another cannibal pleaded. "It won't work without him."

"He's trying to bewitch us and corrupt the minds of our children!" the chief yelled. He turned back to Father Christmas.

"Wait!" the stoutly cook shouted, running over. "He won't taste as good if he's dead before I cook him!"

"It doesn't matter!" the chief confounded. "He must die before he uses his magic to destroy us!"

The chief hoisted up his axe, preparing to bring it down . . . when he heard a loud *crow*!

The tribe looked back, and before the chief could make out anything, he was knocked off his feet with one powerful kick.

Peter Pan and his Lost Boys sprang into action! They were all armed for battle.

"Release the prisoner or pay the consequence!" Peter demanded.

Nana was watching from the woods. This did not seem like a safe thing for the children to be involved in.

"Kill the boy!" the chief ordered.

But the cannibals weren't prepared to fight — they had gathered to dine. As soon as they moved to engage with the interlopers, they realised they didn't have their weapons on them, and the Lost Boys attacked! The cook and the chief were ready, but not the rest of the tribe. The cannibals grabbed frying pans, ladles, femur-sized soup bones, and anything they could find to stave off the advancing foes.

Peter knew they'd be fine as long as they kept the cannibals away from their poison darts.

Peter *crowed* again, excited by the throng of battle!

Nana gasped, covering her eyes with her ears, seeing John and Michael enter the fray. She heard them exchange blow after blow with the Cannibal Killers of the tribe and knew she had to do something. The master and mistress would not have approved of any of this. She would never forgive herself if she let anything happen to her charges.

Peter, of course, fought the chief. The chief was a tall, burly man with a large scar across the left side of his face. He was the strongest warrior and charged at Peter with his powerful battle axe. Peter was fast, and his skill was defter, but when it came to brute strength, he was no match for the sheer force of the chief's deadly blows!

The chief swung! Peter tried to deflect it but was flung across the field — his sword flew out of his hands and embedded itself in the tree behind him.

The chief struck again! Peter ducked, somersaulting out of the way, and the axe cut through the dead tree in one swift slice. The tree toppled, landing on the cannibal Michael was fighting.

Peter flew to his sword! He tried to pry it free, but it was stuck!

The chief advanced on him!

Peter jumped backed away from the tree.

Meanwhile, Wendy had slipped through the field and went to Father Christmas, hoping to loosen his bonds. A cannibal saw her and licked his lips.

" '*Elo pretty!*'" he clicked in a language Wendy couldn't possibly comprehend. But she knew he meant her. She also knew he might have wanted more than just a meal out of her.

The cannibal drew a crude dagger and advanced!

Quickly, she grabbed a rock and pelted him in the head! Then she flew to him as fast as she could and drop-kicked him right in the goolies!

The cannibal *squealed*, dropping to his knees!

Wendy unsheathed the knife she had concealed in her petticoat and touched the blade to his throat, declaring: "Someone needs to teach you the proper way of addressing a lady."

John and Surely were tangling with the wily cook and his assistant. He may have been short and rotund, but he was fast, ferocious, and excellent with blades. The cook had a primitive carving knife in his left hand and a large butcher's knife in the right. He charged the boy, hacking left, right, left, right.

The cannibals drove John back — he scrambled to deflect blow after lethal blow. Then the fat cook turned, kicking John in the chest, and he dropped to the ground. John had dropped his sword!

The cook raised his blade for the fatal blow!

"You'll make an excellent pie!" the cook salivated.

As he swung the blade, he didn't hear Nana rushing toward him from the bushes. With one mighty leap, she was on him! Nothing was stronger or more ferocious than a large Newfoundland Dog defending her pups!

Peter did his best to fend off the chief while trying to re-obtain his sword, but the chief proved too fast and unwavering in his attacks!

Peter dodged out of the way as the axe *whizzed* inches above his head — it tore through the tree, chipping out a chunk of bark. The chief pursued, driving Peter to the beach and further and further away from his sword!

Wendy rushed to Father Christmas.

"I'm going to get you out of here," she whispered.

"Don't worry about me, Wendy," Father Christmas replied with a loving smile.

She froze, turning temporarily into a little child and hearing the angelic chimes of his voice. She couldn't believe it. She was talking to Father Christmas, and he knew her name!

"Get Peter a sword first," Father Christmas added. "Then come back."

She just stared at him, awestruck.

"It's okay." Father Christmas chuckled, then gave a sly wink. "There'll be plenty of time for questions later, but for now, go give them a hand."

The Lost Boys had the element of surprise; unfortunately, the element of surprise only lasts so long, and their momentary advantage was gone. The cannibals had collected themselves. After regrouping, they armed themselves for an organised assault!

Peter was cornered with his back against the bluff. He had been driven away from the woodland part of the cove and gazed up at the ice-covered cliffs towering overhead. To his right, he saw only the sea with its icy waves crashing against the edges of the inlet. He started to reposition himself, then slipped on the rocky surface of the terrain!

The chief closed in!

Peter tried to get to his feet but kept slipping on the wet, icy stones!

The chief hoisted his axe above his head.

"Peter!" Wendy cried

Peter looked, and suddenly, Wendy flung the sword to him! Peter rolled between the chief's legs and leapt, catching the sword's handle in midair.

The chief spun, swinging the axe right at Peter's face! Peter pivoted, whipping his blade around and deflecting the axe's deadly blow. But the force knocked Peter back to the ground!

The chief moved in for the kill, and—

WHAP!!

Wendy struck the chief in the back of the head with a wooden club she found!

Slowly, the chief turned around, startled and angry. He took a step toward Wendy.

Wendy stepped back nervously.

The chief slashed the axe, splitting the club she was holding in two.

Wendy held up the bottom half of the club bravely, preparing to defend herself.

He raised his axe to strike her down . . . then he stopped. As the chief stared at the young woman, he admired her. She was the most beautiful creature he had ever laid his eyes on, and she had the spirit of a warrior! He would kill the others, but the girl was his.

As the chief advanced on Wendy, Peter pounced! With one deft stroke, Peter cut off the chief's arm.

The chief screamed and elbowed the boy in the face, knocking him back down.

The Lost Boys had been driven back; they were surrounded and out-numbered. They called to their captain. Peter looked back, seeing the boys' imminent demise. He kicked the chief in the shin and swept his leg out from under him. Peter rolled to his feet, bringing the tip of his blade to the chief's throat.

"Call them off or prepare to die!" Peter threatened.

"Never!" the chief barked. He turned to his tribe. "Kill them all!!"

Peter snarled: "Prepare to die!"

Peter pulled the blade back to strike when . . .

"That's enough!" a strong voice bellowed. There was no anger or malice in the voice, but it still resonated enough power and authority to stop the world in its tracks. Peter, the chief, the Lost Boys and the tribe stopped, gazing upon the owner of the voice.

Father Christmas was no longer bound. He stood strong and amorous atop a boulder — the sun rays glittered down around him, radiating glory.

"Peter," Father Christmas continued, "put it away."

Peter glanced down at his blade touching the chief's bare throat. He didn't want to put it down.

"But . . ." Peter stammered.

"It's good form to be the better man." Father Christmas smiled. "Or the better *boy* as the case may be."

"But they have my boys," Peter argued, gesturing to the Lost Boys and Michael and John, who were all at the cannibal's mercy.

"He's going to let them go too," Father Christmas assured.

"I'll sooner die than let any of you go," the chief snarled.

"But that is what's going to happen, nevertheless," Father Christmas stated. "Put away your sword, Peter."

This felt horrible to Peter. The old man was either stupid or insane.

"No!"

"Trust me." Father Christmas winked.

Peter had just decided he didn't like Father Christmas very much at that moment; then Wendy placed her hand on his shoulder.

"Peter," Wendy whispered. "Please."

Reluctantly, he withdrew his sword and stepped back.

"Now, let them go," Father Christmas demanded.

"Fool!" the chief bellowed.

The chief kicked Peter, knocking the sword to the ground. He grabbed him by the throat, hoisting him in the air with one arm. He squeezed!

"Did you really think I would miss the opportunity to kill the great Peter Pan?" the chief sneered.

Peter coughed, losing the colour in his cheeks.

"Finish them!" the chief commanded. "We will add them to the stew."

The cannibals hoisted their weapons to strike when Father Christmas' sack suddenly began to twitch. The cannibals gave a distrustful gaze at the bag. Something was moving inside. One by one, toys began to walk out of the sack all on their own . . . and they looked mean!

Next, all the toys Father Christmas gave to the children of the tribe — the ones gathered in a pile to be burned — sprung to life. Dolls chimed "*Mamma*" in a sinister droll; toy soldiers marched to the sound of the self-playing drums; trains, animals, and all sorts of toys imaginable raged on! Not only that, the carved gourds and playthings of the tribe stood up and advanced on them too.

The cannibals were very superstitious and feared magic and evil spirits. They saw the toys and feared the evil spirits that must have been inhabiting them. Evil spirits, coming to devour their souls! The cannibals of the tribe trembled and backed away from the children.

"Get back here!" the chief demanded. "They're just playthings!"

"You've been a naughty boy," Father Christmas declared. "Let him go."

"Never!"

Just then, he heard a clattering. He looked to his left, and the pile of bones began to rumble, spilling to the earth. The bones started assembling themselves; human, beast, and fairy-creatures. Their skeletons stood, casting accusing glares from hollowed-out eye sockets!

"You've been naughty!" they cried in the natives' tongue.

The chief dropped Peter, who tumbled to the earth — he was on the verge of unconsciousness.

"Murderer!" the dead cried. "Cannibal!"

The chief just stood there, a petrified stump. The other cannibals ran!

"I would leave now, chief," Father Christmas advised. "While you still can."

The chief turned and glowered at the old man.

The bones *rattled*, getting closer!

The chief glared at his foes one last time, then turned and bolted!

The children stood victorious, watching their enemy flee in fear. But then took a step back, afraid and awed by the walking toys and skeletons.

"Sorry to scare you," Father Christmas chuckled. His smile could put anyone at ease. "Just a little parlour trick, not so different from marionettes. No need to be alarmed. There are no evil spirits, just a unique way of playing with toys."

Father Christmas looked at the toys. "Okay, playtime's over. Time to go back."

The toys nodded, yawned and made their way back inside the sack.

The bones of the dead looked on, unmoving.

"You too," Father Christmas chimed.

The bones rattled as they made their way back to their pile. They collapsed forevermore.

Wendy went to check on Peter, who was regaining the colour in his cheeks. She knelt down when she felt something tug at her dress. She looked back and beheld an adorable doll. The doll held up a flower to Wendy.

"Why thank you," Wendy said, accepting it.

The doll waved good-bye and ran to catch up with the other toys in the sack. They watched the mountainous bag deflate as the contents inside began to vanish. The mound receded until the bag lay empty on the ground once more.

Pipkin stared at the magic bag and the bone pile, then turned to Father Christmas. "How did you do that?"

"Christmas magic," Father Christmas replied, walking over to retrieve his sack.

Nana felt uneasy. She didn't know what it was, but her whole body tingled; she may have gotten on in years, but her innate sense of danger was stronger than ever. She listened for any strange noises in the woods.

The chief was crouching in the bushes, holding a blow-gun with his only hand. He started to aim for the creature in red when he saw his arm in the clearing. Finally, he turned the blow-dart to Peter. The shift caused him to snap a twig!

Nana *barked!*

Everyone looked but couldn't see anything!

It was too late! By the time they saw the chief, he had already blown the poison-tipped dart. It whizzed through the air!

Being the loyal and dutiful girl she was, Nana saw it and leapt in front of Peter Pan.

She *yelped*, taking it in the shoulder.

"Nana!" Wendy, Michael, and John screamed.

She struggled to stand, then collapsed. Wendy, John, and Michael ran to her. Wendy pulled out the dart, but it was too late. The poison was fast-acting and worked immediately. Nana attempted to stand once more; she looked at Wendy with a loving tear in her eye and then collapsed once again.

Thus perished Nana.

CHAPTER TWELVE
Christmas Magic

He saw her there, lying dead on the side of the clearing. Her tail did not wag, her eyes did not blink; Nana was gone. Wendy, Michael, and John ran to her, desperately trying to wake her from a sleep she would never awaken from. The children began to cry as the realisation settled in. Peter just stood there motionless. He and Nana didn't like each other, never had. But she still gave her life for him, and that showed the kind of dog she was. Without realising it, Peter began to weep.

Then out of the midst of sorrow, a gentle voice called to them.

"What's all this then?" Father Christmas said.

"Nana . . ." Michael's lips quivered. "She's . . . She's . . ."

Father Christmas watched them cradle Nana's lifeless body in their arms. They just sat in the middle of the snowbank, patting and stroking her fur. Wendy was sobbing inconsolably, blaming herself for Nana's fate. She tried to reassure herself that Nana was old and dogs' lives were tragically short anyway, but in the end, if she hadn't insisted on bringing Christmas to Neverland, Nana would still be alive.

Father Christmas knelt beside her and wiped the tears from her cheek; then, as if reading her thoughts, he whispered: "Now, now then." His voice was soft and soothing. "You mustn't blame yourself."

"It . . . it's all my fault," Wendy stammered. "If I hadn't . . ."

"Everything you did was out of love."

She looked up at his warm, caring eyes.

"Your heart is so big." Father Christmas said. "Never lose your compassion. Nana wouldn't want that, and if she could speak, she'd tell you how proud she is of you."

"She didn't even want to come," Wendy cried. "If I would've just left the Lost Boys alone, she'd . . . she'd . . ."

"It's easy to look the other way and do nothing," Father Christmas commented. "A real hero puts the happiness of others first, and that's what you've always done. It's what Nana did. It's what Christmas is all about." His smile beamed reassurance into her heart. "If more people could put aside their differences and learn to work together, the world would be a better place. Not just once a year, but always. This is the one time a year we are reminded of someone extraordinary that showed the world how to live, love, and die selflessly. Nana knew this."

Suddenly his rosy, dimpled cheeks widened with a smile. He got an excited twinkle in his eye — the kind so jolly and sprite-like it could only come from Father Christmas himself.

"There's no greater gift in this world than giving all of yourself to the people you love," Father Christmas declared. He stood up and gave Wendy a wink. "That's the sort of thing that ought to be rewarded."

Just then, he bent down and swooped up Nana's lifeless body in his arms. He turned and started walking away.

The group stared, awkward and confused. They watched Father Christmas' red coat flutter behind him as he strode into the sunset. The golden sky reflected off the white snow, filling the horizon with light and giving his figure an ethereal glow.

Michael turned to the elves. "Where's he going?"

The elves looked at each other and shrugged.

"We don't know," Stanley replied.

They got up and followed after them.

"Hey Boss," Tweedle called out. "What are you doing?"

"What I do best," Father Christmas replied, entering an open grove surrounded by frost-covered trees. "I give presents."

He set Nana's body on the smooth rock surface in the centre of the clearing. It was surrounded by a frozen spring, which almost looked like a natural stone altar — perhaps some ancient ceremonial holdover from some race dwelling in the woods of Neverland.

Father Christmas pulled out his magical red sack and set it down. It was empty when he retrieved it from the recesses of his robe, but now it was full as he set it down with a *thud!*

Wendy and the boys followed close behind.

Father Christmas withdrew an unusual clock from his bag. It looked like a small black grandfather's clock, but instead of a pendulum and counterweights inside the glass casing, there was a small hourglass. Instead of four sides, it had eight wooden columns — each of the octagonal columns contained a hand-carved animal.

The clock did not tick.

The grains of timer-sand in the hourglass were spent.

"Sometimes, the greatest gift a person can give is a little bit of their time." Father Christmas began.

The children watched on with a growing fascination.

"When we take the time to be there for somebody," Father Christmas continued, "we show them that we care. That they matter."

He pulled out a key with a butterfly headpiece.

"Just ask your grandparents what they want most in this world, and when you get right down to it, what they want — what they *really* want — is just a little more time with you."

Father Christmas inserted the key into the keyhole in the back of the strange clock and began to wind it. It was quiet, but the children could hear the tiny gears and springs *click* with every twist of the key.

"People have a lot of funny notions on time," Father Christmas added. "Time is money. Time flies. Time is cruel. Time is borrowed. But one thing is for certain; time is the most precious commodity a person has because no one knows for sure how much they have."

He continued to wind the clock.

"If I could, I'd give Nana some of my time," Michael declared.

"Too bad it doesn't work that way," John muttered.

"What if I told you, it could?" Father Christmas chimed.

"Wait, what?" John asked.

Father Christmas simply smiled, then gazed out at his current surroundings in reverent awe. He let out a tranquil sigh, then replied, "This is truly a remarkable place. Fairies, elves, flying children; they all exist, and yet they don't all at the same time." He grinned. "Even I only exist if you believe I do. In a place like this, children hold a remarkable power they can't possibly understand."

"What's that thing you keep winding?" Michael asked.

"Just a bauble," Father Christmas replied. "By itself, it's nothing."

He took his hand off the key.

Everyone fell silent.

The children leaned in anticipation . . . but nothing happened. The clock was still, and the key did not turn. There wasn't even the vaguest hint of the clockwork trying to *click* or stir inside. It just sat there lifeless.

"It didn't do anything," Surely declared.

"I told you, it's just a bauble," Father Christmas reiterated. "It's worthless . . . without help."

"What sort of help?" Michael asked.

"What if I told you that as long as you're here, you really can give somebody a little of your time?"

Michael took a step closer. "How?"

"You have to believe," Father Christmas said. "If you truly desire to give the gift and truly believe, it can happen."

Michael stared at the clock, then looked at Nana.

"Believe!" Michael willed in his heart.

John stepped up. "And how much time does it require?"

"That's up to Michael," Father Christmas replied. "But she really wouldn't need more than ten or twenty minutes. Just as long as the time given would bring her back to before the poison entered her bloodstream."

"I can give twenty minutes!" Michael proclaimed. "Anything to bring Nana back."

"Wait!" John interjected. "She was already pretty old. What if we wanted to give more than twenty minutes? Could more than one person give a gift?"

Father Christmas turned, facing John. That spritely twinkle in his eye had returned. "I don't see why not."

Wendy understood perfectly. It was something all the Darlings were aware of, but nobody had the heart to talk about. At Nana's age, it was likely to be Nana's last Christmas anyway. So, even if they could revert her body to before being shot, how much time would she have left? What they wouldn't give to hold onto her a little longer.

John figured that there were nine of them, not counting Peter, and if they each gave four months, Nana would get another three years of life, which is twenty-one dog years.

They all heartily agreed.

"Will it make you older?" Peter asked. He wanted to help the noble girl who gave her life for him, but growing up was against everything he stood for. Besides, he knew he would just forget her in a few moments — he was not allowed to remember things that make you grow emotionally or psychologically.

"It would be at the end of your life," Father Christmas explained.

Peter thought it over. He knew he would never grow up, and therefore, if he never grows up, he'll never die, and if he never dies, then what's the harm of giving somebody a part of the end of it?

"Count me in," Peter declared.

Father Christmas patted the boy on the shoulder, then picked up the clock and set it down next to Nana's body.

"Now," Father Christmas whispered. "Close your eyes."

They did.

"And believe."

The children closed their eyes tighter and . . . believed!

At first, nothing happened, and then all of a sudden, they began to hear the *clicking* of the gears spinning inside the clock and causing the key to spin. The clock started to run . . . backwards! The minute, hour, and second hands began to rotate; slowly at first, then fast! The animal carvings on the posts began to revolve around the hourglass-like carousal. The more it spun, the more animated the wooden animals became — bobbing up and down, limbs moving as if they were running.

Faster and faster it spun!

Stanley and Tweedle just stared in awe as the kinetic energy generated temporal sparks of light. The sands in the hourglass began to radiate with a luminescent blue light. The light converged in the centre of the sand, creating rippling dunes. Slowly, a remarkable force rose up like a glorious energy cloud, sparking out what looked like tiny bolts of lightning! The grains of sand rattled in the glass, being pulled by a tremendous force.

Tweedle noticed the key's metal butterfly headpiece begin to wobble fluidly. Slowly, colour grew into the butterfly, and it started to look real. To his surprise, it began to flap and flutter its wings.

Stanley beheld a single grain of sand twitch, struggling to lift up. Finally, it levitated above its brothers and sisters. It continued to rise until it met the glowing energy cloud. There was a blinding flash from inside the glass casing, and the energy escaped the bottom half of the hourglass and shot straight to the top; and with it, more grains of sand trickled up to meet it.

The key kept turning as some of the timer-sand re-entered the top of the hourglass.

Father Christmas was baffled. The clock should have stopped, but it continued to spin, and the sand continued to fill the top of the glass. This was more than three years' worth! He observed the children, and each of the Darlings and the Lost Boys had stopped giving a while ago. Then he saw Peter. It was Peter! He seemed determined to fill that hourglass as close to the top as he could.

Finally, the sands slowed to a stop, just as everything else did. The energy cloud dissipated and vanished, removing its reversed gravitational pull on the sand. The key and the posts were once again lifeless, the clock ticked forward, and the grains of sand dripped down to the bottom of the hourglass the way it should.

The children looked on with growing anticipation, but Nana just laid there as she always had. For a while, nothing happened — just silence and the *whistle* of the wind. Then it happened. Her stiff, hardened muscles began to soften and relax; warmth returned, flowing through her body as the blood flowed through her veins once more. Suddenly, her body twitched. Her thick, well-aged fur started to change, subtly flowing with the soft, colourful locks of youth. Just then, Wendy noticed Nana's chest rumble — softly at first, then deeply as oxygen began to enter her body and inflate her lungs. The breath of life flowed through her nostrils, causing her nose to twitch as it cycled through her body and exhaled out of her mouth.

"Look!" Michael exclaimed.

Wendy gazed down at where Michael was pointing and discovered the playful wagging of her tail.

"Nana?" she called with tears of joy in her eyes.

Nana's lifeless eyes suddenly blinked into consciousness. Then she coughed and blinked again, and with the turn of her head . . . she *barked!*

"Nana!" the Darlings screamed, running to her and lavishing her with hugs and kisses.

"It's a miracle!" Wendy exclaimed.

Father Christmas just smiled with a wink, then turned and walked away.

"WHAT HAPPENED?" Nana's *bark* inquired.

Dogs are much more intelligent than people give credit, but certain things are still beyond them. All she knew was she felt better than she could possibly remember. Her joints were no longer stiff and sore. The arthritis in her paws was gone and no longer bothered her. She was suddenly so full of energy. Her eyesight had returned to its former glory — her cataracts had vanished. Her hearing and sense of smell were as potent as a puppy. She was young again!

She couldn't believe it!

She was young and never felt more alive!

In the end, there's nothing more that needs to be said. We'll let the Darlings share a private moment with their beloved maid.

Father Christmas watched on from a discrete distance, smiling with the pure joy of the children's happiness.

"I didn't know you could do that," Stanley said.

"I can't," Father Christmas replied. "They did."

CHAPTER THIRTEEN

The Cavern of No Return

He had witnessed the whole thing. After blasting the sleigh out of the sky, Hook had made his way down from *The Watch*. After an explosion like that, he knew someone was bound to investigate; but Peter and the boys had gone off to rescue the man in red instead.

He had a lot of ground to cover and so little time to do it in. There was a newfound pomp and stride to his step. He had cleaned up nicely. He wore his finest cologne and his finest black pillaging outfit, with gold cufflinks and a sharp scarlet cravat. He had shaved his beard and groomed his dapper moustache, rounding the tips with wax. When he looked in the mirror, he was overjoyed to see the handsome yet terrifying man of his glory days. Captain James Hook was back! And it would not do for him to greet the world looking anything other than his best.

He polished and sharpened his hook so it glistened elegantly. He was armed with his cutlass in its scabbard, a pistol in his jacket, a blunderbuss at his hip, and a dagger concealed in his freshly polished boot. He glanced at his compass and put it away, next to his spyglass. Finally, he grabbed a few bags of treasure — he had a feeling that when it was time to make his move, he was going to have to move fast.

He trekked to the wreck site, waiting silently from afar — he dared not get too close. He had always been cold and calculating, and now that he was alone, the element of surprise was the most precious commodity he had. He wasn't about to give it up until the time was exactly right. So, he needed to collect as much information as possible.

He peered through his spyglass at the sleigh and the tiny men that Peter and John had rescued. He wasn't sure what to make of them or their funny outfits, but he could tell they were essential to his escape.

When Peter and his crew had dashed off to Cannibal Cove, he had initially intended to ambush the strange little men and steal the sleigh. Unfortunately, the sleigh was damaged, and the reindeer were stuck in a Never-tree. The boys had left the little men behind to tend to the sleigh and to get the reindeer down. Captain Hook, having no experience with flying reindeer and magic sleighs, decided to do the same.

Even though Tweedle and Stanley were never a part of the reindeer department, all elves are born with a certain knack for animal husbandry, particularly reindeer. The real benefit of flying reindeer is that you don't need to get them down from anything, they can fly. The elves merely needed to cut them loose so the reindeer could get themselves down.

The reindeer, unfortunately, were choppy and not particularly graceful in their descent. For instance, the reindeer, better known as Dancer, was flying incredibly crooked and erratic and even lost the ability to maintain flight for random spurts.

The elves believed they had damaged their antlers. Not many people know this, but a reindeer's antlers are crucial to their aviational prowess, which is why only female reindeer can fly. Female reindeer keep their antlers during the winter season, while the male reindeer shed theirs. Also, female reindeer — like females of most species — were bigger and stronger and more coordinated to adjust to all the complexity of aviation. If an antler is sprained or broken, it can throw them off.

Hook understood perfectly. The sleigh needed to be repaired, and then someone with the know-how needed to tend to the reindeer, so stealing the sled was useless until then. Besides, he didn't know how to fly a reindeer-drawn sleigh. He needed to wait.

After the elves had tended to the reindeer, they rejoined the rest of the crew in Cannibal Cove — this was right around the time the toys and skeletons came to their rescue.

Hook had wanted to inspect the sleigh and the reindeer, but they'd see his footprints in the snow — the thing about the element of surprise is, you only get it once, and Hook was determined to make his count. As we're all aware, patience is a virtue, and after four years, he could wait a little longer.

He watched on with a growing fascination as the oddly familiar man in red tempted the cannibals with a magical sack. Next, he witnessed the skirmish with the cannibals and was moved when Father Christmas brought Nana back to life.

Hook marvelled at such benevolent sorcery. This stranger would undoubtedly be a dangerous foe. Still, the thing that puzzled him about this oddly dressed enchanter was the fact that there was something familiar about him — almost comforting.

Well, comforting or not, Hook thought, *this man is a force to be reckoned with!*

The key things he was able to note were these: the magical outsider was not Peter's enemy, there was a magic sack (but only the pure could use it), the sleigh and reindeer could be repaired, and finally, as long as they were in Neverland, the jolly old fat man could bring people back from the dead.

Hook found that last part rather disparaging. If he were to kill Peter Pan, he would want him to stay dead. Of course, Hook's main focus was getting off the island. Still, if he could manage to get hold of the magic bag when he steals the sleigh, then the stranger wouldn't be able to use it to help anyone else.

A sinister smile crept across Hook's face. Eventually, he might even figure a way to use the bag's magic. But he needed to get closer!

Before doing anything else, he decided to stash his bags of treasure just off the path, so he could retrieve them later when the time was right. It also gave him time to think.

Hook was sure they were heading back to their Home in the Trees. He had to discover a way to infiltrate the Valley of the Fairies; unfortunately, there was only one place he could possibly slip through without detection . . .

The Cavern of No Return.

It was dangerous. Hook had only been there once in the four years since he had perished. In the old days, it was believed that evil creatures such as trolls and goblins used to dwell inside, luring unsuspecting victims — victims that were never seen again. Hook didn't fully buy into that nonsense. However, if it would make life more interesting for Peter, perhaps something would eventually show up. But for as long as he had been there, *The Cavern of No Return* was just the outdated moniker for an empty cavern with sulphur pits and a dusty old boneyard.

Empty, that is, until about three and a half years ago.

Now, it's believed to be the lair of the one-eyed killer crocodile of Neverland! He had only been there once, in a manic fit of melancholy, half hoping to encounter his old nemesis, but never saw it. He did, however, encounter several fresh kills. This had become the feeding ground for something big. Perhaps the creature wasn't home, or perhaps it wasn't ready to face him; either way, he had crossed the path undisturbed last time. But the boneyard told him there was something there that needed to be avoided at all costs.

He knew what he had to do. Without delay, he mustered as much courage as he could and headed for the cave entrance on the southern part of the island. When he got there, he stared at the mouth of the cavern with growing trepidation.

Did he dare enter the lair of his greatest fear?

He took a nervous gulp, then stepped into the darkness. He could feel the heat of the cloud of steam billowing out of the mouth of the cave. It made him think of tales of Saint George, entering the lair of the fire-breathing dragon and seeing the bones of its victims littering the path. Of course, he knew it was from the sulphur, but the bones were very real.

Fear began to set in as he stepped along the path. He hated not being able to see what was ahead of him; it was thicker than the London fog rolling in from the harbour. He passed the bones of several unidentifiable creatures. He held his breath, partly from the foul stench of the sulphur — which grew stronger the deeper he went — but mainly because he was afraid of making any noise.

He tip-toed oh so quietly, successfully reaching the bridge. It was old and rickety, and below it was the bubbling sulphur that could roast a man in a matter of seconds. The wooden planks groaned and wobbled beneath his feet, but the rope railing was still sturdy enough. It was a long bridge. He could hear the *squeaks* and *chatter* of the large Never-Bats resting on the stalactite formations above.

He made his way along the bridge. After passing the sulphur pits, the bridge continued across the terrain and over the freshwater pools. That was the place that made him the most nervous. He had no intentions of encountering the creature, but if he did, it'd get a face full of shot — the blunderbuss could obliterate a target at fifteen paces. Even if the blast didn't kill the beast, it certainly wouldn't be feeling particularly well afterwards.

As he made his way deeper and deeper into the darkness, he was aided only by the lantern which dangled limply from his hook. Suddenly, he got a sinking feeling in his stomach . . . that feeling of being watched!

Cautiously, he leaned over the rope railing, using the light to peer into the icy water's surface. It glistened, revealing a thick layer of ice and the watery depths below.

He shined the lantern across the waters with one swift swoop of his claw, then stopped, startled! For a moment, he thought he saw something move. He leaned back over, surveying the water, and then saw what had startled him. There was some large icy log or something beneath the water. He started to dismiss it, then examined it closer. The jagged surface almost resembled teeth.

Curious.

He leaned in closer when all of a sudden, a pair of eyes snapped open! He staggered back, realising he was staring at the toothy grin of the one-eyed crocodile of Neverland!

BAM!!!

It sprang at the captain with a horrifying speed and ferocity! The *thud* rumbled throughout the cavern as the crocodile collided with the icy surface. Hook fought back a *shriek*, nearly losing his balance on the trembling rope bridge.

The creature shot up again!

BAM!!

Hook nearly dropped the lantern in terror, seeing it *snap* its powerful jaws at him! It *crashed* against the frozen surface once more.

Hook fumbled for the blunderbuss at his side. His heart lurched in his chest as he raised the firearm. He glanced up, growing more aware of the stirring of the Never-Bats up above. He raised the lantern; there were thousands of them! They were big, black, hairy, ferocious-looking creatures!

BAM!!!

It snapped for him again!

Hook spun back, turning to fire . . . then stopped. He took his finger off the trigger and began to laugh — a mad, victorious laugh!

"I've got you, you putrid excuse of a reptile!" Hook chortled.

The crocodile went a little deeper.

"Go on!" Hook goaded. "Keep thrashing away!"

The creature shot back up!

BAM!!!

"You can't get me from there!"

Tiny cracks splintered throughout the ice.

Hook turned back. He strode along the bridge when it suddenly occurred to him that the reason the crocodile could have survived in such drastically cold winter conditions was the sulphur pits, making the water warm enough to be comfortable in—

The creature sprang up again!

BAM!!!

The cracks in the ice started to spread and multiply.

. . . and if the water was warm enough to thrive in, then the ice may not be as thick as he had initially—

It shot back up, bursting through the ice!

Hook *shrieked* as it devoured the wooden plank beneath his feet!

He turned and ran!

The croc dove back under!

Hook hurried his way across the unstable bridge, struggling not to trip. He smiled, knowing the egress was just up around the next bend. He ran faster and faster when the ice in front of him exploded by the force of the determined crocodile! It snapped at the bridge, splitting the wooden planks in two!

Hook screamed again, seeing its large teeth and powerful jaws tear through the wood!

It crawled onto the ice. Hook stared at the crocodile, and the crocodile stared at Hook. They had unfinished business.

"Hullo, you detestable old bugger," Hook growled.

It took a step closer, *growling* and *hissing!* It cocked its head and opened its jaws, revealing rows of razor-sharp teeth!

"Don't even think about it!" Hook snarled, raising the blunderbuss. He glanced up at the agitated colony of Never-Bats overheard.

Hook held his breath. Time seemed to slow down. His heart *thumped* in his chest, and he felt a bead of sweat trickle down his forehead.

It sprang at him!

BOOM!!!

Hook fired the blunderbuss while diving out of the way of its snapping jaws!

The blast was deafening and amplified and echoed throughout the cavern!

The captain hit the ice on the other side with a graceful somersault. The creature *squealed* in pain, diving back below the icy depths once more, retreating from the terrified captain!

Of course, the instant he fired the blunderbuss, the Never-Bats swarmed and scattered erratically overhead!

Hook covered his head and rolled underneath the bridge for protection! Their *screech* was horrendous!

As the violent cloud of Never-Bats flew to freedom, Hook peered through the ice, which was stained red by the wounded crocodile. As the water cleared, Hook saw the croc. The croc saw Hook. Their eyes met. Hook knew that if the creature intended to strike, he was done for. Even if he could escape, the hypothermia would claim him.

Fortunately for the captain, the crocodile was too wounded and startled to attack. But through its soulless eyes, it declared, "Mark my words, I will get you!"

The crocodile turned around and swam back to its burrow.

Hook wiped his brow and sighed in relief. When the Never-Bats calmed down, he quickly and cautiously hurried back on the path. He was shaken but all right. He followed the path out of the cavern, but one thing was certain, he wasn't going to take that route back.

Hope once again rose in his heart as he saw the Valley of the Fairies. It was remarkable! He grinned his ghoulish grin, knowing that everything was falling into place.

CHAPTER FOURTEEN

The Home in the Trees

The Never-tree towered up high above the setting sun. If you were to gaze up, higher and higher, so high you may feel that you were about to breach the skyline, there was a large hole near the top of the tree. The hole sloped down into multiple fairy-engineered slides that spiralled and spun down the hollowed-out trunk to the main banquet hall. It was where the Lost Boys ate, held meetings, and played indoor games at night or in poor weather.

Peter and the Lost Boys had initially discussed investigating the noise that blasted Father Christmas out of the sleigh, but they decided to eat something first. Besides, they wanted to start enjoying Christmas and were excited to have Father Christmas with them. There was so much they wanted to ask!

Hook had decided to venture closer to the tree. He knew it was a risk, but it was a risk he was prepared to take. Most of the terrain was ice instead of snow, and ice was more forgiving for hiding one's tracks. Also, the fairies were preoccupied with tending to the reindeer and sleigh — the elves showed them how. He needed to listen in on their conversations, so the risk was acceptable.

Hook had found a large knothole around the base of the tree. He couldn't see anything through it, but when he put his ear against it, he could hear voices. The joyful *caterwauling* of John and Michael's repeated zipping down the slide at the entrance *echoed* through the tree. They marvelled at the remarkable structure, which was far more extensive than their Home Underground.

"Let's eat!" Surely suggested, heading to the table. "I'm starving!"

Hook listened in.

"Capital idea," John agreed. "I'm feeling a bit peckish myself."

The centre of the room contained an enormous round wooden table with chairs — all intricately carved by the fairies. The Lost Boys' names were etched into the back of their chairs. They didn't have time to make chairs for their guests, but when one of the guests happened to have a magical sack, their skills weren't exactly required.

"Excellent!" Peter declared. "We will have a feast to celebrate our honoured guests."

The boys started to sit at the table and then remembered that Wendy had taught them to wash up before dinner. They quickly toddled off and returned with considerably cleaner hands.

Pipkin sat down and licked his lips. "I wonder what the fairies have prepared for us tonight."

"No-no," Peter scoffed with a shake of his head.

The children observed their captain cautiously.

Peter held up his hands, pantomiming a round plate. He held up his imaginary platter to his nose, sniffed it, then smiled, rubbing his tummy.

"Mmm-mmmm," Peter yummed. "It smells so delicious."

Usually, this was the part where the children would all laugh and join in on the game. They would lift their imaginary plates and smile and say: "Mmm, pudding!" or "Roast pork, my favourite!" or whatever it was they pretended to eat; however, today, they were legitimately hungry and had no intention of playing games.

They looked up at their captain, famished and feeling more than a little embarrassed because they had some very special visitors. Nana sniffed at her scentless imaginary plate and rolled her eyes. Stanley and Tweedle sat, each with a knife and fork in hand, and looked at each other, confused. Father Christmas, however, merely laughed his boisterous laugh!

"Uh, Peter," Wendy started.

"Yes?" Peter replied, taking a nibble of his invisible corn.

"Don't you think—"

"Can you pass the salt?" Peter interrupted.

Without thinking about it, Wendy reached out with her left hand, picked up the imaginary salt and handed it to Peter. "Anyway, I was thinking that given the circumstances, it might be best not to play this game right now."

Stanley, Tweedle, and Nana all nodded in affirmation.

"What do you mean?" Peter asked.

"Well, I think everybody is *really* hungry and would prefer to . . ."

"Nonsense," Father Christmas interjected.

Stanley and Tweedle dropped their utensils in disbelief, and Nana snorted out her own quiet displeasure.

Father Christmas ignored them and bent down, inhaling and savouring the overwhelming aroma of the non-existent plate as if he were smelling a well-cooked and hearty meal!

"Mmm-mmmm," Father Christmas declared. "This does look delectable!"

The elves and the Newfoundland Dog all exchanged glances of disbelief.

"Maybe the Boss hit his head a little harder than we thought," Tweedle whispered.

Father Christmas reached down, using an imaginary knife and fork, and cut into an imaginary steak. Next, he brought his pretend fork to his mouth and took his first bite.

"Delicious." Father Christmas declared, still chewing. "Why don't you give it a try?"

The children reached down as they had many times before. They made pantomime cuts with their pantomime knives, but this time, when they pretended to take a bite, something was alarmingly different . . . they could taste something!

Instead of imagining the flavour, they *actually* tasted it! Instead of pretending to chew, they were *actually* chewing! There was solid food in their mouths, food with rich texture and potent flavours. It was remarkable!

They could even see the food now. Somehow, the food materialised before their very eyes. The children gasped in delight and started scarfing it down with a gleeful vigour.

All but Nana and the elves.

"Come on, boys," Father Christmas called. "Dig in. You don't want your food to get cold, do you?"

The elves looked at each other once again. They shrugged and let out a small sigh. When the duo reached down, they immediately withdrew their hands and put their fingers in their mouths.

"Ow!" they exclaimed.

"Something the matter, boys?" Father Christmas inquired.

"It's hot!" Tweedle exclaimed.

The befuddled elves examined the table. They had touched something sizzling but couldn't see anything that could have caused it.

"You should probably use a fork next time," Father Christmas chuckled.

Stanley cautiously picked up his very real fork and gently brought the tines down, not feeling anything. He scooped up the nothingness and glanced over at Father Christmas.

"Go on," Father Christmas gestured.

Slowly, Stanley brought the fork to his mouth, then decided to close his eyes. Clearly, something was going on here, and he felt it might be better if he wasn't distracted by his pesky sight. As the fork entered his mouth, he tasted it!

It was incredible!

He continued to chew, and when he opened his eyes, he saw the food!

"Oh my gosh!" Stanley exclaimed. "I see it! I taste it!"

Tweedle and Nana gasped and looked down at their own serving area. Tweedle closed his eyes and just went for it. Even the perpetually perplexed Nana put aside her pride, closed her eyes, and licked at the nothingness. She *yipped* in surprise, tasting the food and seeing it materialise before her.

The kids laughed in awe. Peter enjoyed the game; however, there was an underlined annoyance. It was fun, but it wasn't the game he had initially wanted to play. He decided not to let it bother him too much, but to be outdone by a grown-up wasn't an experience he was accustomed to.

They all shared a hearty laugh, and Father Christmas taught them how to balance spoons on their nose and stand on their head and all kinds of new games. There was laughing, joking, and all sorts of merriment!

They asked him all sorts of questions. How do the reindeer fly? How does he deliver toys all over the world? How did he become Father Christmas? They asked about the elves, the Workshops, the toys, and everything else they could ever want to know about Christmas.

It was very illuminating for the eavesdropping Captain Hook, who was still listening in from the knothole. When he discovered that Peter's bearded confidant was

Father Christmas, Hook was filled with shock and surprise! He loved the idea that Father Christmas was real! As a little boy, James loved Christmas. When his mother was alive, it was her favourite holiday. But from the sounds of it, a lot has changed over the years. Hook didn't know how he felt about going up against Father Christmas, but he desperately wanted off the island. Luckily for Hook, the children asked all the questions Hook needed to know — particularly about the reindeer.

But there was one more question on all of the Lost Boys' minds.

"Is there *really* a list?" Jojo asked

"A list?" Father Christmas repeated.

"You know," Surely elaborated, "the List."

"Oh," Father Christmas chuckled. "I'm afraid there is."

"Am I on it?" Jojo asked.

"You were put on it when we got Wendy's letter," Father Christmas explained.

"Well," Jojo stammered, "am I on the Naughty List or the Nice List?"

Father Christmas grinned. "I assume you're on the Nice List."

"You mean you don't know?" Pipkin asked.

"I'm afraid," Stanley inserted, "until now, we didn't know any of this existed. Our knowledge of you is only a few hours old."

"Besides," Tweedle added, "the List is open and always changing."

"Changing?" the boys inquired.

"Well, we knew about Wendy, Michael and John," Father Christmas replied. "And as of right now, they are on the Nice List, but they could still do something to be put on the Naughty List."

"We could?!" Michael gasped.

"It's not very likely." Father Christmas giggled. "It takes an awful lot to get on the Naughty List. And for whatever you did, you would have to have absolutely no remorse or desire to change."

"And what gives you the right to go around judging people?" Peter asked bluntly, feeling unsettled by the concept of a grown-up judging children.

"Peter," Wendy admonished.

"It's all right," Father Christmas assured. "Honestly, each person judges themselves. You may not realise it, but you keep a record of all your deeds. One you can't access in the physical realm, but it's still there, nevertheless. The most important reason for this is that you understand the true intentions of your own heart better than anyone else. And I want to make one thing perfectly clear; I do not punish the naughty. I merely reward the nice. Every naughty child knows how it works. Sadly, they cheat themselves out of their own potential."

"Could someone on the Naughty List make it onto the Nice List?" Surely asked.

"Of course."

"What does it look like?" Michael asked.

"The List?" Father Christmas inquired.

Michael nodded.

"Well, I don't have it on me."

"What about the bag?" Pipkin inserted.

"Well, I suppose technically I could . . ." Father Christmas thought for a moment. "Oh, why not?" He grabbed his magical sack and set it in front of Michael. "Go ahead."

"Really?" Michael ventured.

Father Christmas nodded.

Michael reached into the bag and withdrew a bizarre scroll attached to a strange golden roller device and stand. The shimmering gold parchment displayed its contents in the centre of the machine — allowing the user to read the elegant calligraphy — the rest was rolled up at the top and bottom of the massive scrolls. The gold embossed lettering atop of the device declared itself:

THE NAUGHTY & NICE LIST

"Go on," Father Christmas prodded. "Ask it to show you Michael Darling."

Michael leaned in apprehensively and whispered, "Show me Michael Darling." Suddenly, the roller began whirling the top and bottom of the scroll, spinning the golden, glistening parchment. It spun faster and faster before stopping with the exposed section of parchment on the "M. Darling" section. Michael leaned in and read aloud:

"Michael M. Darling: Nice!"

"Ooh! Me next," Jojo requested.

Father Christmas nodded in affirmation.

Jojo leaned in, then stopped. "Wait! I don't know my last name."

"Just say 'of Neverland,'" Stanley suggested.

"Show me Jojo of Neverland," Jojo said to the scroll.

It whirled again, stopping on his name:

JOJO OF NEVERLAND: NICE

"Phew!" Jojo sighed, wiping his brow.

Each child, except one, had their turn. Father Christmas swiftly put the list back in the bag.

"I think we had enough of that," Father Christmas declared. "Time to be going."

"What about Peter?" Wendy asked.

Peter was hiding a sense of unfairness.

"Oh, yes. I forgot. Well, I think we should save that for later," Father Christmas declared. "We have very little time before the reindeer are well enough to leave. I think I should share the most important part of Christmas."

"And what's that?" Surely asked.

"Bringing joy to others."

Hook eagerly listened in and discovered his next move. He knew where the children would eventually end up, so he needed to go prepare some *Christmas Surprises* of his own. He may have survived *The Cavern of No Return*, but he bloody well wasn't about to tempt fate again — at least, not twice in one day. The fairies had decided to have a Christmas party of their own on the other side of the valley. Hook felt that they were preoccupied enough for him to try and slip away through the traditional route.

CHAPTER FIFTEEN

Old Friends

A noise rose in the distance. It started soft and low but grew by the light of the clear night sky. The stars listened in, watching by the light of the vibrant moons, casting their gentle yet brilliant blue beams along the snowy shores of Neverland.

The melodic tones of Peter's flute filled the land. He played with the spirit and childlike joy of Christmas! The Lost Boys were singing in tune with the melody — at least, they were trying to. As they paraded along the path, they handed out goodies and little handmade presents to all the creatures they came across. They were fun, boisterous, and delightful — even if they were a wee bit loud and unsynchronised.

Peter particularly loved the carolling tradition he had learned back in London and was eager to share his new game with his boys. Music was the greatest way to spread cheer as they gave gifts to all. The fairies danced and played, illuminating the land with the colours of

Christmas. They lit torches along the paths to help light their way.

The children carried candles and wore brand new coats as they marched throughout Neverland. Father Christmas knew it would be cold, so he gave each child an early Christmas present. They marvelled at the colourful paper, shiny red ribbons, and bows as they passed out the packages. Inside, Father Christmas provided a fabulous ensemble. There were coats, scarves, hats, gloves, and boots. The children were delighted! For many of them, these were the first real articles of clothing they had ever owned — and they were considerably warmer and softer than fig leaves and pelts.

When Surely asked Father Christmas why he always gave so many gifts, he taught them about the joy and spirit of giving. Father Christmas encouraged them to do something nice for one another. Something to show how much they cared for and appreciated each other.

They all sprang into action, crafting various gifts to give one another — a spear for Jojo, a wicker hat for Pipkin and so forth. Wendy and the boys enjoyed baking cookies for the inhabitants of Neverland. It would have been harder if it wasn't for Father Christmas' magic sack. John had noted it would have been easier to just pull out a box of biscuits instead of all of the ingredients and cooking supplies. But, as Wendy had stated, it wouldn't have felt like Christmas if they didn't make them from scratch.

Everyone had finished wrapping their gifts. They were so excited and impatient, but they knew they weren't allowed to open them yet.

As they trudged along the snowy path, Stanley and Tweedle began to feel like they were wasting a lot of time and energy that could be used trying to get back home. They had nothing against the children, mind you. They just understood what a time crunch they were in; Father Christmas' duties at the North Pole were crucial this time of year — and of course, Stanley thought of Holly.

They gave special bags of seed to the birds, bones to teething wolf-pups, shiny things to the fairies and mermaids, and now headed to their old friends, the Piccaninnies.

Music rang in the distance as the children sang, carrying candles along the hillside. The glow of the lanterns followed the path into the Piccaninny territory.

Father Christmas observed the Piccaninnies — a rather unfortunate name he felt. From what he could tell, just like everything else on the island, they appeared to be caricatures of what a child might imagine a native culture to be instead of the reality of how the cultures *actually* were. They seemed to be modelled after American Indian tribes — not the real Native Americans, nor their customs and culture, but rather the Western/European stereotype concocted by storytellers.

He suspected they had manifested to be what Peter wanted to see after hearing stories of Cowboys and Indians. The magic was truly unique on this island. Much like the North Pole and himself, Neverland was made up of childhood belief and imagination. He supposed that the Piccaninnies might look and sound completely different one day — similar to his own evolving characterisations.

They may even get a completely different name; it would all depend on how future generations of children viewed the world when their time came.

The Indian sentries looked on. At first, they didn't know what to make of the raucous caterwauling from the children approaching their path, but there was no aggression in it. They shared a nod and headed down from their lookout post to intercept the band.

"Peter," the first sentry greeted. The tribe once gave Peter the title of the *Great White Father* after he rescued Tiger Lily from *Marooners' Rock*. They had long since retired that moniker and simply called him Peter. They still regarded Peter and the Lost Boys as friends and allies — and certainly never tried to kill or scalp them anymore — but they didn't fully trust Peter's whims. Peter still got bored and would goad them into fights and trappings — nothing malicious, it was all fun and games. But he would still switch sides mid-fight randomly, leaving the Piccaninnies perplexed.

"What do we owe the honour of your visit?" the brave inquired.

"Christmas," Peter replied. "Me and my tribe come bearing gifts. We wish to bring you tidings of joy and blessings of a prosperous and bounteous new year."

The two braves blinked, then shared an uncertain gaze before the other sentry turned back to the boys.

"We are unfamiliar with this word. What is Christmas?"

Wendy stepped forward. When she first came to Neverland, it was considered impertinent for a squaw to speak out of turn when the men palavered (Tiger Lily didn't count, she was a princess). However, Wendy managed to break them of this mindset when she saved the tribe from the Wendigo that had made its way to Neverland. She even got them to stop referring to her as *squaw*. They tried to call her the *Great White Mother*, but she wouldn't have it. But of course, that was a different story.

"Where I come from," Wendy interjected, "we have a great celebration where we honour friends and allies with gifts of love and appreciation."

"Who's that?" the first sentry asked, motioning to the man in red.

"That's Father Christmas," Wendy replied. "He is sort of the personification of the spirit of giving."

"I don't know what that means," the sentry said.

"It's sort of complicated," Wendy explained. "Please let us give these gifts to the tribe."

Father Christmas stepped forward, speaking in the traditional tongue of the Piccaninny. Although the Piccaninnies knew English and got better at it with each passing year, it wasn't their first language, so they were deeply impressed and honoured by this gesture.

The natives shared a joyous laugh with Father Christmas. The group had no idea what was said, but things were going well. Father Christmas gestured to the snow and offered the sentries new fancy jackets and sweaters to protect them from the cold. The first sentry got a red sweater with a Christmas Tree on it, and the second got a green sweater with a snowman.

"Okay," the second sentry relented. "Forgive us for being leery, but we haven't exactly had the best luck with white men bearing gifts."

Father Christmas put a reassuring hand on his shoulder. "Oh, believe me, I know."

The group followed them to the Piccaninny's camp. The children presented the gifts, and the chief and the tribe were delighted. They were so delighted that the chief announced a massive feast in their honour.

While the banquet was being prepared, the powwow began. There was dancing and games, and the children laughed with joy. There was even talk about passing around a pipe, but Father Christmas put a stop to that before it could get to the children.

Historically, Wendy and Tiger Lily (who had a mutual respect and sympathy for one another) didn't like each other much. But with the spirit of Christmas, even they bonded and became fast friends.

Gentleman Starkey watched from a distance. He didn't know what to make of all the commotion; he was too busy tending to his duties of taking care of the small children of the tribe. He saw the man in red but couldn't hear who he was and what they were doing, but it didn't matter. He knew his place. He quietly put the children to bed.

This was Gentleman Starkey's favourite part of the evening. He had finished watching and tutoring the children of the tribe — along with his other responsibilities — and now he got to spend the rest of the evening uninterrupted with his own family.

It had grown dark, and he had put his daughter to sleep. He had wanted to name her something traditional like Emily or Elizabeth or Mary, but he also wanted her to fit in with the other children. Being the daughter of a white man and a former pirate would be troublesome enough, so he decided on a name that would represent both heritages. He named her Elizabeth "Morning Glory" Starkey — "Elizabeth" after his mother, and "Morning Glory" symbolising not only a lovely flower but also the triumph of a new day and the hope for the future. The tribe mostly called her Morning Glory, but her daddy simply called her Lizzie.

He had done rather well for himself, all things considering. At first, he was mocked and ostracised by the tribe, but he soon won them over. He was good with the children. After all, he was an usher at a school in Yorkshire before becoming a pirate — and let's face it, pirates were infinitely more vexing and childish than children.

Ultimately, Starkey decided he wanted to educate the children of the tribe. He had tried to teach several of the pirates (such as Alf, Noodler, and Skylights) to read and write in the past, but — as Hook had once noted — they were not a particularly teachable lot. The children of the tribe, on the other hand, were bright and eager to learn.

Eventually, he began a friendship with an ageing squaw named Elu, who assisted in caring for the children. She wasn't much to look at and was regarded as something of a spinster, but love can bloom even in the most unlikely of places — and he loved Elu dearly. The chief was distrustful of Starkey but ultimately gave his blessing and consent to the marriage.

As Starkey reflected on his life and how lucky he was, he felt a chill sweep across the land. There was a *rustling* noise behind him. He spun around but didn't see anything out of place. He could hear the *whistle* of the wind and, for a moment, he thought it had called his name.

After a moment of silence, Starkey dismissed it as his imagination. He went back to Lizzie, who, judging by the pungent aroma, needed her nappy changed.

While attending to the child, he felt the change spread across the meadow. Little shivers ran over it, the sun had finished setting, and dark shadows stole across the land, turning it cold and foreboding. It felt as if something dark and sinister had entered the grounds, sending a chill into the night to announce its arrival. He recognised that chill but couldn't quite remember from where.

The hairs on the back of his neck stood on end, alerting him to danger.

What was it?

Again, nothing but the darkness.

He was about to dismiss it as his imagination when he heard two startling words:

"*Mr. Starkey.*"

That ominous yet familiar voice called to him, sending shivers down Starkey's spine. He stood at attention but was too afraid to turn around. With every ounce of his will, he forced his trembling body to turn and face the spectre.

"C-Captain?" Starkey stammered.

From the distant gloom of the woods, he saw two glowing embers flare and rescind. In the flickering of the flame, he saw the outline of a dark and brooding figure — a figure with a terrifyingly familiar face. It was the face of the dead, a face that quickly faded back into darkness and was clouded by a thick plume of smoke.

He'd recognise that twin cigar-holder anywhere.

"A pleasure to see you again, my old friend," the voice called back. "Miss me?"

"But you're . . . you're . . ."

"Dead?" the phantom inserted.

Starkey couldn't speak, he could only tremble and nod.

"Yes," the voice replied in a soft, eerily soothing tone. "I've been dead for quite some time now. But now I'm back."

Starkey had heard the rumours of the ghost of Captain Hook haunting the land but didn't believe it. And he certainly never expected to see his former captain's Spirit standing before him, watching him change a soiled nappy, but there it was!

He could see the glint of the former captain's claw by the pale moonlight. He was terrified. Too terrified for words. He just mumbled.

"Don't think I've forgotten your little mutiny when we last met," the voice stated calmly.

The captain was never more dangerous when he was calm and polite, and Starkey knew it! He also knew the captain didn't forgive, and he didn't forget!

The last time he saw his captain, he had jumped overboard and fled the ship. Something had been killing the crew in the captain's cabin, and he had refused to go in. He remembered the cadaverous face of his captain as Hook approached him. And the murderous red sparks that flared in his eyes — the same sparks that always flared in Hook's eyes just before a kill!

"I'm-a . . . I'm-a sorry, captain!" Starkey pleaded.

"Stop your blubbering!" the voice barked. "I'm not here to kill you! Though you deserve to be garrotted where you stand," he declared, raising his claw aggressively. "I'm offering you a second chance. You, of all people, ought to know that's not something I do very often. So, I suggest you take it."

"What do you want?"

"If you agree to help me now, I am willing to leave the past dead where it belongs," Hook promised. "And if I'm very pleased, I may even let you come with me when I leave this cursed island. Do we have an accord?"

Starkey began to accept Hook's offer, then stopped. He glanced back toward the village and his daughter. Starkey had vowed to be honourable, and nothing Hook had ever done had been particularly honourable. Also, part of him very much wanted off the island, but at the same time, it was his home, and he cared very deeply for these people.

When he turned back, the figure was gone. He had taken a couple of steps closer, surveying the woods for any signs of the spectre . . . but nothing.

Suddenly, he felt the iron claw gently caress his shoulder. He shuddered once more.

He turned and came face to face with his former captain. Hook's features were stern and as dreadful as the dead; then it changed. His eyes softened, and a smile formed; it was warm and inviting but infinitely more frightening to Starkey.

"Well, now," the revenant mused, observing the surroundings. "Hardly the life of a bloodthirsty pirate, but I suppose you've made quite a life for yourself here."

He noticed the sleeping babe.

"Awww," Hook cooed. "Cute little papoose."

Starkey stirred, feeling beads of panic-induced sweat begin to form on his brow. He didn't know what to do. All he knew was he wanted that man as far away from his daughter as possible.

"Yours?" Hook queried.

Starkey just closed his eyes and nodded. "Yes."

"I thought so!" Hook laughed. "She's got your eyes." Gently, he caressed the baby's cheek with his claw. "Hopefully, she won't have to keep them in a jar."

"Captain please . . . !"

"So, you've started a family," James Hook mused. "Simply marvellous! What a coincidence; I was considering starting one myself."

"Don't!"

"Don't what?" Hook asked, almost insulted. "My good man, you're my First Mate. Your family is my family. On my honour, Captain James Hook would never harm his family. Now, are you my First Mate, or are you not?"

Starkey took one look at his daughter and nodded. "Ay, ay."

"Ay, ay what?" Hook bated.

"Ay, ay, captain."

"Good." Hook grinned his dastardly grin, revealing his teeth.

"But . . ." Starkey started weakly.

"But?" Hook's face changed. "But what?"

"If I help you, I want you to take my family too."

Hook silently contemplated when finally, he extended his hook. "Agreed."

CHAPTER SIXTEEN

Peter's Discovery

Time was growing short!

The Piccaninnies were well into their powwow. They celebrated by telling stories through dances. Some wore ceremonial headdresses, while others dressed like sacred animals. Father Christmas and the children were utterly delighted. Starkey, on the other hand, was downright distraught. He was holding the drink with a low-dose sleeping potion for Wendy. He did not want to give it to her, but he dared not defy the captain.

The first part was simple. Starkey would slip the goblet to Wendy while he and the other squaws passed out refreshments to the guests. He had to be careful to put very little potion into the mixture. They didn't want her passing out immediately; it would be suspicious, and they may uncover the plot. No, he would give a very small, diluted concoction to make her drowsy and lie down of her own accord. He would advise his wife Elu — who was still blissfully unaware of what her husband had gotten himself into — to let Wendy use their wigwam and give her a drink containing the rest of the potion.

He just needed the right moment when Wendy was all alone. At that moment, she was looking for Peter. Starkey continued to keep his distance and go about his duties.

Peter was doing his best to enjoy the festivities, but one thing kept grating his mind — he was the only one who didn't get a turn with the Naughty-&-Nice List. He observed Father Christmas and his elves. They were entertaining the children of the tribe. Fortunately for Peter, Father Christmas had left his sack unattended at the seat of honour — the chief had graciously allowed Father Christmas to use his hand-carved chair when he was handing out presents to the children of the tribe.

Peter grinned mischievously. He remembered that Father Christmas stored the List in his magic bag . . . and there it was! Unattended!

He made his way over to the bag. He wasn't sure where the List was lurking inside that seemingly empty sack, but Peter was determined to find it.

"What are you doing?"

Peter was startled momentarily, then turned to see Wendy.

"I have to see," Peter declared, rooting through the sack.

"Have to see what?"

"The List," Peter replied. "He put it here somewhere."

"Peter, I don't think that's a good idea."

"You're probably right," Peter declared, looking over his shoulder and thrusting the sack into Wendy's hands. "People will want to see me. Here, you take the sack behind that tent and look for it. I'll make an appearance and join you shortly."

"But, Peter—"

"Shhhh!" he hushed. "We don't want the others to get suspicious. Just be discreet, and I'll slip away when I can."

Wendy tried to protest, but Peter had already taken off, leaving Wendy with the bag.

"This is ridiculous," she sighed. She knew she shouldn't be messing around with Father Christmas' bag of presents, but she didn't want to disappoint Peter.

Casually, she slipped away from potential prying eyes and began rummaging through the sack. At first, it was just empty. Then she remembered how the List worked. She looked into the bag, closed her eyes and declared:

"Show me what Peter Pan of Neverland needs."

She stuck her hand into the sack and felt a small box. Her fingertips grazed the smooth surface of the wrapping paper. She smiled, gripping the box. When she took it out, she beheld a small present with a red bow. There was a small label dangling below the bow on a string. She unfolded it and read the tag:

For: Peter Pan
From: Father Christmas

She smiled. It wasn't what she was looking for, but she was on the right track. She supposed she needed to be more specific.

She looked back into the sack and was about to call out to it when she was startled by a short, sharp *bark!*

Wendy gasped!

When she turned, she beheld the stern, admonishing gaze of the newly youthful Newfoundland Dog.

"Oh, Nana." Wendy grabbed her chest. "You scared me."

"*Woof?*" Nana *barked*. It didn't take an expert to know she was asking what Wendy thought she was doing rummaging around the bag.

"I was just trying to find the Naughty-&-Nice List for Peter," Wendy explained.

Nana emitted a low series of *yowls*, indicating that it was improper to nose around through someone else's property without their permission.

"I know, but it wasn't fair that Peter didn't get a turn."

Nana *yowled* back.

"I know. But . . ." Wendy sighed. "But it's Peter."

Wendy turned back to the open sack and called out, "Show me the Naughty-&-Nice List."

Nana shook her head and *huffed* her disapproval.

Wendy reached into the bag and retrieved the magnificent golden scroll with its golden rollers and stand. She smiled, gazing into the radiant gold parchment.

"Excellent!" a voice called behind her. "You found it!"

She turned, and Peter had returned.

"Yes," Wendy replied. "I also found this." She held up the package. "It's for you."

"Sweet!" Peter exclaimed, sweeping it up. He set the List on a stump with a lantern to get a better look at the device.

"Peter!" Wendy called, stopping him from opening it. "Father Christmas hasn't given it to you yet. You can't open it now."

"Oh," Peter chuckled. "I almost forgot. That's not what we're here for."

Wendy saw Peter's eyes return to the List. Slowly, he reached out to take it.

Nana began to *whimper*.

"Wait," Wendy pleaded. "I still don't think it's right to use it without Father Christmas' permission."

Nana nodded and *woofed* in agreement.

"But I want to try!" Peter declared with a wide-eyed excitement.

"Well then," Father Christmas called from behind them, startling them. "I suppose you better try it then."

Wendy stood up and stammered. "Oh, sorry. I didn't mean to—"

"It's all right," Father Christmas reassured.

Stanley and Tweedle had joined them and watched Father Christmas turn to Peter.

"Well, Peter," Father Christmas insisted, "I suppose if you need to try it that badly, you should just try it?"

Peter looked over to Wendy, then back to the device. He smiled and swept up the List.

"Show me Peter Pan of Neverland," Peter ordered.

Wendy observed Father Christmas as he and his elves leaned in to watch the golden-scroll swirl. There was uncertainty in his usually ginger face. The tent flickered and flashed by the light of the candles, reflecting off the scroll. A hush fell over the group as the rollers wound down to a stop. They all held their breath as they read his name:

PETER PAN OF NEVERLAND

He didn't know how to read, but he knew the characters were different from the others. Also, the letters weren't written in green . . . they were written in red.

NAUGHTY

The silence continued to grow. Everyone looked over at Father Christmas, then back to the befuddled Peter. He couldn't believe it. The notion transcended all his rational thoughts. He simply stood there in a frozen stupor.

Wendy took a maternal step forward.

"Surely this is some sort of mistake," she cooed.

Suddenly, all eyes were on Father Christmas.

"I'm afraid not," Father Christmas declared. "Originally, I wasn't sure. I wanted to get to know the real you. But the List doesn't lie."

"How can it say that about me?" Peter demanded, unsure if he was going to yell or cry. "Just because I'm not perfect."

"Peter," Father Christmas said, as warm and loving as possible. "Being good isn't about being perfect. Believe me, every child has naughty moments. Now, I don't know what sort of unwritten pact you've made with the island and the fairies, but it's not healthy to always get whatever you want whenever you want it. A good child is teachable and can learn from their mistakes." He shook his head. "Sadly, you will never learn what's truly important in this world."

"But . . ." Wendy interjected. "Peter is a hero. He has rescued us countless times from all sorts of dangers."

Nana *barked* in agreement.

Father Christmas smiled at the sweet old girl. It was a beautiful gesture on Peter's part to give of himself to save her. But then again, what's a few years of life to someone who has lived several lifetimes and will continue to be eternally young?

"He rescues you from the dangers that he puts you in in the first place," Father Christmas explained. "And every evil villain or creature that ends up on the island was summoned out of Peter's boredom. To him, it's just a game. And the adversaries he dispatches of — the *lives* he ends — are merely points on some unwritten scorecard. Just something to boast about."

"That doesn't make sense!" Peter cried.

"Don't get me wrong, you do possess kindness and some very admirable qualities; unfortunately, there is more selfishness and wickedness in you. And it's not just the things you do. It's the things you make other children do. You convince them to run away from home and to engage in wicked behaviour. Your idea of fun and games is killing grown-ups and putting other children's lives in danger." Father Christmas sighed. "I'm afraid that despite all the fun and joy you bring to these kids, what you do is naughty."

Peter's fingers itched for his sword.

"Admit it," Father Christmas added. "You're thinking about killing me right now, aren't you?"

Peter winced. Father Christmas was right! Peter wanted to tear the old, fat *git* limb from limb! He turned away, not wanting people to see him cry.

"But I can change," Peter pleaded.

"Of course you can," Father Christmas said. "Everyone can change if they're serious about changing and are committed to working hard at it. Unfortunately, you have to be able to remember your mistakes in order to learn from them. That's the first part of growing up. And I have a feeling that's not going to happen anytime soon, now is it?"

Peter's shoulders and head drooped. He shook his head. He wanted to be better, but he didn't want to grow up. Unfortunately, it was either one or the other. There was no partial growth — if it started, he wouldn't be able to stop the clock again.

"If you're unable to appreciate the gravity of death," Father Christmas continued, "then you'll never be unable to appreciate the preciousness of life, particularly in others."

Peter's lip began to quiver as moisture overcame his eyes. He averted his gaze, then noticed the present in his hand.

"Oh, yeah!" Peter retorted. "If I'm so bad, why do I have a present?"

"I don't know," Father Christmas replied. "Maybe you should open it."

Peter tore open the wrapping and removed the lid. He froze as he saw the lump of coal.

"I'm sorry, Peter," Father Christmas consoled. "I really am."

Peter was livid! He felt like skinning that fat, *OLD* man like a rabbit! This was why he hated grown-ups! Grown-ups always set up ridiculous rules and stupid standards just so they can judge children and treat them poorly.

But then he began to worry. What if he was right? What if he was wicked? After all, his first instinct to this news was to murder a man who makes children happy.

He felt restless, helpless, and sick to his stomach. He began to weep.

"Peter," Wendy put her hand on his shoulder, trying to comfort him.

"Don't touch me!" he cried, shaking her off.

"Peter?" she recoiled.

"How could you do this to me?!"

"Me?!" Wendy cried. "What did I do?"

"I wish you never told me about Christmas!" Peter lamented. "I was better off not knowing it existed. That's it! I'm banning Christmas in Neverland!"

"But Peter," Wendy interjected. "You can't ban Christmas."

"Go home, Wendy," Peter snarled. "If you want your Christmas, go home! Go home and grow up and be like the rest of them!"

"Peter—"

"I should have never brought you here all those years ago. You're constantly trying to change me. Trying to make me fit into your world. Well, I'm done with it. Go home and leave me alone forever."

Father Christmas took a step forward. "Peter, it isn't her fault."

"Stay away from me, old man!" Peter snarled. "You don't have time for *naughty* children, and I don't have any time or patience for an old, judgmental ass like yourself!"

"Peter—" Father Christmas tried again.

"I mean it!" Peter warned. "You need to back away from me right now, or I *will* hurt you."

Father Christmas shook his head in disappointment. "Very well." He turned to Stanley and Tweedle. "Come on, boys. Let's get back to the party, and then we better start preparing to leave."

The elves nodded and followed their Boss, leaving Wendy and Peter alone once more.

Wendy stood there silently.

"You too!" Peter said.

Wendy frowned. "Surely, you don't want me to—"

"I don't know what I want," Peter snapped. "Please, I want to be alone for a minute."

Peter got up and stormed off into the woods, leaving Wendy cold and alone.

CHAPTER SEVENTEEN

Hook and Peter

Hook's plan to escape the wretched island was in sight, but there was one problem . . . Peter Pan! Hook watched the distraught child mutter to himself, weeping and kicking the snow in front of him. Peter threw his back against a tree and slid down, crying in the snowbank.

He had never seen Peter cry before. As Hook observed Peter, he didn't see his greatest foe. He simply saw a small, vulnerable child. Hook almost pitied Peter as he saw him sob. Considering how much he loathed that cocky brat, sometimes he forgot that he was merely a child.

Remember, he's the enemy, Hook reminded himself. *And right now, he's in your way.*

For a flickering moment, he worried that his years of isolation had made him go soft until a new fiendish plot formed in his mind. Hook grinned, leering at the boy from the darkness.

Peter sat alone in the snow with only his tears for comfort. He was holding the box from Father Christmas' bag. He opened the lid and stared at the coal once more when he heard a voice. It wasn't a voice he recalled hearing before, yet it sounded oddly familiar.

"Boy," the voice called courteously. "Why are you crying?"

He sprung up, alarmed! He looked around but couldn't see anybody.

"Who's there?"

"Just a friend," the voice replied.

Suddenly, a twig *snapped* behind him — the stranger was circling him.

He spun around!

Suddenly, a tall, dark figure emerged from behind the trees in the wintery mist. Peter began to draw his sword.

"No need for that," the man assured with a ginger grin and a chuckle.

Peter slid the sword back into its scabbard.

Captain Hook had concealed his iron claw in his pocket — he had also wrapped it so that if he accidentally took it out, Peter would only see the wrap. If questioned, Hook would tell Peter that he had burned his hand. He supposed it probably wasn't necessary given Peter's memory, but he wasn't about to take any chances. What if Wendy and the Lost Boys had recently shared stories of their past adventures?

Hook was sure he was just being paranoid, but better safe than sorry.

"So," Hook began, "why are you all the way out here instead of enjoying the festivities with everyone else?"

"Christmas!" Peter sneered. "Who cares about stupid ol' Christmas?"

"Well, judging by the way you were crying just now," Hook observed, "I'd say you do."

Peter's lip quivered for a brief instant, then changed. "I wasn't crying."

"I understand perfectly," Hook cooed. "I never really cared for the holiday myself."

"Really?" Peter's eyes widened. "Why?"

"Oh, I don't know," Hook started. "I suppose once you've been placed on the Naughty List, you're no longer allowed to enjoy Christmas. You just have to sit back and watch everyone else enjoy themselves."

"You were put on the Naughty List too?"

"It was completely unfair! I never did anything bad."

"Me either!"

The man was aghast. "You?"

Peter nodded.

"No! You don't mean to say that a fine upstanding young lad like yourself was placed on the Naughty List too?"

Peter nodded again.

"That's outrageous!"

"I know!" Peter exclaimed.

"Why, you don't look like a naughty child to me."

"Neither do you."

"Who are they to judge us?" Hook clamoured. "There are plenty of people in the world worse than us, and they're still getting presents."

"Exactly!"

"And you're Peter Pan, for heaven's sake!"

Peter glanced up, surprised. "You know me?"

Hook just laughed. "Come now, who in this wide world of ours doesn't know the great Peter Pan?"

Peter smiled boastfully. "I suppose that's true."

"If anybody deserves the adventure of Christmas, it's you."

"That's right! It's unfair!"

"Damn right, it's unfair! If the great Peter Pan can't celebrate Christmas, nobody should be allowed to celebrate Christmas."

"Amen to that!"

It's working, Hook thought.

"You're not a bad boy," Hook continued. "And neither am I."

"No we're not."

"You're absolutely right! Let's do it!"

"Yes!" Peter agreed, excited for action, then realised that he didn't know what he was excited about. "Do what?"

"Like you said," Hook manipulated. "Why should everyone else get to celebrate Christmas when you can't?"

"Exactly!" Peter affirmed.

"So, just like you suggested, *we* will make sure nobody gets a Christmas this year."

Peter was a little mixed up. "I said that?"

"Of course you did, lad. And it was brilliant."

Peter smiled, rather pleased with himself. He had always prided himself on his own brilliance.

"Of course it was." Peter grinned. It occurred to him he didn't know where to begin. "How?"

"Gee, I don't know," Hook mused. "I suppose if you could find a way to stop them from delivering the presents. If only we could figure out how the man in red travels around the world, we may be able to take it so he can't leave to deliver the presents."

Peter thought about it a minute and replied, "We can borrow the sled!"

"What a clever boy!" Hook exclaimed. "If you stole the sleigh, you'd be able to get even with them!"

"Yes!"

"And the magic bag."

"Yes!" Peter cried, and then he thought of Wendy. "But . . ."

"But? But what?"

"But wouldn't Wendy be cross with me?"

Hook noticed the box in Peter's hand. "What's that?"

Peter peered down at the present Wendy had pulled from Father Christmas' sack and frowned. "It's coal. They give it to naughty people."

"Wait a minute," Hook declared. "So, not only do naughty children bear the burden of not getting any presents, but the fat man has the audacity to give you *that* to rub it in your face?!"

Peter nodded.

"What kind of sick, twisted mind works like that?" Hook grunted.

"I know!"

"And they dare to call *us* naughty?" Hook exclaimed.

Suddenly, an idea formed in Hook's mind. It was both wicked and shrewd. Perhaps he could trick Peter into destroying the only people on earth who truly liked and cared about him. The idea was so devilishly delicious that he couldn't hide his smirk.

"Say," Hook proceeded, "I've got an idea. Why don't we give them a taste of their own medicine?"

"How?"

Hook grinned. "Follow me."

He led Peter to a bush in the distance where Hook had concealed several large bags. It had taken Hook many trips to sneak them out of his nearest cache and hide them outside the Piccaninny's camp. He had initially intended to give them to Starkey, but getting Peter to smuggle them in was even better. Inside the bags were several small boxes containing the little *Christmas Surprises* he wished to give everyone.

"What's in the boxes?" Peter asked.

"Just little surprises for everyone in camp," Hook replied. "A little Christmas prank. You could sneak them all over the camp."

"What is it?"

"Think of them as several large pieces of coal. To let them know exactly how *you* feel about them right now."

"I like it!"

"There is also a very loud Christmas Cracker inside . . . to scare them and make them jump. It'll be really funny."

Peter began to giggle in anticipation. "I can't wait to see their faces."

"I certainly know what you mean." Hook grinned his dastardly grin. "Of course, we can't stay and watch. While they are distracted, we will take off in the sleigh with the bag of presents. If they catch us, they will try to stop us from taking the sleigh, so you got to be very stealthy."

"I can't wait." Peter giggled excitedly, then stopped. "Will it hurt them?"

"Of course not," Hook lied in an admonishing tone. "Peter, I'm surprised you would even suggest such a thing. But I promise you, they will regret they treated you so poorly."

Peter gazed at the boxes and smiled a wicked smile of his own.

CHAPTER EIGHTEEN

Hook's Plan in Motion

Wendy continued to stand at the edge of the camp, feeling the chill of the cold winter night almost as deeply as the cold glare in Peter's eyes. She had been watching the woods ever since their quarrel. She was waiting for Peter to come back, but she supposed that he wasn't going to.

Wendy was hurt. She felt bad for Peter, but how could he talk to her like that?

Wendy headed back to camp, lost in thought. When Peter first taught her how to fly, he told her that only children could fly as long as they were gay, innocent, and heartless. Of course, children were not heartless by choice — it was just the carelessness that comes with a childlike naivete. Her heart grew after her first adventure, and she learned about consideration and empathy for her parents. Peter, on the other hand, refused to learn.

Perhaps Father Christmas was right. If Peter was heartless by choice, wasn't that the definition of naughty?

Wendy was so lost in her thoughts that she didn't notice Gentleman Starkey when she turned the corner. She ploughed right into his tray, knocking it to the ground.

"Oh, goodness! Sorry, I didn't see you there." she apologised.

"Think nothing of it, Miss Wendy," Starkey replied. "No harm done."

"I'm so sorry I didn't see you." She stamped her foot. "Oh! I'm all mixed up!"

"What's wrong?" He glanced back at the spot where she had been waiting for Peter. "Oh, are we having problems with a certain young boy?"

She gave a guilty smile. "Deep down, I know he's good, but there are times when he can be the most conceited, arrogant and nasty boy in the world."

"Believe me, you're preaching to the choir," Starkey smirked.

She thought about it a minute and laughed. "Oh, yes. I almost forgot that you're a pirate."

"Not anymore," Starkey corrected. "I'm retired, and that *nice* little boy killed the last of them four years ago. I'm just a glorified babysitter, and Heaven knows what's become of Smee." He shook his head. "To be perfectly honest, I have no trouble believing he landed on Father Christmas' Naughty List."

Wendy sighed. "I know."

"Don't look so glum. Why don't you go back and enjoy the party?" Starkey suggested.

"Maybe later. I'm not really in the mood to mingle."

"I understand." He thought a moment, then smiled. "Have you tried that drink those little fellers are passing around?"

She shook her head.

"They call it cocoa," Starkey explained. "It's a warm, rather strange-looking brown confection. But blimey, it's good! Why don't I go get us some?"

She smiled and nodded. "Okay."

This couldn't have worked out better for the captain, Starkey thought. Jas always seemed to have the luck of *Old Nick*.

He turned to leave, and Wendy tapped his shoulder. He turned back.

"Thanks for talking to me," she said. "Sorry I was so uncomfortable around you at first with the whole pirate thing. You're a good listener and a good man."

Guilt flowed through his body. He liked Wendy and didn't want to see anything bad happen to her.

"Thank you," he replied. "You don't know how much that means to me."

He nodded and went to get the cocoa.

Starkey began to wonder how bad it would be if he just *happened to forget* to put Hook's potion in her cocoa. Then he thought of the captain's claw gently caressing Lizzie's cheek and shuddered.

It pained him greatly. He may have liked Wendy, but he *LOVED* his daughter. If he had to choose between Wendy and his daughter, it was no contest.

Wendy had spilt the original drink, so he slipped in a slightly stronger concentration of sleeping potion. He stared at the cup of cocoa. For a moment, he was tempted to spill it out, then remembered the murderous red sparks in Hook's eyes all those years ago. He closed his eyes and took a long breath.

"For Lizzie," he whispered.

When he came back, Wendy happily took her first sip.

"Oh, my," she exclaimed. "This is scrumptious!"

He smiled wryly and sipped his cocoa silently. As they talked, she began to sway and swoon.

"Are you all right?" Starkey asked.

"I feel funny," she replied. "I got real dizzy all of a sudden."

"Maybe you better have a bit of a lie-down," he suggested. "You can use the cot in my tent and take a little nap."

She yawned. "Perhaps you're right. I'm exhausted."

With his help, she staggered to her feet, and he escorted her to his wigwam. Her eyelids continued to droop, but she still saw Lizzie asleep in her bed.

"So precious." Wendy yawned. "Is that your daughter?"

"Yes," Starkey replied. "That's my Lizzie."

"She is beautiful." Wendy smiled. "She takes after her father."

Starkey smiled back, and his heart sank. "Thank you."

She managed to lay down and was asleep before her head could hit the pillow.

"May god forgive me," he uttered aloud.

He watched Wendy sleep for a moment. He brushed a strand of hair off her face in a gentle, fatherly manner. As he observed her, he realised that she was just a sleeping babe, much like his daughter Lizzie. A stronger twinge of guilt and unease arose inside of him once more. But nothing was more important than his family. He only hoped he could find the strength to deliver her when it was time to go.

While Starkey was contemplating Wendy's fate, Peter had surreptitiously placed Hook's special presents all over the camp. It was a very fun game for Peter, to sleuth in the shadows and avoid detection. He had placed them all within five or six metres of each other, just as his new friend had instructed. Now, all he had to do was swipe the bag, but at that moment, it was next to Father Christmas and the two elves. He needed to bide his time and concoct a cunning plan.

If only there were another bag that looked like it, he could apologise and switch them out without anybody noticing. Unfortunately, he had never seen a fabric quite like it before. He would just have to continue to wait until they left it unguarded.

While Peter was watching the bag, Captain James Hook put the finishing touches on his final present for the camp. It was an enormous, round shell filled with spikes, nails, and over twenty pounds of gunpowder.

As a matter of fact, all of the *Christmas Surprises* that Peter had been smuggling into the camp were filled with explosives and sharp metal projectiles that could obliterate anything in a six-metre radius. Of course, those didn't have a fuse. Only the bomb, being carefully crafted by Hook, would be lit. The force of that blast would start a chain reaction. It would ignite the bombs closest to it, and those would ignite the outer layers.

It was a set-up that he had used before. He had lost his first ship to the Spanish Armada but escaped with his best men. At the ceremonial banquet — which was held in honour of the Officers and Admiralty responsible for sinking Hook's vessel — Hook's crew had infiltrated the catering staff. They had smuggled bombs all over the building. He knew he needed plenty of time to escape, so he had developed some unique candles. Hook had ten-minute candles, twenty-minute candles, and some candles that could take up to two hours to melt through the wax before detonating the bomb.

Hook had finagled the lead bomb into the centrepiece at the banquet. After lighting it, it gave him two hours to let everyone settle in and for him to hijack the lightly guarded ship he would later rename, *The Jolly Roger*. He would be well out to sea before the bomb finally went off.

He smiled once more, remembering how he was able to see the building erupt in flames even from his distance in the open waters. It was the assassination that rocked the nautical world. He became world-famous and the most wanted war criminal in Spain since Sir Francis Drake.

Of course, he couldn't risk waiting two hours this time — he couldn't even risk one hour. He had brought several candles with him to give him plenty of options while waiting for Starkey, but with Peter taking his First Mate's place, he supposed he didn't need quite as much time. Hook held up the twenty-minute candle and pondered if it was enough time to get back to the Never-tree and the sled. He supposed he did, then sealed up the bomb with the candle.

Hook was a little nervous because he still didn't know how to fly the reindeer-drawn sleigh, but sometimes in life, you have to just go for it! Besides, he felt that he had gotten the gist while overhearing Father Christmas explain the reindeer to the children. All he had to do was wait for Peter to return.

It wasn't long before he saw Peter Pan flying in, carrying the magic bag.

"All right," Peter called. "We've got everything."

"Excellent!" Hook praised. "Is that really the magic bag?"

"Absolutely."

"You've done a fine job, lad," Hook flattered. He looked down, making himself look contemplative. "Now, I've been thinking. Wouldn't it be nice if we got to keep all of the presents?"

"Well, yeah. But we can't use the bag," Peter replied.

"Why not?" Hook asked, pretending not to know already.

"We're naughty."

"Hmmm . . ." Hook thought a moment. "What if we brought someone who wasn't naughty to get the presents for us?"

"Who?"

Hook paced back and forth, pretending that his next suggestion was spontaneous. "I know! How about the young lady you were talking about earlier?"

"Wendy?" Peter got excited, then frowned. "I don't think she would approve."

"Surely you think she deserves some Christmas presents too, right?"

"Of course. But she'll never come."

"You know, I think I saw her go take a nap in one of the tents. I bet a smart, strong young lad like yourself could carry her back to the sleigh without waking her."

"I don't know."

"Come now, Peter. When have I ever steered you wrong?"

"You're right." Peter agreed. "I'll do it."

Peter turned to fly, but Hook grabbed his shoulder. "Oh, whoa-whoa. Not so fast. I love your enthusiasm, lad. But there is one last thing you need to do."

Peter listened attentively.

"I have one last Christmas cracker." Hook held it up. "It's bigger than the rest. You need to place it in the centre of the camp, and you need to light this candle. Otherwise, nobody will get to see the fireworks. You will then grab Wendy and fly her to the sleigh. I will meet you there, and then we will take off. Remember, don't let anyone see or know what you're doing, or it will ruin everything."

Peter nodded and took the bomb, and flew off.

Hook realised he had made a deal with Starkey, but as everyone knows, deals change. He made his way back to the Never-tree; he had a date to keep with eight tiny reindeer.

CHAPTER NINETEEN

Starkey's Discovery

Starkey had been going about his duties for the Piccaninnies. After cleaning up the remainder of the banquet, he figured he could slip away and retrieve Wendy completely undetected. He had never smuggled anything out of camp before, so he was considerably nervous.

As he cleared away the adobe cups and bowls, he noticed a strange wrapped parcel hidden inside a partially hollowed-out log — which was being used as a bench at the moment. He glanced casually over his shoulder to make sure the coast was clear. He set down the dishes and knelt down to inspect the package.

He stayed low and unwrapped the gift as cautiously as possible. He managed to keep one eye out in case someone happened to venture near. When he drew back the lid, he gasped! He immediately recognised that the big black orb inside . . . was a bomb!

"Oh, dear god," he moaned to himself.

He noticed that the bomb didn't have a fuse, and in that instant, he knew Hook's plan. He had helped him execute it on many occasions. It was the ceremony at the Spanish Court all over again. He knew that if there was one, then the whole camp would be infested with these deadly parcels.

He felt sick to his stomach. Hook had told him about stealing the sleigh and leaving the owners stranded, but he had no idea he had planned to kill everyone!

He supposed he wasn't entirely surprised, but he still didn't want to see anything bad happen to his new family!

Now the thing that struck him was . . . how could Hook have possibly infiltrated the camp without detection? He wouldn't exactly blend in with this crowd.

"Maybe he really is a ghost," he muttered. He knew that if these were in place, there would be a lit bomb somewhere in the centre of the camp.

He didn't know what to do.

His conscience rippled throughout his body, causing him to tremble once more. It was his home. They were his wife and daughter's family, and he loved the tribe.

Starkey knew that if the candle had been lit, then the bomb could go off at any moment — it could be a few hours or just a few minutes. He had no idea how much time was left until the candle's wax was spent.

Starkey set the bomb down.

Time was *ticking* in his head! It *ticked* like the clock that the murderous crocodile had eaten all those years ago. But for him, it was counting down; and once it got to zero . . . !

Starkey dashed off to search for his wife!

Elu was still assisting with the refreshments for the powwow. Starkey rushed to her. He instructed her to swaddle up Lizzie and to wait for him at the grove outside of camp. Elu started to protest, but he was so scared and insistent that she complied without question.

Starkey immediately rushed to his wigwam to check on Wendy. He drew back the entrance flap, and when he entered, he gasped!

His cot was empty!

It was impossible!

"Wendy?" he called.

It didn't make sense; he gave a strong enough dose that she should be out for several hours.

"Wendy?"

He continued to search the room. When it was clear that she wasn't there, he dashed outside, looking for any signs of Wendy.

Did she wake up?

Starkey rejoined the party and searched through the crowd. He kept surveying the grounds, but she was nowhere in sight. He took a breath and saw the candles on the table. As he watched the hot flames, he noticed the wax slowly drip onto the table, and he remembered the bomb!

Part of him knew he needed to get out of there as fast as he could, or he'd be blown up with the rest of the camp. At the same time, he knew that if he showed up without Wendy, there was no telling what Hook would do to him — or his family!

He continued to search the other wigwams and felt the growing weight of fear and anxiety pulsate through his body. Many of them had Hook's *special* packages hidden in them as well.

Suddenly, it hit him!

If Hook was crafty enough to smuggle the bombs into camp, why couldn't he figure out a way to smuggle Wendy out of camp?

As he stood in a tent, he decided that he had pressed his luck with the bombs long enough and took off into the woods to regroup with his family.

At that exact moment, John and Michael began to realise that they hadn't seen their sister in quite some time.

"Has anyone seen Wendy?" Michael asked.

Everyone shook their head.

"No, not since Peter yelled at her," Tweedle replied.

"Peter yelled at Wendy?" John asked. "Whatever for?"

Stanley shrugged. "Honestly, Peter was so angry when he found out he was on the Naughty List that I don't think he knew what he was saying."

"He what?!" John and Michael exclaimed in unison.

"Oh, boy." Stanley groaned. "I probably shouldn't have said anything. But if you promise to keep it to yourselves, I'll tell you what happened."

The elves told them everything they knew but whispered softly to avoid being overheard by casual eavesdroppers. You see, Father Christmas and his workers all adhere to a strict Child/Christmas Confidentiality Policy.

"Should we go look for Wendy and Peter?" Michael asked.

"I think we should probably give them some space," Stanley advised.

The group agreed that Wendy and Peter needed time to work out their issues. Nana, on the other hand, wasn't so sure. She decided to do a little sleuthing of her own. Nana retraced their steps back to where Wendy and Peter had their quarrel. As the nervous Newfoundland Dog brought her nose to the ground, she immediately picked up their scent — all of them! She could easily distinguish the unique aromas of Peter, Wendy, Father Christmas, and the elves — even in the snow!

Nana was pleasantly surprised at how keen her sense of smell had gotten ever since the incident at Cannibal Cove. She decided to focus on Wendy's scent. Wendy had followed Peter into the woods. After lingering there, Wendy's fragrance headed back to camp.

Soon the smell led Nana to a spot where Wendy had bumped into a stranger. It was a man, but Nana didn't recognise his musk. After interacting with the stranger, Wendy staggered to a wigwam in the back. Nana followed her nose to the cot where Wendy had laid down to take a nap. She could tell the stranger had left the tent, but someone else entered the room shortly after. It was Peter! Peter had approached the cot, and suddenly, their smells vanished!

Nana was baffled. How could their scent simply disappear like that?

Nana pondered this for a moment when she realised that Peter must have flown Wendy out of the tent. But why?

Nana let out a soft *whine*. She was beginning to fear for Wendy's safety once more. All of her canine intuitions indicated danger! She supposed that Peter and Wendy could have made up and flown off somewhere innocently together, but she didn't think so.

As Nana left the tent, she got her first strong whiff of gunpowder!

While Nana pursued the new scent, Peter flew the unconscious Wendy straight into the clutches of Captain James Hook.

"I lit the candle and grabbed Wendy," Peter reported back.

"Excellent job, my boy!" Hook praised, placing the last bag of treasure into the sleigh. He managed to retrieve his stash on his way back to the Never-tree.

The former captain sighed, gazing at his meagre bounty. It was a little disheartening for Hook to leave his vast fortune behind. Still, it was reassuring to know that this booty was still enough to make him wealthier than most kings.

"Now, I've prepared the reindeer," Hook informed. "Put Wendy in the back, and let's be off!"

"Right away!"

Peter set Wendy down gently and covered her with a blanket. He knew how cold Wendy got with high altitudes. He got in the front seat with Hook.

"All right," Peter said. "Let's go!"

Hook whipped at the reins, and . . . nothing happened.

He tried again.

"Why aren't they moving?" Captain Hook asked.

"I don't know," Peter replied.

Hook whipped the reins again, and the reindeer remained motionless.

Hook turned to Peter. "Is there something we're forgetting?"

"I don't know."

"Think, lad. Think carefully."

Peter had never ridden in the sleigh, so he had no idea how to operate it. However, Wendy had told him all sorts of stories about Father Christmas. He tried to remember what she had said about the reindeer. That's when Peter remembered the poem she had read. He liked it so much that he had her re-read it several times.

What did they do?

"Well?" Hook asked, exasperated.

"The names!" Peter replied. "In the story, Father Christmas called out the reindeer's names." He smiled, so proud of himself.

"Excellent!" Hook replied. "And what are their names?"

Peter turned to answer, then stopped. "I don't remember."

"You don't remember?!"

Peter shook his head.

Suddenly, Hook remembered who he was talking to and sighed. They thought for a moment when Peter broke the silence.

"Look." Peter pointed. "They have them written on the name tags."

"Well spotted, my boy!" Hook exclaimed, patting Peter on the back. Hook leaned in and squinted, trying to make out the words. "I'm afraid my eyes aren't what they used to be. What do they say?"

"I'm not sure," Peter replied. "I can't read."

Hook took a deep, exasperated breath to maintain his composure. "One moment," he declared, hopping out of the sleigh.

Hook inspected each reindeer one by one. He wanted to make sure he didn't forget their names, so he wrote them down on a piece of parchment. After examining them, he studied the completed list.

What peculiar names, Hook mused to himself.

After remounting the sleigh, Hook took the reins once more. "Okay." Hook declared, addressing the reindeer. "Now, Dasher! Now, Dancer! Now, Prancer! Now, Vixen! On, Comet! On, Cupid! On, Dunder and Blixem!" He turned to Peter. "I sure hope I said it right."

Hook whipped the reins again, and the reindeer began to trot.

Peter and Hook laughed with excitement and delight!

"We're really doing this!" Peter exclaimed. He was elated to be embarking on another awfully big adventure.

Suddenly, Starkey and his family entered the clearing. Starkey gasped, seeing the reindeer pick up speed. He started running for the sleigh. "Captain, wait!"

Hook glanced back, still concentrating on guiding the reindeer.

"Wait for me!" Starkey cried.

"Ah, Starkey," Hook replied without looking back at him, "almost forgot about you."

"Stop the sleigh so we can get on!" Starkey begged, running faster.

"Sorry, dear boy, but I'm afraid there has been a change in plans."

"What?!"

"I'm afraid we have a full sleigh, and we're just not able to fit all of you."

"At least take my wife and daughter. You don't know what they'll do to us when they find out what we've done."

Hook let out a loud, ghastly laugh. "Starkey, me ol' mate! Somehow, I don't think anyone will come looking for you." Hook turned to face Starkey and grinned. "Remember the Imperial Court?"

Starkey stopped running.

"No need to thank me," Hook said. He whipped the reins harder, and the reindeer began to take flight once again.

Panic and guilt filled Starkey's face.

"Oh, and Starkey," Hook called down. "Happy Christmas."

Hook laughed his wicked laugh once more.

"Don't go," Starkey muttered weakly as the sleigh flew off in the distance.

Starkey stood there, feeling scared and betrayed. He couldn't move, watching them shrink in the distance. Finally, something flared in his mind. At that moment, he had a choice. The bombs were still at the camp. If they found out that he had helped Captain Hook again, they would surely scalp him and tie him to four wild horses.

He grimaced at the thought.

As Hook had suggested, he could simply stay there and leave everyone to their fate. As the old pirate maxim went: *Dead Men Tell No Tales* — or as Captain Flint was prone to say: *Dead Men Don't Bite!*

On the other hand, he loved his people. He didn't think he could live with himself if he were responsible for the death of the people that he considered family.

Once again, he felt the pressure of the incessant *ticking* of time in his mind. He supposed that even if he were to come back, there was still no guarantee he could get to them in time.

His wife put her hand on his shoulder. He looked at her, and she smiled, rubbing his back. When he saw the look of concern and love in her eyes, he felt ashamed. He didn't deserve her. Then he looked at Lizzie, curled up and sleeping peacefully in her mother's arms.

These were Lizzie's people. And she deserved a father she could look up to. He may have begun life on this island as a pirate, but he was determined to leave it as a man of honour.

He stood tall, full of resolve to protect his new family. Even if it was too late, he still had to try. He told Elu to stay there with Lizzie — far away from danger. He would have liked to stay to help her kindle a fire, but there was no time. Besides, he knew his wife could manage easily enough — she was a strong and wonderful woman.

He sprinted off, rushing to return to the tribe.

CHAPTER TWENTY

Starkey's Redemption

Father Christmas and the elves were surprised by the sound of sleigh bells *jingling* in the distance. When they spun around, they saw the sleigh ascend into the sky.

"What the devil?" Father Christmas grumbled. "They wouldn't leave without me."

Father Christmas *whistled* to his team, but they were too far away. He reached into his coat and magically produced a pair of high-powered binoculars — the likes the boys had never seen.

"There's a man with a hook flying my sleigh," Father Christmas declared.

"A hook?" John repeated. "Let me see those."

Father Christmas handed the binoculars to John. John was astonished at how clear and powerful the images were. After a moment, he turned to the group with a shocked, horrified expression on his face. "Blimey! It's Captain Hook!"

The group gasped.

"I thought he was dead," Michael replied.

"Clearly, not dead enough," Tweedle proclaimed.

"But how did he—"

Before Michael could complete his sentence, Starkey burst into the clearing.

"Everybody, flee!" Starkey called, rushing past. "It's Captain Hook! He and Peter took Wendy, stole the sleigh, and planted bombs all over camp."

"Peter?!" the group gasped.

They couldn't believe it. Peter may have had his faults, but they could never imagine such a betrayal. John looked back through the binoculars, and his heart sank when he saw Peter at Hook's side.

Nana started *barking*, alarmed for Wendy.

"But why would he do this?" Father Christmas asked.

"He didn't seem particularly happy when he found out he was on the Naughty List," Stanley replied.

"Even so, he isn't the sort to just do something like this."

"The captain must've tricked him," Starkey replied. "He knows how to manipulate people. He preys on them in their weakest moments — he's a master at that! Anyway, it doesn't matter. Everybody needs to start running! I got to find the bomb!"

"Where?!" Stanley asked.

"They're all over the place!" Starkey declared. "But the one I'm looking for is hidden in one of the packages."

"Like this one?" Michael asked, picking one up.

"Yes, but that one doesn't have a fuse! There are many bombs in the camp, but only one has a lit fuse, and when it melts through the candle wax, it will go off, and that blast will cause a chain reaction, detonating all the others."

"My god," Stanley uttered. "Peter's hidden them all over the camp."

"Yes! So, you need to start running now! I'm going to look for it, but if Hook took off, then the bomb could go off at any moment!"

"Can I help?" Father Christmas asked.

"Just make sure everyone evacuates the camp safely," Starkey advised. He started to turn, then stopped. "Oh, and, if anything happens to me, find my wife and daughter and make sure they're safe and looked after." He paused, getting emotional. "And let them know . . . that I did the right thing in the end."

Father Christmas gave a reassuring pat on the shoulder. "You're a good man, Gentleman Starkey."

John made sure Michael went with the other Lost Boys but stayed behind.

"What are we looking for?" John asked.

"It's somewhere in the centre of camp, so its blast radius can trigger the rest," Starkey panicked. "I just can't seem to spot where."

They searched the grounds but came up empty. Time was running out, and the Lost Boys and the tribe weren't far enough away yet.

"I don't know what to do!" John cried.

"Me neither!" Starkey admitted.

Nana had been looking after Michael when she noticed that John was still in danger. She *barked* to him, but John didn't seem to hear it.

Suddenly, Nana remembered that she had been gifted with a new nose. She could find the bomb!

Nana took off *barking*.

"Nana?" John called.

She hurried to them and *barked* for John to get away from the danger.

"But I need to help," John explained.

Nana *barked* again.

"What did she say?" Starkey asked.

"She said she could find it."

Nana nodded, then put her nose to the ground and began sniffing for the aroma of *fire, melting wax,* and *gunpowder.* After a moment of concentration, she *barked* and then took off!

"I think she's caught the scent," John declared.

"Good," Starkey replied. "Now, you got to get out of here!"

John nodded and ran to rejoin Michael and the rest of the boys as fast as he could! Starkey hurried to catch up with Nana.

Nana frantically sniffed around, hoping to find it in time. The scent led her to the seat at the head of the table. Starkey didn't see anything, but Nana buried her nose into the earth and *barked!* Nana began digging! When Starkey saw what she was doing, he got on his hands and knees to help. As he reached into the earth, he could feel the soil was loose!

How did he get it down here? Starkey wondered.

They frantically dug into the earth, pulling up large handfuls of dirt. Finally, Starkey saw the box. It was tall! He supposed it was to prevent the container from burning — but even if it did catch fire, the soil on top would quell the flames but still allow the candle to burn inside.

Gently, Starkey opened the lid — if he was lucky, there was still time to blow out the candle. When he saw the bomb, he saw strands of melted wax dripping down its shell. He immediately realised he couldn't see the flame, but he could still smell the fire burning on the wick.

It had dropped below the surface!

He *gasped*, knowing it could go off at any moment!

Starkey grabbed a clay goblet from the table and poured its contents over the hole. He didn't know if it worked, but he wasn't about to wait around to find out! There was a stream to the north of camp. He was going to try to dump it.

"Good job, ol' girl!" Starkey said, commending Nana. "Now, you need to get out of here as fast as you can!"

Starkey picked up the bomb and took off running to the north — Nana bolted off to the south. The tribe still hadn't reached the end of the perimeter! If the bomb went off now, they still couldn't escape the fallout explosions!

Starkey ran faster! His heart was racing in his chest!

The metal casing began to heat up in his hands.

"Come on!" Starkey begged. "Just a little further."

The group looked on from Father Christmas' binoculars. They saw Starkey and the stream up ahead.

"Come on," Father Christmas cried. "You can do it."

Starkey reached the stream! He stopped, swinging the heavy bomb back and flinging it forward with all his might.

The bomb soared through the air. To Starkey, it felt like it was moving painfully slow. As it began to drop back down, he was afraid his toss would come up short!

The bomb continued to drift downward but managed to hit the water.

Starkey breathed a sigh of relief as it sank into the stream. He was about to turn back to the camp when—

BOOOOOM!!!

The water splashed up, erupting with the full force of the explosion! It worked! The stream had muted the blast and prevented the other bombs from detonating.

At the far end of camp, the others watched on and cheered!

Starkey smiled and then realised how bad his body felt. When he glanced down, he discovered his clothes were drenched in blood.

He felt weak. Suddenly, he dropped to his knees and collapsed on the floor.

Father Christmas and the group ran after him. When they got there, he was lying in a pool of his own blood.

"Starkey?" Father Christmas called. He drew back Starkey's garment to assess the damage. When he did, he saw Starkey's body was riddled with many hot, sharp nails and pieces of shrapnel. They had penetrated most of his vital organs.

"Do something!" John cried.

"I'm afraid there's nothing we can do," Father Christmas declared solemnly.

"What about back there with Nana?" John asked.

Nana *barked* in affirmation.

Father Christmas shook his head. "That's not going to work this time. They stole my bag when they stole the sleigh." He turned to Stanley and Tweedle. "Boys, do you have any spare magic on you?"

Stanley shook his head, heartbroken.

"*Nooooo!!*" Elu cried. She had heard the explosion and hurried to investigate. Her heart sank, seeing her husband lying at the edges of the stream — his blood stained the white snow with a bright red. She rushed to his side.

The rest of the tribe had gathered around.

"Him, a grand warrior," the chief declared. "Him shall be buried with honour and join mighty warriors in Happy Hunting Ground."

Starkey stirred.

"I think he's trying to say something," Tweedle observed.

Starkey gestured to his wife, Elu. He wanted to see her and his beautiful baby girl Lizzie one last time.

"When she gets old enough . . ." He coughed and sputtered blood. ". . . old enough to understand, tell her that her daddy loved her very much. And in the end . . . he did the right thing.”

He gently reached up and touched Lizzie’s head. With his remaining strength, he reached out to Elu. His hand was cold and trembling, but he still managed to wipe her tears with the ball of his thumb and smiled.

“Hey, it’ll be okay,” he assured. “I love you.”

Elu sobbed, “I love you too.”

He gasped and closed his eyes.

Thus perished Starkey.

CHAPTER TWENTY-ONE

Taking Flight

Soaring up, high in the sky, Captain Hook and Peter Pan shared a devious chuckle. Feeling the wind whip at their faces was exhilarating. It was the perfect heist and the perfect getaway.

Even though the reindeer were well trained and did most of the work, Captain Hook still had difficulty controlling the sleigh. It was, after all, his first time flying magical reindeer — it was his first time flying anything for that matter.

They had found the breathing apparatuses that Father Christmas had made for the elves. It didn't take long for Hook to understand their importance. He put it on quickly and was impressed at how light and comfortable they were to wear. Peter also chose to wear one — he didn't physically need one, but it was all part of the game and helped make it fun.

Hook wasn't used to the speeds or altitudes, but he discovered that he was fine so long as he didn't look directly over the edge. As for navigation, he didn't have a map, but as a devoted sailor who had lived many lifetimes, he did a fine job navigating by the stars.

Hook was unaffected by his difficulties; he had a wide, childlike smile on his face. He was having the time of his life! He hated to admit it, but being on the same side as Peter Pan was oddly thrilling and, dare he say, fun! Peter was surprisingly more competent than Hook's previous crews. And Peter's youth and enthusiasm were surprisingly infectious — even for an old *blaggard* like Hook.

Once again, Hook had to remind himself that Peter was the enemy — and more importantly, he had a sneaking suspicion that he still needed Peter.

They had also discovered a small bag that Father Christmas kept in the front seat. It was scarlet with gold lettering reading: *Sandman Powder*. Hook had a feeling he knew what it was but didn't have the chance to test it yet. He simply advised Peter not to open it.

"So, what do we do now?" Peter asked.

"I don't know," Hook admitted. "I suppose I'll head back to England. I'll find a nice Inn and start opening presents."

Peter nodded in agreement. He desperately wanted to open presents too.

Hook glanced offhandedly. "Also, I suppose it's high time I start planning my wedding."

"You're getting married?" Peter scrunched up his nose — he found the whole concept both unpleasant and distasteful.

"Well, I'm not exactly a boy anymore," Hook explained. "It could be nice to have someone look after me in my old age."

"Like a mother?"

Hook gazed down at the boy and grinned. "Well, I suppose a lot of men think that way. For them, a wife is more of a substitute mother. Then others view their spouse as more of a Partner in Crime."

"Which one are you?" Peter asked.

Hook thought about it a moment. "I suppose I'd like a Partner in Crime. But I'm willing to settle for a mother."

Hook glanced back at Wendy. He suspected Wendy would be more like a mother than a partner, but he supposed that was all right by him — he had intended to retire anyhow. She wasn't going to be too keen at first, but he had once been renowned for his ineffable charm. It was going to be challenging to woo her, but he felt that she would come to her senses . . . eventually.

"I want to do something fun," Peter declared.

"Like what?"

Peter thought for a minute. "We can pretend to be delivering toys to children all over the world."

"Come now, lad," Hook sneered. "We're stealing presents, and you want to play Father Christmas? If anything, we're pirates of the sky!"

Peter's eyes lit up with excitement.

"Pirates of the Sky?" Peter rubbed his hands together with delight.

That sounded like an excellent game! Peter had completely forgotten how much fun he had playing pirates. When he and the Lost Boys had initially defeated Captain Hook and his crew, he took over the *Jolly Roger* and sailed out to the open ocean. Peter had imagined that they were the scum of Rio and the Gold Coast, and Captain Pan treated his men like dogs. He kept switching between a pirate ship and an honest vessel — but deep down, it was much more fun to be a pirate. But since all those memories were lost to Peter, this was a new and exciting experience.

"Shouldn't we plunder and seek out treasure?!" Peter exclaimed heartily.

"I like the way you think, lad." Hook chuckled, gripping his shoulder with pride.

Hook realised that his good fortune wouldn't last forever. He had been gifted with the opportunity of a lifetime, so he needed to act fast! After all, it wasn't every day that you have a flying sleigh, a magic bag, a boy who could fly, and a bag of *Sandman Powder* just fall into your lap. He couldn't waste this opportunity, but what incredible caper was worthy of this crew?

He knew he couldn't waste it on just any old heist . . . it had to be spectacular! It had to be something impossible!

He thought about it, and it didn't take long to realise that there was one last score to settle. One great heist he had always wanted to undertake, but he didn't dare to attempt it . . . until now.

"Tell you what," Hook mused. "I know a place to plunder once we get to England. And if we happen to come across a cargo barge or a fishing lorry along the way, we can practice pillaging it for fun. I want to test out this *Sandman Powder* and see what it can do."

"Awesome!"

While they were contemplating their new airborne piracy, Father Christmas and the others on the island had mourned the loss of Gentleman Starkey. Now their main priority was to get off the island and to get Father Christmas' sleigh back.

Some of the boys had initially tried to fly after the sleigh, but it was long gone. Besides, Father Christmas' reindeer were infinitely faster flyers than the Lost Boys or any of the fairies. There had been talks about Father Christmas and the elves learning to fly with pixie dust, but they had too far to go and too little time.

"Thank you, boys," Father Christmas started, "but I'm afraid it's just not going to be good enough. We don't even know where they're going, and it would take too long to get to the North Pole flying this slow."

Father Christmas reached into his coat. He still had a small pouch with magic feed for the reindeer. The feed not only helped the reindeer fly but also allowed them to achieve speeds only possible when Father Christmas was in his pure state. He always carried a spare pouch in case the reindeer's magic ran down prematurely, and they needed a quick pick-me-up.

"I suppose I could always give this magic feed to something else to pull my sleigh," Father Christmas began. "But I don't see any large animals around here smart enough to handle flying without years of training."

"You can give it to us," Pipkin suggested.

"Yeah," John agreed. "We've had plenty of flight training."

Father Christmas scratched his beard and shook his head. "I don't know."

"Well," Stanley interjected, "technically, it's possible."

Father Christmas pondered long and hard. "Theoretically, yes. But it's still too risky. We've never tested it on mortals before — particularly children."

Nana *barked*, and its intent was clear: "You can test it on me."

Father Christmas turned and smiled. "Are you sure?"

Nana let out a brief series of *yowls*, *yips*, and *whimpers*. Again, the message was clear. They had Wendy. Nana loved her as if she were her own pup. It was her sworn duty to protect her charges safe at any cost.

Father Christmas nodded. "Very well." He reached into the pouch and offered up a small handful of magic feed.

Nana approached the feed cautiously. It smelled enough like regular feed, but there was also something unusual about its fragrance. She was nervous, but she'd do anything for the children.

She opened her mouth and lapped it up.

Everyone leaned in close to observe her.

Well, it tastes normal enough, Nana thought, scarfing it down.

"Now what?" John asked.

"Now, we test her," Father Christmas replied. Quickly, he fashioned a harness out of rope and fastened it around Nana securely. "All right, are you ready?"

If Nana was perfectly honest, she most definitely wasn't ready for this. She was so terrified that she couldn't stop shaking — it was worse than going to the veterinarian. But she loved Wendy and was willing to do whatever was necessary.

Nana looked back at Father Christmas. She nodded and *woofed*, "Yes."

Father Christmas saw how much she was trembling. He walked over and scratched her behind the ear. "It'll be okay."

After patting her on the back, he returned to his spot. He gripped the rope firmly and called out. "All right, Nana. Up!"

Suddenly, Nana and Father Christmas levitated.

"Just a quick jaunt around the island," Father Christmas declared. He whipped the reins and called, "Ho!"

Suddenly, they vanished, and the boys' mouths were agape.

"What are you boys looking at?" a voice called from behind them.

They turned and saw Nana and Father Christmas standing there as if nothing had happened.

"How'd you do that?" Michael asked. His eyes were like saucers.

"We flew around the island," Father Christmas replied.

"The entire island?" John inquired. "I didn't even blink."

"I needed to know if it was safe to go full speed with a carbon-based life form on this dimensional plane," Father Christmas explained. "After testing the transfiguration process with Nana, I feel it should be safe enough for the rest of you."

"And what does that mean?" John asked.

"Oh, it's just magic stuff," Stanley dismissed. "Nothing to concern yourself with."

"Everyone always says that," John complained. "It would be nice, just once, to hear a scientific explanation."

"Very well," Tweedle conceded. "Father Christmas is made up of pure belief, which means when you see or hear him in a solid state, magic is generating a mass so he can exist and interact with matter on this plane of existence. But whenever he needs to fly at full speed, the magic is diverted, and his mass is reduced back to absolute zero. Then the magic sort of generates its own *true* zero-gravity field, compelling him and his travellers to move . . . well . . . impossibly fast."

The boys just stared at him blankly.

"And the magic feed allows the reindeer to do all that?" John asked, scratching his head.

"Exactly," Stanley affirmed. "It also gives the reindeer a molecular fluidity that allows their mass to reduce to zero too without, you know, killing them."

The boys gulped, suddenly feeling afraid.

"Wait, if we need the magic feed to go full speed," John clarified, "does that mean Peter and Wendy can die up there?"

Father Christmas stepped forward. "I wouldn't worry about that," he assured. "They can't travel outside the limitations of this dimensional plane on their own."

"He's right," Tweedle confirmed. "The reindeer can't go full speed or transfigure without Father Christmas."

"So, if we eat the magic feed and go with Father Christmas . . . *we* can do all that?" John inquired.

"Yes," Stanley replied. "And aside from surviving those speeds, the feed will give you strength and allow you to maintain control of your movements and coordinate what direction you're travelling in."

"That sounds incredibly dangerous," John declared.

"We know," Tweedle said. "Which is why we never tested it on any non-magical beings before."

"Which reminds me," Father Christmas uttered, kneeling down to check on Nana. "How are you feeling?"

Nana *woofed* and licked his cheek, indicating that she felt fine. She was surprised that she didn't feel sick this time. Whatever was in that feed prevented her from feeling the effects of flying.

"Boys," Father Christmas called to his elves. "I'm going to stay and look after Nana for a little while — just to be safe. The Piccaninnies should have a large canoe we can borrow. You should be able to modify it into a sleigh easy enough."

"Will do," Tweedle replied, and the elves went to work.

Father Christmas gave Nana a complete examination, checking her eyes, ears, and reflexes. He made sure she was in perfect health after the transmogrification.

Father Christmas turned to the Lost Boys. "Traditionally, there are eight reindeer. Nana has already eaten the feed, so that's one." He looked at his elves. "Stanley and Tweedle need to take the feed in order to come with me on this journey. So, that makes three."

"Wait, what?" Stanley exclaimed.

Stanley and Tweedle looked at each other. They were both concerned with the metaphysical ramification of taking the feed.

"I think I can just wait here," Tweedle added.

"No, no," Father Christmas insisted, shaking his head. "I need you boys with me."

The elves shared a grimace.

"So, there are five spots left," Father Christmas declared. "Who all wants to pull my sleigh tonight?"

The boys looked at each other, nervous and unsure.

"I'll go," John declared.

"Me too," Michael volunteered.

Father Christmas turned to the Lost Boys. "Anyone else?"

Surely, Pipkin and Jojo raised their hands reluctantly.

"Excellent." Father Christmas clapped his hands together. "Get in the harness and take the feed."

"Wait," John said. "I don't understand. Why do we need to be harnessed? Can't we just take the feed and fly together?"

"Of course not," Tweedle replied. "Our bodies need to transfigure, and that can't happen without a physical connection to Father Christmas."

"A physical connection?" John inquired.

"Exactly," Stanley elaborated. "Father Christmas' form touches the sleigh, the sleigh touches the harnesses, and the harnesses touch whatever they're attached to."

"What if you accidentally break your harness?" Michael asked.

"Then your mass will immediately return, and you'll most likely explode," Tweedle replied.

"EXPLODE?!!" the children exclaimed.

"Well, we don't really know that for sure," Stanley stated to ease their concern. "It's never happened before."

"But even if you were to survive," Tweedle added. "You'd shoot off randomly and decelerate. And if that didn't kill you, you could wind up lost anywhere in the world or even the cosmos."

"Thank you, Mr. Tact." Stanely chided.

"You'll be just fine, boys," Father Christmas assured. "I'll take very good care of you."

The elves finished fashioning a sleigh out of the canoe, and Nana took the lead. The boys strapped themselves into the harnesses as Father Christmas passed around the magic feed. The boys and elves sniffed at it, then very cautiously ate it.

"All right," Father Christmas said as he mounted the craft. "Now, Stanley! Now, Tweedle! Now, Surely! Now, Pipkin! On, Jojo! On, Michael! On, John and Nan'kin!"

"Nan'kin?" John asked.

"Sorry," Father Christmas apologised. "It was a horrible attempt to rhyme it."

He tugged on the reins once more, and they were compelled to trot. They raced faster and faster, beginning to leave the ground.

"To the top of the porch! To the top of the wall!" Father Christmas recited. "Now dash away! Dash away! Dash away all!"

They watched the small island shrink away as they left Neverland. Father Christmas wasn't ready to go full speed just yet. He called to Stanley and Tweedle, who were positioned closest to the canoe. "Boys! Can we track them?"

Stanley shook his head. "I'm afraid not. Our tracking system is still in the sleigh."

"That's what I was afraid of," Father Christmas sighed. "We need to go back to the North Pole, so we'll have to go full speed. Brace yourselves, boys. This is going to be a little rocky."

He whipped the reins, placed his finger alongside his nose, and suddenly, they disappeared from the Neverland sky!

CHAPTER TWENTY-TWO
The Old Sea Dog

It was a cold, bleak winter night in London. The thick London fog rolled in from the Thames, bringing a crisp chill to the air. It was hard to make out an inch in front of your nose, but the boisterous sounds of the tavern at the edge of the docks filled the night. The lamps were a beacon to all wary sea dogs who needed a drink and a place to unwind after a long day at sea.

The tavern was decorated with some garland, tinsel and pixie-lights to help give a more Christmassy atmosphere. It may have been a bit of a dive, but the regular patrons were a tight-knit band — and when they were drinking together, they were the closest things any of them had to a family. They told funny stories, sang songs, and gathered together, so they weren't alone for the holiday season.

One of the regulars was a stout, slightly portly man with a greying beard. He was regaling them with another one of his tall tales of sailing with pirates on the high sea. Of course, no one believed his stories, but they sure loved hearing them — and if you buy him a drink, he'd be more than happy to oblige.

"So, there we were," the jolly man began. "We had been lost in a thick fog and an unsteady tide. You see, the captain had found a treasure map for a long-forgotten cluster of islands in the Aethiopian Sea."

"What's the Aethiopian Sea?" Millie, the plump barmaid, asked.

"Well, in the old days, they used to refer to the southern half of the Atlantic as the Aethiopian Sea," the man replied. "Anyway, the island we were looking for happened to be somewhere between Africa and Brazil, in the middle of nowhere really."

"What kind of map would have that?" one of the other patrons asked.

"An ancient map," the storyteller replied. "Forged long ago, in the age of titans and ancient gods. Back when Poseidon still ruled the sea. But it was a dangerous route, fraught with terrors of the deep, clamouring to swallow the ship whole. It was not a route you wanted to get lost in."

"Poppycock," an older gentleman exclaimed.

"It's true!" the man insisted. "Anyway, we gets to this small cluster of islands. The map said that the island had a volcano that looked like the face of some hideous woman surrounded by snakes. I had initially thought it was all nonsense, but then we saw it.

" 'There!' the captain had called. He ordered us to drop anchor and ready the longboats. We made our way cautiously through the water and into the jungles until we saw the Temple's entrance carved into the base of the volcano. The stone was carved to look like a regal-looking entrance, with high-reaching pillars etched on either side of the opening. And leering up above was the face of an enormous Gorgon, chiselled in stone."

"A Gorgon?" Millie asked.

"You know, like Medusa," the man explained. "Fangs, snakes in the hair, a serpent's tongue. That sort of thing. Anyway, at that moment, the crew was terrified. The captain demanded we go in, and we were trying to decide if we were more afraid of what might be inside the cave or what the captain would do to us if we disobeyed."

"Oooo. It gives me the shivers," Millie said playfully.

"If you like, you can sit here, love," the jolly man replied, slapping his knee. "I can keep you warm, Millie."

"Oh, get on with the story." She winked playfully.

He grinned. "Anyway, we traversed deep into the heart of the volcano. And it was hard to see because the steam of the sulphur pits clouded everything. And the smell was ghastly. Anyway, we finds it. The room was filled with treasure — gold, diamonds, emeralds, and such."

"Blimey," one of the patrons exclaimed. "I couldn't imagine seeing so much wealth."

"What happened to it?" another sailor asked.

"Well," the man continued, "as we loaded up the treasure, we began to hear a loud, angry *hissing* sound. It was followed by the ancient *snarling* voice of some creature lurking in the darkness. We turned and saw the silhouette of six strange figures approaching us. One of them spoke."

"What did it say?" Millie asked, enthused.

"Well, Tobias, one of me ol' shipmates," Smee clarified, "he said it sounded like ancient Greek. And he ought to know, he was from Crete. He listened in and said: '*The Punishment for Trespassers is Death.*'

"The first figure emerged from the shadows, and the captain shouted: 'Quick! Avert your eyes!' And we all looked away. Well, all but Bob the Butcher. He takes one look at the creature, and he turns to stone!"

"Wait a minute!" the old sailor called from the back. "You actually expect us to believe you met Medusa?!"

"Well, I don't know if it was *actually* Medusa. It's not like I stopped and asked, 'Oh, by the way, does your name happen to be Medusa perchance?' No! But it was a Gorgon." Smee saw the group's disbelieving gaze and held up his hand. "I swear to god. And anyway, it wouldn't have been Medusa. She was killed by that Perseus bloke, wasn't she? But she had two immortal sisters see? And they were still women, weren't they? And being that there were more than two of them, they must've mated at least once in the thousands of years that story had happened."

"Then what happened?" the barkeep asked with a chuckle, sliding him another round.

"Well, we were frightened. And I thought this was the end. But the captain was a brilliant and well-educated man — I think that's what made him so dangerous. He knew the story of Perseus. So, he picked up a shiny gold shield from the treasure and held it up. You see, he knew he would be able to keep an eye on them in the reflection. He stood up and pulled out the blunderbuss.

" 'Tobias,' he called. 'Tell them that, unlike Perseus, I come with a magic *Boom Stick*. And to consider this a demonstration of my power.'

"He whipped the weapon over his shoulder and blew the head off the approaching Gorgon! The snakes *shrieked* and *hissed* as the body collapsed to the floor.

"The biggest creature slithered forward and spoke. Tobias translated, 'That little toy may work on my daughters, but not me. You cannot have *all* of the treasure, but you can leave with your life and whatever treasure you've gathered already . . . if you're willing to make a trade.'

"The captain thought a minute and then asked, 'What do you want?' "

"What did she want?" the patrons asked.

The storyteller began to blush. "Well, it can be pretty lonely living on an island for thousands of years with no men and no way of making more daughters. And, truth be told, the youngest daughter took a fancy to me."

"What?!" the group asked.

"Yep. She wanted a mate for her daughter, and that daughter wanted yours truly."

The group began to snicker and chuckle.

"What did the captain say?" Millie asked.

"He said, 'What the hell, you've been with worse.' "

The group howled with laughter.

Smee continued. "And I was like, 'There's no way I'm getting near that thing. She'll turn me to stone.'

"He just looks at me and says: 'We can get you a blindfold.' "

The group chortled louder.

"I couldn't believe it! A blindfold? What about them poisonous snakes in her hair, eh? Also, only her top half is human; the bottom half is a serpent. How in the blazes was that supposed to work?

"And the captain says to me, 'Quit your whining, Smee. It's our only hope to get out of here alive. Really, you need to start being more open to new experiences.'

"And I says to him, 'Well, excuse me for not being sophisticated. And if you don't like it, you can just take care of her yourself.' "

The barkeep laughed. "You must've been terrified if you had the guts to speak to Captain Hook that way."

"Nah, it wouldn't matter," Smee replied smugly. He held up his hand and crossed his middle finger and forefinger. "Him and me were like this, you see. Besides, not many people know this. But I was the only one ol' Jas Hook was afraid of."

The group shared another hearty laugh.

Smee took a big swig of his drink. "Anyway, I ended agreeing, and they held a primitive sort of . . . uh, well, I think we'll call it a marriage ceremony. And while the men were loading up the treasure, I was taken back to her lair to, uh . . . make the union official. And . . ."

The group leaned in anxiously.

"I had never been more terrified in my life."

"I'll bet," Millie snorted. "Most men are afraid of commitment."

Smee smiled at Millie. "So, I just sort of laid back there with my blindfold on, and the moment I felt her large, snake-like scales slither next to me, I was done! I managed to distract her, then bolted out of there as fast as my legs could carry me. She was furious! She *shrieked* and *wailed,* chasing after me. I kept me eyes fixed on the floor and ran away as fast as I could. I could see me mates loading the longboat, and I yelled, 'Leg it, boys!' I caught up to them, and we took off!"

The group clapped.

"So, you got the treasure?" the barkeep asked.

"Yep."

"And jilted your Gorgon bride in the process," Millie added.

"When you put it like that, it sounds kind of bad," Smee replied.

The old patron clapped him on the back. "Well, being that it never happened, I wouldn't worry about it too much."

Smee just flashed him a weak smile.

"Good story, mate," another patron declared.

Millie gave Smee a peck on the cheek and went back to serving the customers.

Smee, of course, knew they didn't believe him — they never believed him. He still had the amulet that was given to him that day. He could show it to them, but what was the point? Besides, that was his retirement fund. As a former pirate, he knew it was best not to let people know he had anything valuable — otherwise, he might not have it for long.

Life had been good for Smee ever since leaving Neverland. It wasn't as deep or emotionally rewarding as Starkey's, but he enjoyed it nevertheless. He had managed to escape the island with several small bags of treasure. He had an old Tudor Mansion in Hyde Park and plenty of money to eat and drink himself to death if he wanted. Of course, he found that he and the upper-classes weren't the most compatible, which is why he always found his way to the docks, with the salt-of-the-earth, sea-fairing people . . . his people!

In the end, Smee didn't need much, just a pint of ale, some good company, and the smell of the sea and a gentle breeze. He just hung out at the tavern, and whenever he felt the call of the sea, he'd spend a day on a fishing lorry. None of his new mates knew about his wealth or where he lived — it was best to keep a low profile.

The night had wound down, and Smee reckoned it was time to be shoving off. He wished the group a Happy Christmas, thanked them for the drink, and then headed out.

As he stepped into the cold winter air, he realised he needed to relieve himself — several large pints will do that to you. Unfortunately, the loo was occupied, but the sky was black, and the fog was thick. Smee glanced over his shoulder and made his way to the edge of the pier. He figured, why not? He had relieved himself over the docks before.

It was a brisk night, and he was mid-stream when he heard a voice in the fog.

"Mr. Smee."

He knew that voice. It didn't even register with him how much time had passed when he had last heard it. Instinctively his buttocks clenched, and he stood at attention.

"Ay, ay, captain!" Smee replied, saluting the darkness. He was unaware that his trousers had fallen to his feet.

Hook grabbed his head, embarrassed by the sight of Smee's bare bottom. "Pull up your pants, Smee."

"Ay, ay, sir."

"Honestly, Smee, one full moon is all I intended to see tonight."

As Smee hitched up his trousers, his brain fully registered the situation. "Oh, my god!" he exclaimed. "It's the ghost of Captain Hook!"

He turned to run and smacked right into the lamppost.

Hook just rolled his eyes and chuckled. "Oh, Smee. How I've missed you." He walked over to his former bo'sun, who had collapsed on the ground.

"You're just a spook!" Smee cried. "Keep away from me!"

"I'm not a spook, you dolt!" Hook retorted.

"You're not?"

"Of course not. I survived the crocodile attack," Hook explained. "Now get up so I can get a good look at you."

"Ay, ay," Smee muttered, getting to his feet.

Hook looked his former bo'sun over. "My word, you've really let yourself go, haven't you? You're a regular landlubber now, aren't you?"

"The last few years have been particularly kind to me," Smee replied.

"So I've heard." Hook grinned. "And I suppose that's why you were the only pirate the illustrious Captain James Hook was afraid of?"

Smee's face went bright red with embarrassment. His head drooped near his shoulders as a big sheepish grin appeared on his face. "Uh, you heard that?"

James nodded — his face was expressionless, except for the wisp of amusement out of the corner of his mouth.

"Well, uh . . . that was just tavern talk," Smee muttered. "Everyone knows not to take it too seriously. Besides, didn't you used to go around tellin' everyone that Barbecue was afraid of you?"

"Smee. Barbecue *was* afraid of me," the captain stated.

"Well, it's not like anyone believes anything I say."

"Never mind. I have a job, and I require the assistance of my trusty bo'sun."

Smee didn't particularly fancy the idea of teaming up with the captain on another one of Hook's dastardly plans — not at this stage of his life anyhow. However, he knew what happened to people who told Hook *no*. Smee looked around nervously, making sure they were unobserved, then turned back to the captain. "What's the job?"

Hook simply grinned his dastardly grin. "Follow me."

Captain Hook led Smee to the sleigh. Smee did a double-take, aghast at the sight of eight tiny reindeer.

"Is that . . . ?" Smee asked. "Is that what I think it is?"

Hooked nodded boastfully.

"Does this mean that . . . Father Christmas is real?"

Hook nodded. "I know; who would've guessed? But Father Christmas has changed an awful lot since we've been on the island."

"Don't I know it," Smee acknowledged. "Christmas has changed a lot since then. Life in general, for that matter. Just look around at how much the world has progressed while we were piddling around in Neverland."

"Yes, but if we weren't — as you so eloquently put it — piddling around on the island," Hook stated dryly, "then I'm afraid none of us would have lived long enough to see it anyway."

"I know. It was a lot to take in. But I think I'm starting to get the hang of it now." Suddenly, it hit Smee. "Wait a minute. If that's Father Christmas's sleigh, then where's Father Christmas?"

"I don't think he'll be bothering anyone anytime soon."

Smee looked around sombrely. "You didn't . . . *off* him or anything, did you?"

"No, of course not." Hook seemed almost insulted. "There may have been an explosion or two, but he's most likely temporarily marooned. I had a little help swiping the sleigh while he was entertaining the Never-Brats on the island."

"Help?" Smee asked. That's when he noticed the boy who wouldn't grow up, sitting in the sleigh. "*Wha—! Is that—?!*"

Hook nodded.

"He . . ." Smee emphasised. "Helped you?"

"Yes. His pesky memory forgot all about us after our last duel, and I've more or less been in hiding until now. Remember, I am not Captain Hook the pirate. And you have never seen Peter before. Is that clear?"

Smee nodded. "If you say so, captain."

Hook escorted Smee to the sleigh, and Hook greeted Peter Pan. "Aw, Peter. I'd like to introduce you to an old mate of mine, Mr. Smee. Mr. Smee, this is Peter Pan."

"Pleased to meet you," Smee greeted nervously.

Pan studied him carefully. For a fleeting moment, the name Smee seemed oddly familiar to him, but he couldn't recall from where. The moment passed, and Peter greeted him.

Hook stepped forward, addressing Peter. "He's going to help us get the treasure we had talked about."

As Hook guided Smee to the back of the sleigh, Smee noticed a figure under the blanket. He drew back the sheet and gasped, seeing Wendy.

"Is that—?" Smee mumbled.

Hook nodded. "Yes. You see, we ended up absconding with Father Christmas' magic sack as well." He lifted up the bag, presenting it to Smee. "Unfortunately, you can't get any presents out of it if you're on the Naughty List." He gestured to Wendy. "That's where she comes in."

"Fair enough." Smee shrugged, leaning against the sleigh.

"Also, I've been thinking about settling down," Hook muttered.

"What?" Peter asked.

"Nothing, just another game," Hook dismissed. "But first, our young friend Peter has this jolly fun idea about being Pirates of the Sky. We think Wendy will be more susceptible to playing along with us if we got her a gift."

"What sort of a gift?" Smee asked, feeling a little uneasy.

"The diamond kind." Hook grinned. "The exceptionally large and expensive diamond kind that are kept in a very special tower here in London."

"You can't be serious." Smee groaned.

"Nothing but the best for my future bride."

"I'm starting to feel a little uncomfortable with this plan," Smee confessed. "You know, nobody knows who we are. No one's out to get us. We're free! Everyone we ever knew is dead, and as far as the world is concerned, so are we." He thought for a moment. "Didn't you smuggle any treasure with you?"

"Of course I did," Hook scoffed. "But it's not really about the money."

Smee sighed. "Yeah, I suppose it never really was, was it?"

"See, I knew you'd understand," Hook smirked. "We have a once-in-a-lifetime opportunity to do something truly remarkable. It'd be a shame to waste it." Hook turned, stepping onto the sleigh. "Well, we should be taking off. But first, I'm terribly thirsty. You wouldn't happen to have anything to drink on you?"

"Not on me, I'm afraid."

The three began looking around, and then Smee smiled, handing the captain a bottle of Cognac.

"There you go," Smee declared joyously.

"Where the blazes did you find that?" Hook asked.

"It was in that bag over there," Smee replied.

Hook started to dismiss it until he realised that Smee was pointing to the magic sack. "Wait!" Hook gasped. "You mean to tell me that you pulled this bottle out of that bag?"

Smee looked at the sack, then back to Hook, and shrugged. "Yeah."

"Smee, what the devil are you doing on the Nice List?"

"Sorry, captain. I didn't mean to be."

Peter stepped forward. "Well, at least it's one more person that can pull out presents if Wendy refuses."

"Excellent point," Hook declared, proudly placing his hand on Peter's shoulder.

Hook realised how fortunate they were for Smee to be on the Nice List; unfortunately, he also realised that as soon as Smee committed any crimes, he would be deemed Naughty and may lose the ability to use the bag. It was clear to Hook that if they needed anything from the magic sack, Smee would need to get it before the heist. He also supposed that motivation might also be an issue.

"Smee," Hook added. "Remember, you're not doing these things for fun or profit; you're doing them because we'll kill you if you don't. Is that understood?"

"That's pretty much what I figured," Smee replied.

"Good. Do you have a place of your own nearby?"

Smee twitched at the question. His muscles tightened at the prospect of the captain knowing where he lived, but he didn't really have a choice. "Yeah."

"Excellent. Now, we need a place to drop off the Neverland treasure and to plan and prepare." Hook smiled triumphantly. "All right, boys! Let's shove off. I have a bunch of crazy ideas, and we have a long night ahead of us."

CHAPTER TWENTY-THREE

The Pirates of the Sky

It was late. While Father Christmas and the crudely constructed craft raced to the North Pole, the Yeomen Warders patrolled the grounds of the Tower of London. It was a quiet night, and the guards ignored the fog and the chill as they made their rounds. Even the ravens had gone to sleep in their roost. They were all blissfully unaware that there was a reindeer-drawn sleigh flying silently above them — shrouded in mist.

It was the perfect setting for the Pirates of the Sky to make their debut. Captain James Hook hadn't been to England in ages. His biggest concern was making sure he knew which one of the towers in the compound contained the treasure.

The crown jewels had moved around the grounds of the Tower of London a lot over the years. Hook had Smee bring out a map from the magic sack, and he discovered their current location. At the moment, they had constructed a new chamber on the upper level of the *Wakefield Tower.* With the map, they knew where to go.

The fog was the perfect cover for them. The sleigh flew across the Thames, over *Traitors' Gate*, and past *St. Thomas's Tower* completely undetected. After crossing the Outer Ward, they hovered secretly above the *Wakefield Tower.*

Hook had toyed with the idea of getting rid of Peter before the heist — after all, Wendy would eventually wake up, and things could get ugly rather fast. But he was enjoying himself too much. Besides, it was an extremely treacherous heist — even with the *Sandman Powder* they had found and tested. He poured the powder into three separate bags at Smee's house. Hook was thrilled to discover that the bag generated a never-ending supply of powder. Luck was certainly on his side, but he still needed Peter.

"All right, my boy," Hook began, showing Peter the map. "Now, take the bag of sleeping powder. Go down — make sure no one sees you — and throw the powder in the face of everyone you see. To them, it will seem like a bizarre dizzy spell, but they will be out for a few hours."

Peter nodded.

"And search the entire compound," Hook continued. "There are a lot of people living here, and we want to make sure that we are completely unobserved. It doesn't matter if they're young or old — even if they're already asleep — I still want you to throw it in their face. Do you understand?"

"Absolutely," Peter replied.

"Marvellous. And be sure you don't trigger any alarms that might be down there. If you see any in the *Wakefield Tower* or the *White Tower*, disarm them."

Peter was starting to get excited. This seemed like a challenging game — a game that would test all of his craft and cunning!

Hook held up the map. "Now, here is the bed chambers of General Sir Arthur Wynne, the *Master of the Jewel Office*. He is also the current *Keeper of the Crown Jewels*. Make sure that he and his household are asleep. Then find his official keys and come back here."

Hook stopped and peered down, hearing footsteps approaching. "Here comes a couple of Beefeaters now. All right, go down and start with the guards."

Peter nodded and flew down with great stealth.

Hook and Smee watched Peter descend. Hook had observed the uniforms of the Yeomen Warders approaching; their uniforms had changed since he had been in England last. They still had the hats, but the uniforms were now dark blue with red trim.

"So much has changed. Hasn't it, Smee?" Hook whispered.

The guards were oblivious as the powder struck them, incapacitating them instantly. Peter slipped into the mist and vanished out of sight.

"Oh, I know," Smee agreed. He continued to stare. "You know, it's a very large compound; he'll be gone for quite some time."

"Good thing Father Christmas' bag has a limitless supply," Hook added.

"Do you want to tell me what this is all about?"

Hook looked to Smee. "I'm sure I don't know what you mean."

"I may be retired, but I know you. You're a big picture man." Smee gazed back down where Peter had been. "Not that I want anything bad to happen to anyone anymore . . . but why is Peter Pan — your mortal enemy — still alive?"

"It's easier for him to fly down and take out the guards."

"Are you sure that's the only reason?"

"Smee," Hook replied. "I've been improvising this whole thing as I've gone along. The fact that I've made it this far is a testament to ingenuity and dumb luck."

Smee glanced back, getting his first real look at Wendy. She was no longer a little girl. She was a full-fledged woman — and a stunning one at that.

"Oh, yes. I believe you, captain." Smee nodded. "Still . . . it seems to me that you didn't need to kidnap her to convince Peter to help you. Now that you have me, you don't need her for the bag anymore. What's up?"

"Smee," Hook replied, flashing him a gentle but threatening smile. "I have a feeling that after you help me inside, you won't be on the Nice List anymore."

"You're probably right there."

"So, the less you know about my plan, the better." Hook declared. "Now, when we land, I want you to stay back while Peter and I go ahead. I need you to retrieve a few more things from that bag without asking any questions. There are things I don't want Peter to know about yet. Once you're done, bring over Wendy and rejoin us."

"Ay, ay, captain," Smee replied out loud.

After Peter made a full sweep of the Tower of London, he returned to the sleigh. It was now safe to land, so Hook gently brought the team back down. Hook and Peter hopped out and strolled to the entranceway. Hook was elated and felt at ease. He had started a conversation with Peter to buy Smee time to complete his tasks. When Smee was finished, he carried Wendy and regrouped with the others.

As they entered the Jewel House, they discovered the Crown Jewel display was in the centre of the room and surrounded by an enormous cage. The cage had thick, intersecting bars to ward off potential thieves. At the top of the pyramidal display was *St. Edward's Crown.*

"There it is!" Hook declared with a childlike twinkle in his eye.

Smee noticed an uncharacteristic reverence and a sense of national pride in Hook's smile. It gave him a glimpse of what James was like as a little boy. Smee turned his glance to Peter, then back to Hook. He supposed Peter might have been right. In some ways, it was a shame that children had to grow up — even the captain must have been cute as an innocent child. Smee began to wonder what sort of a man Peter would grow into if Peter would ever allow himself to grow up. He also wondered what sort of child Jas would have been had he stayed a child. In the end, he wasn't sure how different they really were.

Captain Hook motioned across the room with his wrapped hand. "Here lies the most precious artefacts and symbols of power in the whole of the British Empire."

"Wow!" Peter muttered.

"Wow is right," Hook agreed. "Now, do you have the keys?"

Peter nodded and retrieved the key ring from his pocket. "I got them right here."

"Good job, my boy," Hook congratulated. He turned to his former bo'sun. "Smee, set Wendy over in the corner, then get the keys from Peter and see if you can find the one that opens the cage."

"Ay, ay, captain," Smee replied, setting Wendy down.

He managed to open the cage on his second try.

"Excellent!" Hook gave his team a warm smile. "All right, boys. Let's start loading up."

Smee and Peter sprang into action.

Slowly, Wendy's head began to clear. She didn't know where she was. The last thing she remembered was talking to Starkey and taking a nap in his tent. It certainly didn't feel like a tent. She began to stir, attempting to sit up.

"Greetings, my dear," Hook's voice called to her. There was a charm and elegance to the voice that disarmed her.

Hook had concealed himself in the shadows so she wouldn't be too alarmed by his presence. At first, she looked around and saw nothing she recognised! She was sitting in a beautiful old tower. When she turned her head, her eyes beheld the most beautiful assortment of jewels and royal regalia she had ever seen.

"Where am I?" Wendy asked.

"The Tower of London," Hook answered, still in the shadows.

She sprung up!

"The Tower of London?!" Wendy cried. "Where's Father Christmas?! Where's the camp?!"

"Still in Neverland," Peter replied, approaching her. He was wearing the *Imperial State Crown*, which was too big for his head, and a royal robe draped over his shoulders. In his fist, he was clutching a sovereign's sceptre.

"Peter?!" Wendy gasped. "What's going on?"

"We decided it wasn't fair that we were on the Naughty List," Peter pouted. "So, we took the sleigh and magic bag so no one can have a Christmas."

"Peter, that's horrible!"

"No it's not!" Peter exclaimed. "It's horrible that there's a holiday dedicated to making children feel judged and persecuted!"

"Peter, I know you're upset," Wendy muttered. "But this isn't the answer."

"We were hoping you could help us retrieve the presents from the bag," Peter said softly.

"I'm not going to help you with this!" Wendy snapped. "Peter, it's not right to take something that doesn't belong to you. You need to take it back right away."

"No," Peter replied. "Anyway, we don't need you for that anymore. We have Smee."

"Smee?" She looked and saw the loveable former pirate — he was also playing dress-up with the royal regalia.

"Pleasure to see you again, Miss Wendy," Smee greeted with an embarrassed wave and a curtsy.

She turned back to Peter. "What have you done?"

"We're the Pirates of the Sky now!" Peter declared with pride.

"This isn't like you," Wendy cried. "Not only did you steal the Christmas presents from every child in the world, but now you're robbing the Tower of London?" She turned to Smee. "Is this your doing?"

"No, ma'am," Smee replied, shaking his head. "But I agree, it does sound a little like overkill for one night."

"Then why?" Wendy demanded.

"That was my fault," Captain Hook declared, stepping out of the shadows. He was carrying a silver platter with two glasses of champagne in his good hand.

She gasped. "But I—"

"Thought I was dead," Hook brushed off. "Yeah-yeah. That's what everyone says. Care for a drink?"

"No!" Wendy growled.

"Well, I hate to toast alone," Hook said. "How 'bout you, Peter?"

Hook spun the tray, and Peter happily grabbed the glass.

"What about me?" Smee asked.

"Honestly, Smee, I only have one hand," Hook dismissed. "Just pour yourself a glass. It's on the counter."

Smee nodded and helped himself.

"Peter," Wendy called. "Do you know who that is?"

"My friend," Peter replied, downing the whole glass in one gulp.

"No!" Wendy cried. "It's—"

"The former Captain James Hook," Hook finished with a bow. "At your service."

Peter's eyes widened. "You mean, that cad you talk about in your stories?"

"*Cad?*" Hook frowned, feeling insulted. "Don't you think that's a little harsh?"

"You tried to make me walk the plank," Wendy retorted.

"Please, it was just a game," Hook fibbed. "I knew Peter would rescue you. You know how much Peter likes games." Hook took a step closer to Peter. "If it's any consolation, I *really* did enjoy having an adventure with you."

"Well, I—" Peter gasped, feeling dizzy.

"Peter?" Wendy called.

Suddenly, Peter collapsed, hitting the ground!

"*Peter!!*"

CHAPTER TWENTY-FOUR

Back at the North Pole

While Hook and the others were raiding the Tower of London, they were completely unaware that Father Christmas and the boys were racing to the North Pole.

The boys were astounded! They were hurtling at speeds they never dreamed possible. At first, the colours and lights of the world seemed to swirl and blend together like water on a wet oil painting. They were worried that everything was moving too fast for their brains to process, but eventually, their bodies adapted — stabilising as they became one with their velocity. Everything cleared in their minds.

To the outside world, they were moving imperceivably fast; but to them, they were moving normally, and the rest of the world seemed to be moving incredibly slowly. So slow, in fact, that it hardly seemed to be moving at all. The team were in complete control of their movements and surroundings. It was a surreal and truly remarkable experience.

They also didn't have to worry about where to go. Nana instinctively knew where to lead the team. Some unseen inner force was guiding her way. Perhaps it was some primal animal instinct — the same sort of instinct that led the salmon back to the spawning grounds of their birth. For whatever reason, she knew exactly where to go.

The North Pole had been on red alert ever since Father Christmas broke through the barrier to Neverland. As far as they could tell, the sleigh had vanished off the face of the earth. The elves tried not to worry — they had an unwavering faith in Father Christmas. However, Father Christmas had been gone for far too long, and there was no way to track him — no way to know if he was all right. Barnaby, the Grand High Elf, had tried to search for him in the mystic Watching-Pools, but it was useless.

The elves feared the worst and were beginning to panic. They were relieved when they detected Father Christmas' new craft approaching.

Father Christmas pulled back on the reins as they reached the Arctic Tundra. As they approached the heart of the Polar Ice Cap, Nana slowed the team down to a crawl. Suddenly, Father Christmas whipped the reins, and Nana shot them down through a series of chasms and shimmering ice-chutes, leading to the magical kingdom hidden below. The large icy tunnel opened out into the lush valley. It was not exactly what the kids had imagined, but it was still wondrous nevertheless.

When they arrived at Father Christmas' glorious palace, they were greeted by a host of Christmas elves. The local elves were surprised and a little shocked to see a converted canoe being pulled by five children, two elves, and a large Newfoundland Dog in the lead.

Clearly, Father Christmas had encountered some pretty dire circumstances, but the elves were relieved to have him home.

"What happened?" the Grand High Elf asked.

"No time to explain," Father Christmas replied. "We need a new sleigh loaded up and ready to go. The fate of a young woman and my reindeer are at stake."

"But—?"

"No buts. We need to get going right away."

Father Christmas had Barnaby and Lakky bustling to get a new sleigh and stocking it with supplies. Another group of elves took the Neverland crew to warm up by a roaring fire. They needed to re-hydrate and rest. Father Christmas also sent his medical staff to give the group a quick check-up to ensure everyone was healthy and unharmed after all they had gone through.

"Tweedle," Father Christmas called.

"Yes, sir?" Tweedle replied.

"Are you feeling well enough to join me for a minute?"

"I think so." Tweedle nodded.

"Good." Father Christmas grinned, placing his hand on the elf's shoulder. "I need you to swing by your department and get us some new tracking equipment. After that, meet me in the Watching-Pools. We need to get a fix on the reindeer and the sleigh as soon as possible."

"Right away," Tweedle declared.

"What about me?" Stanley asked. "Do you want me to go with him?"

Father Christmas shook his head and gave him his warm, knowing smile. "No. I asked for Miss Bellringer to come and keep the children occupied while we figure things out."

Stanley's heart fluttered at the sound of Holly's name.

"I thought you might want to give her a hand," Father Christmas continued.

Stanley couldn't hide the enormous grin forming on his face. "Thank you!"

Father Christmas winked, patted him on the back, and started to leave. He stopped. "Oh, and in case you're wondering, she's not that sore about you missing your date. By now, she knows what happened, and she's just happy you're safe."

Stanley looked up. "How did you know about that?"

He chuckled. "I'm Father Christmas. I see everything."

"That's kind of disturbing when you think about it."

"Don't worry." Father Christmas laughed louder. "I'm good at respecting privacy. Believe me, there's a lot I elect not to see."

Father Christmas turned and left with Tweedle as Holly hurried into the room.

"Stanley!" she called, running into his arms. "I was so worried when I found out what happened. It must have been terrifying."

"You know, as harrowing as this whole adventure has been, there was only one thing I was truly frightened of," Stanley replied.

"And what was that?"

"Missing our picnic."

She smiled, wrapping her arms around his neck. Suddenly, she gazed up and pointed at the decoration above the door frame. "Stanley. We're standing under the mistletoe."

Stanley's smile widened as he started to blush. "So we are."

Holly's eyelashes fluttered coyly.

Slowly, Stanley leaned in, and they shared a long, passionate kiss.

Suddenly, they were interrupted by the loud *hooting* and *whooping* from the boys watching from the hall.

"Gross!" Pipkin exclaimed at the sight of the lively lip-lock.

"Oh, you won't mind it so much when you get older," John replied.

Both Stanley and Holly giggled — their cheeks were flushed and turning bright red from embarrassment.

"Oops," Holly mumbled, facing all of the children. "I almost forgot what I'm here for." She turned back to Stanley. "Stanley, would you like to introduce me to everyone?"

"Absolutely!" he declared.

Stanley gave her a formal introduction, and the boys were excited to tell Holly all about their Christmas adventure! Shortly after the group settled in, Lakky returned.

"Stanley," Lakky called, "the Boss wants you to join him at the Watching-Pools."

"Okay, tell him I'll be right there," Stanley replied. Lakky nodded and left.

Stanley turned back to Holly. "Well, it looks like I have to go again."

"I know," Holly replied, wrapping her arms around his neck once more. "Just promise to be careful."

She kissed him one last time before Stanley left.

Stanley hurried to rejoin Father Christmas. When he got there, Father Christmas approached the water. He touched the tip of his staff to the clear blue liquid and watched the billowing cloud form from beneath the surface of the water. As the ripples began to subside, he called out, "Where is Wendy Darling and Peter Pan?"

The thick black cloud flowed out once again and began to change colours. The darkness gave way to light ripples. The new scene revealed that they were in London. Images began to form as ramparts and parapets appeared around a tower. There were several unconscious Yeomen Warders. As the images cleared, he realised they were in the Tower of London.

"Show them to me," Father Christmas commanded.

The water bubbled and flowed again, revealing a dim chamber. He saw Captain James Hook and Wendy. As the image cleared, he saw Peter lying face down on the floor.

CHAPTER TWENTY-FIVE
The Proposal

Wendy turned to Hook. "*What did you do to him?!*"

"I suppose some people just can't hold their ale," Hook smirked, sipping his champagne.

"*You poisoned him!*" she cried.

"He's perfectly safe, my dear," Hook assured, unwrapping his claw. "It was just a dash of Father Christmas' patented *Sandman Powder.* Believe me, he'll be right as rain in a few hours. I just need him out of the way for a little while so I can talk to you."

"I have nothing to say to the likes of you," Wendy snapped.

"If you ever want Peter to wake up," Captain Hook declared, "then I'd say that you have plenty to say to me."

She peered up at him.

"Am I being clear enough for you, Miss Darling?" Hook asked gingerly. He offered his arm with the same debonair suaveness that had charmed her and overcame her apprehensions of him all those years ago.

She knew better but relented. Wendy nodded and took his arm. Hook scooped his claw through the metal ring atop the lantern and escorted her outside into the fog. Smee stayed behind. He needed to finish loading up the sleigh — plus, the captain had given him further instructions that he needed to carry out before he was permitted to join them.

"My dear, Wendy," Hook cooed as they continued their stroll. "I assure you, I am not the same loathsome monster that I used to be. And I want to start by apologising for all of the pain and heartache that I've caused you and your brothers. As a matter of fact, I have completely forgiven Peter for doing this to me," he added, raising his claw. "You know, I never tried to hunt him or his Lost Boys until he cut off my hand. And do you know why he did it?"

Wendy shook her head.

"He did it because of a dare," Hook replied. "Imagine that! The little bugger ruined my life, all because of a dare."

Wendy began to feel sorry for James.

"But of course, the dare wasn't the real reason," Hook continued. "In the end, I grew up. Just like you and every other creature on od's green earth, I couldn't stop the hands of time until it was too late. But to Peter, that's an offence punishable by death. I ask you, is it fair to be punished for something you can't control?"

She shook her head *no*.

"He really did deserve to be on that Naughty List," Hook added. "Me too, I'm afraid. But you like him for some reason." He stopped, giving her a sober gaze. "As a matter of fact, you love him, don't you?"

She froze, feeling embarrassed, but deep down, she knew it was true.

"You love him," Hook continued, "but you hate me. I find that a little ironic because, honestly, what is the real difference between him and me?"

"Well," Wendy ventured, "he's much younger than you for a start."

"Is he?" Hook mused. "We measure age based on how long we've existed on this planet, and Peter has been here longer than any of us. I don't know how long he was in Neverland before we arrived. But one thing is for certain; that boy is hundreds of years old. He only looks and acts like a child." He took a breath. "No. Do you know the real difference between us?"

She shook her head.

"Fairies didn't come and rescue me as a boy," Hook proclaimed. "I had a father who denied my existence and a mother who died when I was very young. Oh, what I wouldn't have given to be whisked off to Neverland. To fly off and be carefree. To not be burdened with painful memories and the constant feelings of rejection. To have noble blood but remain a dark secret."

Wendy watched Hook, feeling pity for him for the first time. She couldn't have imagined what sort of childhood could have created a man like Captain James Hook.

Hook looked up and gazed into her gentle eyes. "I think I would have been exactly the same as Peter if the fairies had found me instead. Perhaps that's what I despised about him the most. He reminded me of me at that age. I was a cocky little bastard too." Hook chuckled. "But I was also brave, strong, honourable, and a born leader. Had the fairies found me, maybe you would have fallen in love with me instead."

Wendy was quiet, feeling suspicious as he led her to the *White Tower* in the centre of the Tower of London grounds. They passed more unconscious Yeoman Warders in the square.

"If you're curious," Hook stated, gesturing to the incapacitated guards, "this was Peter's work, not mine."

She observed them closely. For a moment, she thought they were dead but noticed that they were still breathing.

"Peter would have just as soon as killed them," Hook added. "Fortunately, Father Christmas has a limitless supply of *Sandman Powder.*"

They entered through the large doors and continued into the great hall.

"Still, it makes you think," Hook continued, "if I would have been like Peter, what sort of a man do you think Peter would have been if the fairies didn't find him?" He waited for a response, and when none came, he proceeded. "Hmm? A boy who likes to fight, order people about, and seeks out adventure." He paused. "I don't know about you, but it sort of sounds like the makings of a pirate to me."

Wendy tried to protest, but Hook held up his good hand.

"I know," Hook interrupted. "He may have enlisted in the King's Navy first, but he hates authority, and without noble blood, he wouldn't have been fast-tracked to be an officer. My guess is that he would have either led a mutiny or hijacked a ship and gone into business for himself. Either way, you're looking at the makings of a blood-thirsty pirate. Maybe even worse than me."

Wendy stopped and turned to Hook. "What do you really want?"

Hook grinned. "Feisty and direct. My kind of woman." He chuckled again. "The answer lies up ahead."

Smee had completed his duties. As he was wrapping up, he was startled by a movement in the distance. For a fleeting moment, he thought he saw two small boys watching him. He rubbed his eyes, and they were gone.

He supposed his mind was playing tricks on him in the fog — after all, this caper had left him all nerves. Peter had put everyone to sleep, so there shouldn't be anybody watching them. There wasn't anything to worry about.

Wasn't there?

Across the square, he saw the light of Hook's lantern at the *White Tower*. He looked back one last time, then hurried to catch up with them.

"Everything's all taken care of," Smee reported, catching up to the captain and Wendy. "We're ready to go whenever you are."

"Ah, Smee," Hook called, "you're just in time. I think you need to see this too."

Hook took them down the *Line of Kings*. He took off his hat as they walked along the rows of royal armour.

"The *Line of Kings*," Hook spoke with reverent awe. "These were all worn by some of the greatest rulers in English history."

Hook led them to a wall of carved and painted wooden heads. To Wendy, they looked like the decapitated remains of some eerie life-sized marionettes. Each face was crafted in the likenesses of a former King of England. Hook stopped walking. He turned to Wendy, bowed, and gestured for her to take a closer look. "After you, my dear."

Wendy was nervous but stepped up to the display. She hated to admit it, but the wooden heads gave her the creeps in the dark. They looked vibrant, almost alive by the flickering of candlelight. She observed them closer, trying to figure out what Hook wanted her to see.

"Earlier, you said it's not right to take what doesn't belong to you," Hook reminded her. "But what you don't understand is . . . all that you see belongs to me."

Wendy looked up at him with a sceptical raise of the eyebrow.

"Or rather, they should *rightfully* belong to me," Hook elaborated. He gestured to the wooden busts of the ill-fated Stuarts with his claw. "They look oddly familiar, don't they?"

When Wendy studied the face, it hit her! She looked back to Hook, then back to the head — the eyes, nose, and jaw-line were uncanny.

"It can't be," Wendy muttered.

"My family," Hook confirmed with great pride.

"Blimey!" Smee exclaimed. "They really do look a little like you, don't they?"

Smee was dumbfounded. He had been sailing with the captain for centuries and had never been told. Hook always talked about being a nobleman, but he never imagined this.

"You know," Hook started, "the only reason the Stuarts didn't keep their crown was because the only heirs they knew about were Catholic and not Anglican. If they had found a direct descendant willing to side with the Anglican Church of England, they might still be in power."

Wendy and Smee were in shock.

"And to think, we gave the world the *King James Bible*." Hook shook his head. "But an heir did exist," he declared. "Now, suppose the true King of England had a pirate's ruthlessness and devious cunning. There would be nothing to stop him from reclaiming his birthright."

"What are you saying?" Wendy gasped.

"I should be the rightful King of England!" Hook declared. "Imagine, *King James the Third*. Has a nice ring to it, don't you think?" He smiled gingerly and stepped forward. "Of course, every good king needs a queen."

"Are you mad?!" Wendy exclaimed.

"You're a woman now, Wendy," Hook declared. "Anytime now, a young suitor can swoop in and ask for your hand. But I can offer you everything you've ever wanted. I can offer you the world!"

"What are you saying?!" Wendy cried.

"Monarchs come and go," Hook explained. "The Prime Minister and the Houses of Parliament can be dealt with. And if you want, I can make you the next Queen of England." Hook took off his hat and got down on one knee. "Wendy Moira Angela Darling, will you marry me?"

He held out his hand, and inside was the biggest diamond ring she had ever seen.

Wendy and Smee were both stunned! She was momentarily mesmerised by the size of the diamond, then she shook her head.

"*Never!*" she screamed, running back down the hall.

Smee turned. "Do you want me to run after her?"

"Did you do what I asked of you?" Hook asked.

"Yes."

"Then it won't be necessary," Hook replied, walking past Smee.

Smee took one last look at the wooden heads. "Ughh! These things give me the creeps."

Suddenly, the wooden bust of *King James the First* turned and winked.

Smee gasped and ran after the captain. "Wait for me!"

Wendy ran out into the fog. She was mortified! She could have never imagined such a situation in a million years.

She saw the figure of the sleigh up ahead. She ran to it and gasped, seeing Peter!

Peter's unconscious body was propped with his head fastened to a wooden executioner's block. Heavy chains connected the shackles on his wrist to the manacles on his ankles. Wendy whimpered, seeing a large, glistening axe leaning against the sleigh.

"It doesn't have to end this way," Hook assured as he rejoined Wendy.

"You're a monster!" she cried.

"Don't exaggerate," Hook said calmly. "I don't intend on using that axe. I just want to talk to you." He took a breath. "I'm not such a bad man, really. I just need the right influence in my life." Hook took another step closer. "You could do so much good. You aren't just some beautiful object. You are smart and wise, and compassionate. I would be your humble servant. Without you, I wouldn't be much of a king. But if I had you, I could use my power to help others and make the world a better place."

As she looked at his humble, vulnerable face, he no longer seemed scary to her. He looked like a scared little boy. She felt pity for him once more. Also, she had to admit there were many injustices in the world. Given the opportunity, could she actually make a difference?

"We can even adopt Peter," Hook offered.

Wendy couldn't believe her ears, and neither could Smee.

"I need to stop drinking," Smee muttered, scratching his head. "I think I'm starting to hear things."

"I mean it," Hook insisted. "Behind every great man is a great woman, and Wendy, you're the greatest. You shouldn't waste that greatness on just anybody. If you say yes, I know I can be an honest man. I know I can make you happy."

Wendy was quiet. She couldn't believe that a part of her was honestly considering it.

She shook her head to regain control of her thoughts. This was Captain Hook, after all! And he was talking about treason!

"Of course," Hook added, "if you were to say no, I might lose my ability to be a good man. I may go back to being a heartless scoundrel. Who knows, I may even decide to introduce Peter to Anne Boleyn."

Wendy grabbed her neck nervously. Her eyes returned to Peter on the chopping block, then the axe. Captain Hook may have been chivalrous and polite, but she understood his threat perfectly well. She knew what would happen to Peter if she refused.

"So, you're saying," Wendy verified, "that if I don't marry you, you will cut off Peter's head?"

Hook shrugged. "I don't know what will happen. All I know is that without you at my side, influencing me for good . . . I can't really be held responsible for my actions."

Wendy closed her eyes. Her head drooped, and she took a deep breath. "Okay."

"Okay?" Hook persisted.

"I'll marry you," Wendy declared.

Hook smiled. "Excellent."

CHAPTER TWENTY-SIX

To the Rescue

Father Christmas had seen enough! They needed to act, and they needed to act fast!

"All right," Father Christmas declared. "We have to go right away." He turned to Stanley and Tweedle. "Did you get the new tracking equipment set up?"

Tweedle nodded. "Yes. The boys have located the sleigh and are tracking it as we speak."

"Excellent!" Father Christmas replied. "Now, this may come as a shock, but I need you to fly the sleigh to England for me."

Tweedle froze, then looked Father Christmas in the eye, feeling as though he had misheard him. "Excuse me?"

"It's very simple," Father Christmas explained. "I need you in the driver's seat, guiding the team. Just follow your tracker and take the team where they need to go."

"You're not coming?!"

"I may have another way to get there faster. I haven't tried it yet, but in theory, it should work. Sadly, I'm the only one that can physically complete the journey. So, just do your best and meet me there as fast as you can."

Tweedle and Stanley exchanged nervous glances. Tweedle started to protest, but Father Christmas cut him off.

"No time to explain," Father Christmas declared. "We have to leave right now. Saddle up your gear and hurry to the sleigh. I'll send Barnaby to explain everything to everyone. Now remember, you won't be able to go full speed without me, but you all ate the magic feed. So, you'll still be able to manoeuvre and fly faster than you ever thought possible. So stay alert."

Tweedle tried to protest once more, but Father Christmas left, and the Grand High Elf helped usher them out of the Watching-Pools and to the sleigh. Barnaby instructed the group and prepared them to take off. He gave Tweedle a special radio to keep in communication with him at the North Pole. Barnaby would be using the Watching-Pools and a team of trackers at the North Pole Command Centre to keep Tweedle abreast of any sudden changes.

Father Christmas had other things to work on in the Present Room. Hook still had his magic bag. It was common knowledge that he could retrieve any non-living item he wanted from the North Pole using the bag, regardless of where in the world they may be. They had been trying to develop a way to transport pets, but the technology just wasn't there yet. But being he was made up of pure belief and not solid matter, in theory, someone could possibly retrieve him — if he allowed it. He believed that there must be a way for him to connect to the bag from there.

He stood in the centre of the room. He closed his eyes, trying to feel for the magical connection to the bag.

He felt it! His body began to vibrate with energy as it started to connect. He concentrated and felt his body transform, matching the same magical frequency. Slowly, his physical form faded away as it became one with the astral current of the bag.

"Well," Father Christmas muttered to himself, "here goes nothing."

He laid his finger alongside his nose and leapt into the unknown.

The elves watched Father Christmas vanish and hurried back to the Watching-Pools to see how it all played out.

While Father Christmas took a leap of faith, Smee had put Peter back into the sleigh — he was still unconscious with his hands and feet shackled behind his back.

"All right," Captain Hook called. "It's time we be shoving off."

"Ay, ay, captain," Smee called in response.

Suddenly, the magic bag began to twitch!

Hook turned. The sack continued to rattle and rustle around spontaneously in the back of the sleigh.

"Smee," Hook called. "Are you doing that?"

Smee glanced over, and the bag continued to jiggle and rumble more fiercely.

"N-not me, captain," Smee answered, shaking his head.

It rustled and bounced around more rapidly!

Hook approached the restless bag. "What the devil is going on?"

Slowly, he reached out with his claw and cautiously pulled the bag open. At first, he saw nothing — just an empty sack. Then all of a sudden, it began to spark and glow inside!

Hook stepped back, alarmed!

The bag began to inflate and stand up. Wind and arctic snowflakes swirled around inside and sprinkled up into the sky. A soft yellow glow shone through the sack as the winds picked up more wildly. A blurred figure began to form from the particles being whipped up from inside the bag — each particle was independent and radiating with light.

"Ho! Ho! Ho!" a deep, booming voice called out.

As the whirl of the wind swirled around the bag, the particles fused together and dimmed, forming the image of Father Christmas.

Hook, Smee, and Wendy all watched Father Christmas materialise before their very eyes. Father Christmas stared at the group, then looked over to the unconscious Peter, who was bound with heavy chains in the back of the sleigh. He turned back to Hook and held his gaze. "Clearly, someone's been very naughty."

Smee's lip began to quiver, feeling the weight of his guilt rushing up to him.

"Father Christmas, I presume," Hook replied with a courtly bow. "Glad to see you're still with us. I take it you're not here to give us coal."

Father Christmas shook his head. "Well, you're right there."

"Oh, Father Christmas!" Smee cried, falling to his knees and crawling toward the jolly man in red. "Please forgive me! I didn't mean to get sucked into all this!"

"Smee!" Hook snapped. "Get a hold of yourself! You're a pirate, for god's sake!"

"It's okay, Smee." Father Christmas chuckled. "Deep down, I know you have a good heart."

"Was everyone amused by my little going-away present?" Hook asked.

"Not Starkey," Father Christmas admonished.

"Starkey?" Smee inquired.

"He died a few hours ago," Father Christmas declared. "Hook left Starkey's wife a widow and his daughter fatherless."

Wendy's heart sank. She turned to Hook. "You killed Starkey?"

"Of course not," Hook replied. He turned to Father Christmas. "You don't mean to tell me that idiot went back to the camp?"

Father Christmas nodded. "He saved them all."

"I knew he was weak," Hook muttered. He turned back to Wendy. "Oh, and Peter was the one that planted those bombs and lit the fuse. Peter killed Starkey, not me."

"What?!" Wendy gasped.

"Yes," Hook acknowledged. "Your precious Peter planted bombs all over the camp. "Yes," Hook acknowledged. "Your precious Peter planted bombs all over the camp. If it weren't for Starkey, they would all be dead now."

"He wouldn't!" Wendy cried.

"He did!" Hook declared.

"Only because you tricked him!" Father Christmas clarified. "He didn't know what they were or what would happen."

"Well, they didn't die," Hook rebuked. "In the end, Peter killed another pirate. Big deal!"

"Starkey was a good man!" Father Christmas declared.

"So, what's your plan?" Hook asked.

"I plan on taking my sleigh, my bag, and the children with me," Father Christmas replied. "And I intend to return all of the jewels that were stolen using my magic."

"And what about Smee and I?"

"I'd like to do more," Father Christmas sneered. "But I am forbidden."

Hook pointed his pistol at Father Christmas. "I don't suppose this would do too much good on you, would it?"

Father Christmas shook his head.

"All right," Hook bartered. "Take the sleigh and the presents. That wasn't what this was all about anyway. I'm actually rather fond of Christmas, and I hope you can salvage it. You can also have Peter. I just want safe passage out of here. I want to keep the jewels that rightfully belong to me. And as for Wendy," he looked at her and grinned, "she has just consented to be my wife."

"That's not going to happen," Father Christmas declared.

Hook looked at the pistol. "This may not work on you, but I'm sure it will work on them."

The pistol swayed back and forth between Peter and Wendy.

"You know what?" Smee declared, backing away. "This is a little more than I can handle right now. I think I'll just find my own way out of here while everyone is still asleep. Thanks."

"Smee, get back here!" Hook ordered.

"Really, captain. Strange things always happen to us. This is another one of those situations where we should just cut our losses and go."

"You can't just jump ship on me now," Hook admonished.

"It's Christmas. I think we should just go home and pretend this whole thing never happened. And . . . ." Smee stopped, seeing the two little boys standing behind Father Christmas. "What in the blazes?"

The group turned and saw the translucent figures of two small boys wearing old-fashioned clothing.

Hook looked to Father Christmas. "Are they with you?"

Father Christmas shook his head in surprise. "No."

Smee turned to run for it when he heard a noise up ahead.

"What was that?" Hook asked.

"I don't know," Smee replied. "Everyone should be asleep."

They saw a figure in the fog.

"Who goes there?!" Hook demanded, raising his pistol.

There was no response. But the figure moved closer.

"I'm warning you," Captain Hook barked, "I have a loaded pistol aimed, and I don't mind using it."

Suddenly, the stranger hurled something at them. Something with hair! It bounded and rolled, stopping at their feet. The group *gasped*, realising it was a woman's head!

"What the devil?!" Hook cried.

Instantly, the eyes on the severed head snapped open!

Hook jumped back, startled—

BANG!

He fired his pistol, but the blast passed through the spectre as if it wasn't even there!

The woman's head looked up at them and shrieked, *"Who took my head?!"*

They all staggered back in alarm!

The woman's headless body approached the group.

Hook looked back to Father Christmas. "I saw what happened with the cannibals. Is this another one of your tricks?"

"No," Father Christmas replied. "I don't know a lot about the spirit world, but they are attracted and energised by magic. And right now, we have both Christmas magic and Neverland magic. Not to mention the fact that we have a direct descendant to the former King of England."

"How'd you know that?" Hook asked.

"I'm Father Christmas, James. I know everything," Father Christmas declared. "And you just disturbed the grounds of one of the most haunted places in England."

The headless corpse lunged forward!

"Is that the ghost of Anne Boleyn?!" Smee asked, turning his attention to Father Christmas.

Father Christmas shrugged. When Smee looked back, the revenant was gone!

"Where'd she go?" Smee asked.

Suddenly, Smee felt a pair of cold, rotting hands grip his shoulder.

"*Captain!!*" Smee screamed.

The headless woman materialised, lifting Smee off the ground and throwing him across the square! He hit the cobblestone surface, skidding with a *thud*. He let out a loud *grunt!*

"Can a ghost harm anyone?" Hook asked.

"Normally, I'd say no," Father Christmas replied. "However, I don't think they've ever had this much energy to feed on before."

Father Christmas was especially worried. He was mostly safe against mortals because he wasn't entirely a physical being. Unfortunately, ghosts weren't physical beings either.

The group backed up and saw another headless body approach with its head tucked underneath its arm.

"*Aaahhhhhhhhhhhhhhhhhhhh!!*" the head shrilled like a banshee.

They looked to the left and saw more ghastly apparitions emerge from the fog. They turned to the right and *gasped*, seeing an even bigger crowd of corpses converging on them. They were surrounded, and the angry spectres were closing in!

"How many bloody ghosts does this place have?" Hook snapped.

"Well, considering that there were over a hundred documented executions," Father Christmas replied, "there could be quite a few."

"*Who took my head?!*" the woman wailed again, approaching Hook.

"I believe it was your husband, Henry," Hook replied. He glanced over his shoulder at Father Christmas. "You know, a big fat guy with a beard. Used to wear funny red clothes."

She lunged at Hook, and he dodged her hands.

Hook turned and pointed to Father Christmas. "Hey, isn't that him over there?!"

The spectre looked and *shrieked!* She turned and charged Father Christmas!

"*Henry!!*" the phantom roared!

Father Christmas ran and saw another hoard of spirits *shriek* and *howl* and *hiss* at him! They turned, rushing him!

Father Christmas was terrified! He slammed the tip of his staff to the ground, and a bright wave of light erupted, pushing the spectres back with a great force.

Smee had tried to slip away unnoticed. He saw the gate up ahead and smiled, feeling relieved. As he approached the gate, he heard a deafening *ROAR!!*

Slowly, he peered into the shadows and beheld an enormous, dead grizzly bear lurking in the entranceway.

"You gotta be kidding me," Smee groaned.

The bear stood on its hind legs with its claws raised, ready to pounce. It let out another fierce, slime-filled *ROAR!!*

"*Caaaptaaaainn!!*" Smee screamed, sprinting back for the sleigh as fast as he could!

The group saw Smee running, being chased by the phantasmal bear. It swiped at him and chomped at him, but Smee kept narrowly evading the beast's deadly jaws.

"*Why is there a bear chasing me?!*" Smee cried.

Hook recalled that they used to keep animals at the Tower of London when he was a child — as a matter of fact, his aunt took him to see the Royal Menagerie on several occasions when he was a child. He hadn't thought about it in years, but he supposed that an animal could be a ghost too.

"*Leg it!*" Hook called.

Smee increased his velocity.

So did the bear!

Hook raised his pistol and fired at the creature!

BANG!

Once again, the bullet passed right through the entity.

Suddenly, they began to hear other animal noises in the fog.

"Quick, into the sleigh!" Father Christmas commanded.

The bear was gaining on Smee!

Up ahead, Smee saw the sleigh in sight.

Father Christmas ran toward Smee and the bear.

Smee passed Father Christmas, and Father Christmas turned, slamming his staff to the ground again! A bright light shot out with a seismic wave. The phantasmal bear ran into it and flew backwards.

Hook whipped on the reins. "*Now, Dasher! Now, Dancer! Now, Prancer! Now, Vixen!*"

Smee leapt and gripped the back of the sleigh.

"*On, Comet! On, Cupid! On, Dunder and Blixem!*"

The reindeer began to trot.

"*Wait for me!*" Smee yelled.

"Ah, Smee," Hook called, helping him inside. "So glad you can join us."

"See, this is what I was talking about," Smee complained, climbing into the back seat. "Who else meets Father Christmas and gets attacked by headless ghosts and a dead grizzly bear?! Nobody! That's the sort of thing that only happens to us!"

"Stop your whining, Smee," Hook baulked. "Now, hold on tight!"

The sleigh began to ascend into the sky.

"What about Father Christmas?" Smee asked. "After all, he did save us."

"He'll be fine," Hook assured. "I'm sure we'll see him again soon enough."

Father Christmas saw a line of ghosts between him and the sleigh. He ran past them, deflecting their attacks with his magic staff. He touched his finger alongside his nose and leapt into the sky after the sleigh. He rocketed up high — nearly halfway up the tower — and grasped the sleigh's left runner.

The sleigh jerked momentarily from the weight of Father Christmas. It stabilised and flew over the outer walls, leaving the ghosts and the Tower of London far behind them.

CHAPTER TWENTY-SEVEN
The Chase

Tweedle and the boys had nearly reached Scotland when they were alerted by the tracking beacon. Tweedle observed his guidance equipment, and the other sleigh was leaving the Tower of London. They had a separate fix on Father Christmas, and it appeared that Father Christmas was currently travelling with the other sleigh. They had no way of knowing if Peter and Wendy were with him, but the sleigh was heading southwest.

"That doesn't seem right," Tweedle mumbled, getting a lock on the other sleigh's trajectory. He turned and shouted to the team, who had trouble hearing him over the whipping winds. "Okay, guys! They're moving in the wrong direction. Let's pick up the pace and be prepared for anything!"

He *snapped* the reins, and the team sped up, bursting into action! They knew they were closing in.

Meanwhile, Hook glanced back at Father Christmas, dangling from the runner. He pulled up on the reins, and the reindeer shot up into a sharp vertical incline.

Father Christmas slid back fast, struggling to hold on!

Suddenly, Hook yanked the team down, causing the reindeer to drop, diving down rapidly!

Father Christmas flipped! His body slammed against the metal runner, but he managed to hang on! He tried to wrap his leg around the runner for support but—

Hook brought the team back up, swerving from side to side, trying to shake the old man off, but Father Christmas clung on tight.

Hook whipped the reins harshly, and the sleigh plunged into another terrifying nose-dive! Father Christmas' legs flew up as the sleigh hurtled faster and faster to the sea. At the last second, Hook levelled out, bringing the sleigh to the waterline — the bottom of the sleigh skimmed the ocean's surface.

Father Christmas struggled with his grip, feeling the force of the ice water pounding against his face and body! The powerful *crash* of the water hit him like a freight train! He was still in his physical form and couldn't concentrate enough to switch out of it, so he had to endure the elements — but he still didn't let go!

Hook glanced back and *growled*, frustrated that he couldn't shake the old geezer off! Hook pulled up on the reins, and the reindeer shot back up into the sky — Father Christmas managed to wrap his legs around the runner. Then Hook brought it down, slamming Father Christmas back into the water!

Father Christmas gasped, taking the water in!

Hook did it again!

And again!

"Stop it!" Wendy cried.

She found the reindeer whip in the front seat and grabbed it. She flung it back to Father Christmas, who caught it and wrapped it around his hand.

"Smee," Hook called. "Will you take that thing from her?"

"I don't know, captain," Smee declared defiantly, watching Father Christmas struggle to pull himself out of the water. "It doesn't seem right to leave a man to drown, especially after he saved me from a bear."

"For heaven's sake!" Hook growled. "I keep trying to tell you, he's Father Christmas! I don't think he can die! The only thing we can do is slow him down!"

Father Christmas gripped the back of the sleigh with one foot on the runner.

Hook held on to the reins with his claw, reached into his coat pocket and produced his pistol.

Father Christmas climbed over the back seat and—

BANG!!

The shot caught Father Christmas in the shoulder. He recoiled back, tumbling over the edge and plummeting into the sea.

"There!" Hook huffed, concentrating on flying the craft. He whipped the reins, and the team took to the sky once more.

Father Christmas sunk into the freezing depths of the ocean. At first, he was too shocked to move. He had inhaled a lot of salt water. In his physical form, he could feel a little pain. He closed his eyes and concentrated.

Slowly, his shoulder healed itself as the water evacuated his lungs, and like that, he stopped feeling the chill. He opened his eyes and swam to the surface.

Nearby, Tweedle watched the lights on his tracking device. The light that represented Father Christmas stopped moving, and the light that represented the other sleigh maintained its course.

"Something just happened," Tweedle muttered.

The radio *clicked* on, and the garbled voice of Barnaby came over the speaker.

"Tweedle," Barnaby said, reporting from the Watching-Pools. "Father Christmas has been shot and dumped in the ocean nearby. Over."

"Thank you," Tweedle replied, speaking into the microphone. "We're almost there! Over."

They flew low to the sea. All eyes were peeled for any sign of movement in the water; unfortunately, it was too dark to see.

Father Christmas heard them approaching. He gazed up, and his keen eyes spotted them. He watched as the sleigh passed overhead and realized they missed him!

Father Christmas tried to call out, but they were too far away to hear. He looked around to see if there was any way of attracting their attention, then remembered Nana was in the lead. He let out a loud, piercing *whistle!*

Nana's ears perked up. She slowed the team down, surveying the ocean floor below.

"Thank god!" Father Christmas muttered to himself. He took a breath and brayed out another harsh *whistle!* It was even higher-pitched and longer than the last one.

Nana *barked!*

Everyone stopped, struggling to look for the yuletide gift-giver. The stars and the moon reflected on the rippling waves, making them feel like they were soaring through the limitless beauty of the Milky Way.

"Over here!" Father Christmas yelled.

Nana *barked* and turned the group around, following the voice.

Father Christmas called out again, and this time, the rest of them heard it.

Finally, Nana spotted him! They skimmed the waters and stopped the sleigh next to the man in red. Tweedle reached out, taking Father Christmas' hand. With a bit of heft, Father Christmas managed to pull himself up and climb into the sleigh.

"Are you all right?" Tweedle asked.

"I'll be fine," Father Christmas assured. "Thank you, everyone. You've done a magnificent job."

Everyone watched him silently.

"Well," Father Christmas replied, "what's everybody waiting around for? We've got a sleigh to catch."

They nodded. Father Christmas took the reins, and they were off!

They were in hot pursuit. Hook was going fast, but Father Christmas was going faster!

Smee glanced over his shoulder and noticed the other odd-looking vessel approaching. He did a double-take, then turned to Hook and tapped his shoulder "Uh, captain . . ."

"Yes, Mr. Smee?" Hook replied.

"Don't look now, but there's another sleigh approaching," Smee warned.

Wendy and Hook turned and saw the Lost-Boy-drawn canoe gaining on them. Hook reached into his coat and retrieved his spyglass. He got a good look at Father Christmas in the driver's seat.

"They're more resilient than I thought," Hook griped, collapsing the spyglass and putting it back in his coat.

Nana, who was still in the lead, *barked* at the sight of the sleigh!

Wendy smiled in relief and excitement. They were getting closer!

Hook whipped the reins, trying to pick up the pace!

They had reached a city with tall buildings. Hook flew low, weaving in between the structures rapidly, hoping to make Father Christmas crash — but to no avail!

They passed the city and flew through the woods, then into the mountains! Hook flew erratically, dodging cliffs and peaks and canyons — anything he could do to shake Father Christmas off their trail. But they were gaining!

There was a tall peak up ahead in the centre of the canyon. Hook went right, and Father Christmas went left, kicking up speed! By the time the canyon converged, Father Christmas had pulled beside Hook's sleigh.

"You can't keep this up forever!" Father Christmas called.

Hook turned. "You're probably right. But . . ."

Crack!

Hook picked up a whip and snapped it at Father Christmas' head.

". . . I'm afraid I am an unbelievably stubborn man," Hook finished.

Father Christmas winced!

Hook whipped him again!

And again!

Father Christmas grabbed his whip and struck back at Hook!

Hook recoiled, grimacing at the lash!

Both men went back and forth, exchanging stinging blows of the whip until Hook tugged the reins to the left, pulling them apart. Then he whipped the reins back, ramming Father Christmas!

The canoe wobbled.

Hook rammed it again!

And again!

Hook pulled away, retrieving the blunderbuss from his coat. He turned and—

BOOOM!!

—fired at the other sleigh!

Wendy screamed!

Hook blew an enormous hole in the side of the canoe, causing it to spin out of control and fall back.

Hook whipped on the reins, and his sleigh pulled away, lengthening his lead.

Father Christmas had re-stabilised and regained control of the makeshift sleigh. His body had been riddled with shot, but he knew he would be okay — he was more concerned with Tweedle and the others. When he saw that everyone was all right, he whipped the reins, determined to catch back up.

Hook glanced back and saw the other sleigh was back on their tail.

"Smee," Hook called. "Reload the blunderbuss and prepare to fire again."

Hook tossed the gun to his former bo'sun, and Smee fumbled it as he caught it.

"I don't know, captain," Smee mumbled. "It just doesn't feel right."

Hook spun his head around, facing Smee — the red sparks of death flared in his eyes.

"Right on it, captain!" Smee declared, rapidly reloading the gun.

Hook turned back to flying the sleigh, then looked back.

"On second thought," Hook declared, "why don't you take the reins for a moment? I don't think I can trust your aim just now."

Smee took the driver's seat, and Hook took back the blunderbuss.

Hook sat in the back, waiting patiently for his next shot. He turned to Wendy. "Wendy, my dear," Hook called gently. "I'm going to need you to procure something for me from out of that bag."

"No!" Wendy snapped.

"It's nothing bad," he assured. "It's just something I think you and I will need very shortly."

Father Christmas was closing in.

BOOOM!!

Father Christmas and his team evaded the blast more gracefully this time, but it still slowed them down for a minute.

"What do we do?" Stanley asked. They were over another ocean.

Father Christmas wasn't sure. He may be okay with gunshots — in the long run — but the children, Nana, and the elves could still die if they were shot! He thought for a moment and slowed the sleigh down.

"Are you giving up?" Tweedle asked.

"Nope." Father Christmas shook his head.

Hook, Wendy, and Smee watched the other sleigh shrink in the distance.

"Are they giving up?" Smee asked.

Hook watched the other sleigh fade away in the distance. "Not bloody likely. Keep a sharp eye!"

As soon as Hook's sleigh was out of sight, Father Christmas brought the canoe up high into the sky — higher than the clouds. As soon as they reached the altitude Father Christmas wanted, he whipped the reins, and the sleigh shot forward at full speed. It was only for a second or two, but that was all he needed to shoot ahead of Hook.

He waited, then dropped the canoe down fast on top of Hook's sleigh. Father Christmas leapt and landed in the sleigh, kicking Captain Hook over the railing. As he flew out of the sleigh, Hook barely managed to catch the cross-section to the runners with his claw. He watched the blunderbuss fall out of his hands, forever lost to the sea.

Father Christmas turned to Smee.

Smee looked up sheepishly, then stood up, holding out the reins. "I was just keeping the seat nice and warm for you."

"That's okay," Father Christmas replied. "I've got a few things to do back here. You keep flying it for a few minutes and start heading back to Neverland."

"Ay, ay!" Smee replied.

Hook continued to hold on and fought to swing his leg back onto the runner. He was struggling to pull himself up with the high winds.

Father Christmas reached into the magic sack and retrieved the magical-smelling salts. He waved it under Peter's nose, and Peter woke up instantly.

"Whoa— Wha—?" Peter looked around. "Where am I? What happened?"

"You were tricked into helping Captain Hook," Wendy explained.

"Captain Hook?" Peter exclaimed.

"Yes! He betrayed you, and now Father Christmas is trying to rescue us."

Suddenly, the captain's claw pierced the back of the sleigh as he crawled inside.

"Bad form!" Hook cried to Father Christmas. "Good move, but still . . . bad form."

"I'll take your word for it," Father Christmas replied. "After all, you are the expert."

Hook went for his sword, but Father Christmas held the tip of his staff to his neck. Suddenly, the wooden tip transformed into a spearhead — Hook felt the metal point press against his throat.

"*Touché,*" Hook replied.

"Are you ready to concede?" Father Christmas asked.

"Almost," Hook admitted. He glanced over at Peter. "I see the boy's finally up. How are you, Peter?"

Father Christmas glanced back, and Hook turned and kicked Peter — whose hands and feet were still manacled together with thick iron chains. Peter flipped back, falling out of the sleigh!

"*PETER!!*" Wendy shrieked.

Father Christmas turned, hearing Peter cry as he plummeted below.

Peter couldn't free himself, and he couldn't fly. He hit the cold water with a big splash! It hurt, but Peter desperately tried to hold his breath as the water filled his nostrils. The water was freezing as he sunk deeper and deeper into the ocean.

Father Christmas turned back to Hook, who shrugged boyishly and smiled. Father Christmas grit his teeth, suppressing the urge to run him through.

"Now who has bad form?" Father Christmas declared. "I'll be back."

"I'm sure you will," Hook replied.

Father Christmas turned and dove over the side of the sleigh, preparing his body to hit the water.

Hook sat up. "Well, that went rather well!"

Wendy lunged forward and began hitting Hook. "You said you wouldn't hurt Peter!"

Hook grabbed her hair and twisted it back.

"Peter is fine!" Hook cried, pulling her off. "Do you honestly think Father Christmas will let anything happen to him?"

Tweedle turned their vessel around to stay with Father Christmas.

"My apologies for being a little rough," Hook said, letting Wendy's hair go. "I assure you it will all turn out fine for everyone." He turned to his bo'son and handed him the breathing apparatus they had found when they first stole the sleigh. "Fly wherever you want as fast as you can. We'll be getting off shortly."

Down below, Father Christmas dove into the sea. He swam as fast as he could, desperately trying to locate Peter before it was too late! He couldn't see a trace of the boy, so he closed his eyes to let his magic hone into Peter and guide him there.

Peter held his breath for as long as he could — much longer than any average person — but even his breath eventually went out, and his lungs failed him!

Father Christmas saw Peter in sight and swam faster. Once Father Christmas reached Peter, he touched the chains. The metal rings on Peter's hands and feet snapped open and sunk deeper into the watery abyss.

Father Christmas was worried about the water filling in Peter's lungs. He also worried about the crushing pressure of the ocean depths and the lack of oxygen going to Peter's brain!

Father Christmas held Peter's nose and breathed as much air and magic into Peter's lungs as he could before surfacing.

Tweedle, Stanley, John, Michael, Surely, Pipkin, Jojo, and Nana waited nervously to see if they would resurface.

Nana saw a bubble rise to the surface. She *whimpered*.

Finally, Father Christmas emerged with Peter. He swam to the canoe and was helped inside. He stopped to check on Peter, who was not breathing.

Immediately, Father Christmas applied skilful chest compressions. Next, he tilted Peter's head back — placing one hand under the chin and the other pinched the nose close — and gave two slow, gentle breaths into Peter's mouth.

They all watched nervously, waiting and . . .

Nothing.

He applied more chest compression, followed by two more rescue breaths, and . . .

Still, nothing!

"Come on, Peter," Father Christmas called.

He started the compressions up again until . . . Peter coughed up salt water!

Peter continued to cough and hack up everything he had swallowed, but he was still cold and in pain.

Father Christmas swaddled him up in a warm blanket. "We need to get him back to the North Pole right away! His lungs are collapsing, and we don't want hypothermia to set in."

"Will he be okay?" Michael asked.

"Only if we get him to the North Pole in time."
Father Christmas declared, gripping the reins.

"What are we going to do about Hook?" Tweedle
asked.

"I will deal with him later," Father Christmas
replied. "Peter hasn't eaten any of the magic feed, so we
can't go full speed without killing him! Now brace
yourselves, it's going to be a very stressful flight!"

Father Christmas whipped the reins, and the
children flew off as fast as Peter was physically able.

"*Stay with me, Peter!*" Father Christmas cried. It
was very touch and go, and his one hope was to keep Peter
awake and breathing until they reached the North Pole.

CHAPTER TWENTY-EIGHT

Hook and Wendy

Hook had put on the parachute that he had asked Wendy to retrieve from the magic bag. From the moment Father Christmas had emerged at the Tower of London, Hook knew he couldn't win — not entirely. He knew that Father Christmas was tracking the sleigh and that Father Christmas could use that bag as a portal. He decided to leave the bag in the sleigh and make Smee fly it as far away as possible until Father Christmas finally caught up again. Smee would surrender, and Hook and Wendy would be long gone, having already parachuted several continents away.

Smee had protested at first, but Hook assured him Father Christmas would never harm or implicate him in any crimes to the authorities. He also promised Smee that his loyalty would be greatly rewarded once Father Christmas turned him loose. Smee had seen the stash Hook had left at his house, so he knew he wasn't bluffing.

"Won't they still come after you and Wendy after they find me?" Smee asked.

"Once she's legally my wife, it won't matter," Hook replied.

"I'm not marrying you," Wendy huffed.

"We'll see," Hook replied.

"She doesn't seem all that keen," Smee interrupted. "Besides, Father Christmas is quick. How do you plan on getting hitched that fast?"

Hook grinned. "The captain of a ship is often authorised to perform legally binding marriage ceremonies. I am a captain, and for all extensive purposes, this is my vessel, and we are currently out at sea. And since we are currently citizens of Neverland and Neverland has no restrictive rules or waiting periods, there's nothing stopping me from officiating my own marriage ceremony right now." Hook smirked. "And I can just write up a quick Neverland wedding certificate."

Hook pulled out a parchment from his jacket. "Like the one I had drawn up before I left."

Wendy and Smee looked at it. It was simple but succinct. Hook had already signed and dated on the lines for the groom and the officiator, but there were still two blank spaces that needed signatures:

The Bride:

____

The Witness:

Smee shook his head. "Got to hand it to the Captain. He's got more tricks up his sleeve than the devil in a poker tournament."

"Well put, Smee," Hook replied. "Now, if you'd be so kind as to sign your name as the witness."

Wendy looked over at Smee. Smee was guilt-stricken.

"I'm sorry," Smee apologised, taking the document and signing it.

"Well, none of it will matter," Wendy declared. "Because I will never . . . *EVER* . . . marry you!"

"Madam," Hook addressed, "I was to believe that you were a woman of honour. You gave your word."

"Honour?" Wendy huffed with a snide chuckle. "You promised you wouldn't hurt Peter. What do you know about honour?"

"I never once used those words," Hook corrected. "I said if I had a woman like you as my wife, I could be a good and honest man." He leaned in. "You're not my wife yet."

"I'd rather die than marry you!"

Hook stood up furiously. *"That can be arranged!"*

Hook's bellow frightened Wendy. His face was red, his cheeks were flushed, and, for a fleeting moment, she saw those red sparks return to his eyes. He closed his eyes and took a long, slow breath, regaining his composure.

"My apologies," Hook said, sitting down, in complete control of himself once more. "I did not mean to lose my temper. And I can assure you, Peter is perfectly safe. It was never my intention to kick him over the edge. Alas, it was all I could think of at the moment to make Father Christmas go away."

Wendy's eyes darted to the magic bag, then back to Hook before he could notice.

"Of course, when I am King—"

"There you go again!" Wendy snapped. "You're always on about being a king. Well. I don't want a king! And I don't want to be a queen! I am loyal to my country and will not be party to treason. I want a nice, normal life with a nice, normal husband."

Hook was quiet and contemplative. Finally, he spoke. "Okay."

Wendy blinked in confusion. "Okay?"

"To paraphrase *Richard the Third* 'My Kingdom for a Wife,' " Hook replied. "You were prepared to marry me for Peter. Would you be willing to do it for your country?"

Wendy shook her head in disbelief. "What is wrong with you?"

"I know I can make you happy if you give me a chance."

"Why is this so important?"

"Wendy," Hook began. "I was just a boy when my mother died. My father abandoned her. He abandoned me too. My legacy was stolen from me, but that's not what mattered to me as a child. What mattered was that my mum deserved better. I vowed that if I was ever blessed enough to meet a woman as wonderful as my mother, that I would not only marry her, but I would love her and treat her with the same respect and devotion my mother never got. The sort of love and devotion she deserved!" His stern expression softened. "I wanted to make my bride happy. I would strive to be the sort of man she could be proud of." He looked up at Wendy. "But that's not the sort of man I am right now, is it?"

Wendy shook her head.

"If it's not a kingdom or a crown you crave . . ." Hook reached into the bag where Smee had stashed the crown jewels and retrieved the *St. Edward's Crown*. He handed it to Wendy. "They can keep the jewels, and I can forget my birthright. If what you desire is a simple, quiet, honest life with an honest man, I can give that to you instead."

"I'm afraid it's not going to happen," Wendy replied.

"Has anyone ever been able to offer so much to the woman he adores?"

Wendy shook her head. "I'm sorry . . . but no."

"Very well." Hook shrugged. "Smee!"

"Yes, captain?" Smee replied.

"Throw her overboard."

Wendy gasped!

"What?!" Smee exclaimed, looking back at the captain.

"You heard me."

Smee peaked over the edge of the sleigh and observed the long, lethal drop below. "Surely, you don't mean that!"

"I certainly do," Hook insisted, standing over his reticent bo'sun. "Either you throw her over, or I'll throw both of you overboard!"

Smee watched Hook's claw inch closer to his neck and took a long, petrified gulp.

Wendy took advantage of the distraction and slipped her hand into the magic bag. She concentrated and retrieved a loaded *Webley Mk IV* service revolver. She swung it fast, lining it up with Captain Hook's face!

Hook recoiled in shock and alarm!

"Don't move!" Wendy demanded.

Hook gazed down the barrel of the most unusual looking pistol he had ever seen and replied, "Well, it looks like someone has an interesting Christmas wish list."

"Well, there is a war on." Wendy theorised.

"That would explain it," Hook grinned. "I suppose some things never change."

He shifted in his seat, and Wendy's arm shot up aggressively! "I swear if you move, I'll blow that smirk off your face!"

Hook threw his head back and laughed. "Again, you show that fighting spirit! So strong and determined. That's why I wanted you. My future children and I deserve the best. And you, my dear Wendy, are the best."

"Smee," Wendy commanded. "Take this sleigh down."

"Ay, ay," Smee replied, lowering the sleigh.

"Don't be stupid, Smee," Hook retorted. "She's not going to shoot."

Wendy pulled back the hammer on the revolver.

"Okay, fun is over," Hook mused. "Give it here."

He lunged forward and—

BANG!

She shot him in the thigh.

Hook *wailed* out in pain as he collapsed to the floor. He gazed up at Wendy. "You shot me!"

"The next one will be in the face!" Wendy threatened. "And this is a modern pistol, so it doesn't need to be reloaded after one shot!"

"Good form, Wendy." Hook nodded. He was curled on his side, gripping his wound. He did his best not to let the sight of his hideous blood distract him. "So, what are you going to do now?"

"I don't know," she admitted.

CHAPTER TWENTY-NINE

Peter's Revelation

By the time they reached the North Pole, Peter was in critical condition! Father Christmas had his best medical staff on standby to receive Peter as soon as they landed. Peter had drifted in and out of consciousness during the flight. His vision was blurry, and he was only vaguely aware of his surroundings. He heard strange voices and loud machines as Father Christmas swooped him up and placed him on the rolling hospital bed.

Father Christmas watched the team spring into action, connecting as sorts of magical machinery to the boy. He wanted to stay with Peter while the elves worked on him, but there was no time. Wendy needed him. Peter's fate was in the hands of the elves, and he had faith in them.

He took one last look, noticing Peter's heart rate stabilising, and then excused himself. Father Christmas didn't even bother to go to the Watching-Pools. He hurried straight to the Present Room. He had to get to Wendy fast. He had a date with an incredibly Naughty Boy with a hook!

Still, it didn't take long for the elves to get Peter's vital signs under control. Barnaby, the Grand High Elf, personally looked over Peter's care. Slowly, Peter started to come around. As he woke up, he felt weak, but his head and vision cleared. Then Peter remembered what had happened and the betrayal of a man he thought was his friend.

Serves me right for trusting a grown-up! Peter's mind screamed. He wanted to cry.

It was unfair! It was Father Christmas' fault! Him and that damned List! And Wendy too! All anybody ever did was hurt him.

As Peter gazed up, he discovered an old, wise-looking elf sitting beside the bed. The elf gave the boy a warm, loving smile.

"How are you feeling?" Barnaby asked.

"Terrible," Peter declared, wanting to weep.

"Well, the doctors are doing all they can," Barnaby replied. "It'll take time for you to fully recover."

"It's not that,"

"What is it then?"

"Why does everyone I love always leave me?!" Peter cried.

"What?" the Grand High Elf asked.

"My mom, Wendy, the Lost Boys, the Pirates of the Sky. Even Father Christmas and that horrible List have turned their backs on me."

Barnaby's heart wept for the poor boy. As the Grand High Elf, he possessed certain magic and insights into children's minds. Peter's abandonment issues ran deep and never healed. It made him distrustful. It made him controlling — especially of the Lost Boys. It made him want to forget things. Perhaps, his bad memory was something he secretly wanted and not just a side effect of staying a child.

"You've never forgiven your mother for closing her window to you," the Grand High Elf uttered.

"What?" Peter replied. "How do you know about that?"

"I can read it in your eyes," Barnaby declared. "I can hear it in the moans of your heart." He gripped his staff for support as he stood up. "Come. Let me show you something."

The medical staff unlocked the wheels of Peter's hospital bed and pushed it, following the Grand High Elf. Peter was confused but got excited as they led Peter down a large tunnel that opened out into the caverns below. Peter loved to explore caves. For him, it was an adventure. He was in awe, seeing the torches on the walls spontaneously erupt with flame as they drew near.

Finally, his eyes lit up at the sight of the mystic Watching-Pools.

Barnaby touched his staff to the liquid below, then turned to Peter. "Watch the water."

A white cloud emerged below the depths, rising close to the surface. Figures began to take shape — figures Peter recognised! Peter saw himself as a baby, frolicking with pixies in Kensington Gardens. Peter grinned arrogantly, thinking he was the most remarkable baby the world had ever seen.

When Peter saw his mother's face, he felt a twinge of unease in his heart — the kind he had never felt before. His mother's face was sweet, caring, and beautiful. His mother had only turned away for a moment when the baby flew off with the fairies, leaving the young woman alone. She began to panic, looking around everywhere for her child.

For the first time, Peter felt guilty for causing his mother such pain.

The water continued to bubble and ferment, changing from one scene to the next!

His mother was crying. She had alerted the constable and spoke with an Inspector of Scotland Yard but was told that she would likely never see her son again. Peter was pained to see the sorrow and anguish his mother went through.

Next, he witnessed as she sat beside an empty crib in front of the open window of the nursery. She sat there night after night. Peter's father tried to comfort her and have her close the window, but she refused. She knew it made no sense, but she would leave her window open in case their son would return. The weeks became months, and the months became a year, and still, she waited.

Peter looked at Barnaby with guilt-ridden eyes. Barnaby nodded and gestured for Peter to keep watching.

There was a quick flash under the water, and it showed Peter as a toddler. He was playing selfishly without a care in the world in Neverland. There was another flash, taking them back to his mother. Another year had gone by. She was sitting in the chair, looking miserable. Peter peered closer and noticed that she looked different somehow. Her stomach was swollen. She was expecting another child, yet she continued to sit by the open window, waiting for Peter. Peter's parents reluctantly agreed that Peter was never coming back. His mother clutched her swollen tummy tight and closed her eyes. She had lost one child and vowed never to lose another. With a single tear dripping down her cheek, she went to the window and closed it. She locked it forever, ensuring that her new baby would never leave.

"She waited as long as she could," Barnaby declared. "Losing a child is a parent's greatest fear, and she had to live with it for the rest of her life. Your mother didn't lock the window because she didn't want you anymore. She locked it because she was terrified of losing your brother in the same horrible way. Believe me, she thought about you every single day you were gone."

The water continued to ferment, and there was one last flash. Peter saw himself a little older. He had decided to fly back home, but when he got there, he found the window was closed. The young boy's face twisted in shock and heartbreak. Peter remembered that moment all too well. He watched his younger self gaze inside the nursery, only to discover a new baby in the crib.

Peter remembered feeling his heart shatter in his chest. He thought his mother had forgotten about him — had replaced him! But as Peter watched the whole incident unfold in the water, he began to realise that he was wrong about everything.

"Why didn't you knock?" Barnaby asked.

"I didn't know," Peter whimpered, trying to choke back the tears. "I was sure they had abandoned me. That they didn't want me anymore."

"They would have let you in," Barnaby declared. "She would have been so happy to see you. She would have hugged you and never let you go."

Peter shook his head. "I didn't know."

"I know."

Peter gazed up at Barnaby. "Is it too late?"

"I'm afraid so," Barnaby said with a woeful sigh. "That was a long time ago. Your mother, your brothers, and sister—"

Peter's eyes flashed in surprise.

"That's right," Barnaby clarified, "she did have more children. But I'm afraid they are all gone now. But you should take comfort in knowing that they never abandoned you. You were always loved and wanted. Even the Darlings offered to adopt you."

The water bubbled up, recreating that moment in the Darlings' nursery. Peter had felt that Wendy and the Lost Boys had abandoned him, but once again, he saw that he was loved and wanted.

"No one abandoned you," Barnaby continued.

"I abandoned them," Peter declared, realising the truth. He closed his eyes, and another teardrop rolled down his cheek. "It was my fault."

"Don't be so hard on yourself. You were only a child — you're still a child! You weren't old enough to know better. Now, the one thing you need to take away from this is that you made a choice. For better or worse, you made a choice, and you have to live with it and move on. You need to forgive your mother. And you need to forgive yourself. Your heart needs to move on so it can heal, and you can start taking chances on the people who care about you the most."

"I have to make up for what I've done," Peter declared. Suddenly, it hit him! "Where's Wendy?! Is she all right?!"

The Grand High Elf tapped the water, and the images cleared. Suddenly, a new image formed, and they beheld Wendy in Father Christmas' stolen sleigh. Captain Hook was clutching his leg as Wendy held a firearm to him.

CHAPTER THIRTY
A Final Showdown

"Fire, Wendy," Hook suggested, gazing down the barrel of Wendy's revolver. "But aim true." He opened his shirt, baring his chest. "Aim for my heart. The very heart you have broken."

"I probably should, after all you've done." Wendy wasn't sure if she had it in her to pull the trigger.

Suddenly, the bag stood up on its own. The soft yellow glow filled inside it once more as the winds picked up more wildly. A blurred, shimmering figure began to form from the particles swirling up from the bottom of the sack.

"Well, that was fast." Hook sighed, watching the glowing particles swirl and merge once more. "I really should've thrown that bag overboard."

"Ho! Ho! Ho!" the voice bellowed once again.

Wendy watched and smiled, feeling relieved as she witnessed Father Christmas' form begin to materialise.

Hook observed Wendy's attention shift. With what little strength he could muster, he rolled and sprang forward like a cobra striking its prey! His hand launched forth, ripping the gun out of Wendy's hand! It happened too fast for Wendy to react.

Instinctively, she lunged back at him, pawing for the revolver! Hook grimaced as her knee stuck his bullet wound! The pain surged through him as she crawled on top of him! Hook's back arched, pressing hard against the floor as he kicked Wendy off with his good leg. When she looked up, she saw the pistol pointed at her head.

"Thank you, my dear," Hook muttered, trying to catch his breath from the shooting pain in his thigh. "I think I'll hold onto this for now."

Her fingers itched to go for the magic bag.

"And keep your hands where I can see them," Hook warned. "It was a nice trick, but not one I'm going to fall for again."

The glittering sparks of light subsided, and Father Christmas had fully materialised onto the physical plane.

"Well, hullo again," Hook greeted. Even while sprawled out on the floor of a sleigh, Hook still exuded elegance and grace.

"Hullo," Father Christmas replied.

"You know, we really need to stop meeting like this," Hook quipped.

"I couldn't agree with you more." Father Christmas declared. He noticed that Hook's thigh was bleeding. "Looks like you're a little worse for wear."

Hook smiled with an unblinking gaze. "Just a little domestic dispute. You see, Wendy wasn't too keen on me kicking Peter out of the sleigh."

"I wasn't too keen on that myself," Father Christmas said.

"Would you do me a favour?" Hook asked. "Will you just let her know that Peter is going to be just fine so she can calm down?"

"He could've died," Father Christmas declared.

"But he didn't," Hook rebuked. "I knew he was going to be all right."

"He's still in critical condition!" Father Christmas hissed. "Fortunately, my elves have the greatest medical staff in history. But we almost didn't make it to them in time."

"In other words . . . *yes*, he's going to be just fine," Hook reiterated.

Father Christmas took an aggressive step forward.

Hook raised the revolver. "And how well is that staff at removing bullets from a pretty young girl's brain?"

Father Christmas took a step back.

"Like I said, hang tight, and you'll get the sleigh back," Hook proclaimed. "But if you don't mind, I just want to finish my conversation with this lovely young woman." He turned his attention to his former bo'sun. "Smee."

Smee turned around and stood at attention. "Yes, captain?"

Hook kicked Smee with his good leg, sending him hurtling over the edge of the sleigh.

"Thank you, Smee," Hook replied. "That will be all."

Father Christmas quickly grabbed the whip in the front seat and leaned over the side, flailing the whip out.

Smee screamed as the whip wrapped around his leg, catching him before falling out of range.

As Smee dangled below the runner, Hook shifted his body on the floor and kicked Father Christmas over the edge as well.

Father Christmas grabbed the runner with his left hand while still holding the whip and Smee with his right.

Smee *whimpered*, staring at the ground far below.

They were no longer over an ocean!

"There!" Hook grinned despite the throbbing pain in his leg. "That's better. Now we can have a little privacy to finish our conversation."

"That was horrid!" Wendy hissed.

"If I wanted to be ruthless, I could've shot Father Christmas' hand and made them fall," Hook pointed out, propping himself up to a sitting position. "I only need them out of the way for a moment."

"I've said all I need to say to you," Wendy growled.

"You know," Hook added, "for a moment, I thought you were truly interested. After all, you could have flown away at any time you wanted, but you didn't."

It had never occurred to her. After her nap and waking up in a strange environment, she had completely forgotten she could fly.

"See?" Hook smiled. "Even when I asked Smee to throw you overboard, I knew you'd be perfectly safe. Just like I knew Peter would be all right. Just like I know that the two men hanging on for dear life right now will be all right as well."

"It must be nice to know everything," Wendy sassed.

"Don't patronise me, Wendy," Hook admonished.

"Heaven forbid," she smirked.

"Well, I suppose this is the end of the line." Hook sighed. "I just want you to know that I wasn't such a bad man, really. And I wasn't lying about my mum. She was a wonderful woman. But there is something else I remember . . . she loved Christmas. And I loved Christmas too, which is why I never intended to ruin it. It just sort of happens when you're a . . . well . . . when you're a cad." He smiled with a nostalgic twinkle in his eye. "My last real memory of my mum was a wonderful Christmas we shared. I was hoping to feel that way one last time. A Christmas wedding. But . . . that's not going to happen." He shrugged and sighed once more. "Very well, keep the crown jewels. Keep the kingdom. It is Christmas, after all."

Wendy raised her eyebrow in surprise. "Excuse me?"

"If my mum was still alive, I'm sure that's what she would want me to do," Hook explained, pushing the hammer of the pistol forward. "And she would have liked you too."

Wendy smiled. "I'm sure I would have liked her."

"In honour of my mother, I'm giving this back to you." Hook handed the pistol to her. "Happy Christmas, Wendy."

"What am I supposed to do with this?"

"Whatever your heart tells you."

Wendy was at a loss for words. Peter had shown her many truly unique and extraordinary things, but nothing she had experienced could compare to the sheer unpredictability of Captain James Hook.

"Is this real?" she asked. "This isn't just another one of your tricks?"

"No tricks, my dear," Hook assured. "I've had an incredibly long day, and I'm all tricked out for the moment."

She gave him a distrusting stare.

"I know when I've been beaten," Hook declared. "It's funny. When I began this, all I wanted was to leave the island with enough money to start a new life. Unfortunately, I am a pirate, and when all those other things just fell into my lap, I couldn't resist. And besides, whether I get to keep it or not, I did successfully steal the crown jewels." He smiled proudly. "A feat no other criminal can claim."

Wendy shook her head. "You know, it's amazing how someone with the makings of a great king also has the potential to be a brilliant monster."

Hook grinned. "You think I could have made a great king?"

"It could have gone either way, to tell the truth," Wendy replied. "When someone has greatness in them, eventually they must choose to use it for good or evil." She gave him a kiss on his cheek. "You just need to start using your greatness more wisely."

Hook's smile widened. "So, you do think there's greatness in me?"

Wendy rolled her eyes, nodded, then returned his smile.

"Are you sure you don't want to become Mrs. Captain James Hook?"

"Positive."

She tossed him the box with the wedding ring he had given her. It was a heavy ring with the most enormous diamond she had ever seen.

"That's worth a lot of money," Wendy stated. "You can keep that, along with the treasure you brought from Neverland. You can have that quiet, honest life. And maybe you'll even find someone who will appreciate you."

"So, you're not going to kill me or turn me in or anything?" Hook inquired.

"Like you said, it's Christmas. Consider it a present," Wendy replied. "Just make sure you leave some treasure for Smee."

"Of course. We're Gentlemen of Fortune. What kind of a captain would I be if I stiffed me old mate?" Hook struggled to his feet. "I don't suppose someone asked for a crutch or a splint for Christmas?"

Wendy reached into the magic sack and produced a sturdy crutch and a splint.

"Much obliged." Hook smiled.

"One more thing," Wendy added.

"Yes?"

She pointed over the edge. "Will you please pull them back up?"

"Oops." Hook laughed. "Almost forgot about that."

Hook hobbled to the edge. He reached over the side and looked at Father Christmas.

"Okay," Hook called down. "We're done. You can come up now."

Hook held out his hand. Father Christmas didn't trust it and shook his head.

Hook turned to Wendy. "Call me crazy, but I don't think he's buying it." He thought for a moment. "Why don't you get a rope ladder or something from the bag?"

Wendy did. Hook tied it off on the brass rail and then tossed the rope ladder down to them.

"There," Hook proclaimed. "You can try that."

"How do I know this isn't a trick?" Father Christmas asked.

"Because I won't be here to sabotage it," Hook explained. "Oh, and Smee?"

Smee looked up.

"We're giving the crown jewels back," Hook declared. "But I'll still leave you your share of the treasure I brought with me from Neverland. Happy Christmas!"

"Uh, Happy Christmas," Smee replied. He glanced over to Father Christmas. "Did we just miss something?"

Father Christmas shrugged. "You know, I am the greatest judge of the hearts and minds of every mortal who ever lived, and even I don't know what the heck is going on in Captain Hook's head at any given moment."

Hook tugged on his parachute's straps, ensuring they were still secure. He prepared to jump when he felt a tap on his shoulder. He turned around and saw Wendy.

"Happy Christmas, Captain Hook."

"Call me Jas."

She smiled. "Happy Christmas, Jas."

"Happy Christmas, Wendy," Hook replied warmly.

With those words, he dove over the edge to begin the next big adventure of his life.

Father Christmas and Mr. Smee climbed back into the sleigh. They watched the figure of Captain James Hook fade from sight as he approached the land below.

"Do you think he'll be okay?" Wendy asked.

"Oh, I'm sure he will," Smee replied. "If there's one thing you can say about the captain, he always lands on his feet."

And Hook did land safely in the marshlands below. From the scent in the air, he knew it was connected to the sea. He didn't know where he was or where he was going to go, but he was determined to find his way back to England.

For the first time in ages, he felt warm and Christmassy. Captain James Hook was going to celebrate Christmas and was determined to enjoy it, even if he had to do it in a swamp.

Suddenly, he heard something rustle in the water.

He turned his head and beheld the face of the one-eyed crocodile emerge from the water.

"So, we meet again," Hook greeted. He drew his sword from its scabbard. "I don't suppose you're here to wish me a Happy Christmas?"

The crocodile snapped its jaws and *ROARED!!*

"I guess not," Hook replied. "Well, let's get this over with."

CHAPTER THIRTY-ONE

Back Home

It had been an exceptionally long night for everyone. Before heading back to the North Pole, Father Christmas returned the crown jewels and the keys to the Tower of London — he was careful not to disturb the ornery apparitions. Eventually, the guards would wake up, but they wouldn't remember a thing. Most weren't even aware that they had fallen asleep, and the ones that were weren't going to say anything — they knew their position would be terminated immediately if anyone knew they had fallen asleep at their post.

They also dropped Smee off at his house. Father Christmas rather liked Smee and didn't figure he'd be on the Naughty List for too long. Wendy liked Smee too, but there was something surreal about seeing Smee's house and knowing it was just over in Hyde Park.

By the time the group returned to the North Pole, Peter had made some significant improvements. He still wouldn't fully recover for a few more days, but he was safe to travel, and the worst was behind him.

The children enjoyed exploring Father Christmas' Workshops and playing with the elves. But as much as they loved the wonders of the North Pole, they knew it was time to go home.

Father Christmas was happy to be reacquainted with his reindeer. They were a little fatigued from the whole ordeal but were more than capable of giving the children a ride home. There wasn't enough room for everyone to ride inside the sleigh, so Nana was added as the lead, and the rest of the children — the ones who had eaten the magic feed — rode on top of the reindeer.

Eventually, the magic feed would wear off, but until it did, he was going to take advantage of the children's metaphysical abilities. With the magic still in their system, they were more than capable of staying on the reindeer no matter how fast they went.

He offered to drop Wendy, John, and Michael home on the way to Neverland, but Wendy shook her head.

"No, we need to go back to Neverland first," Wendy replied.

When they arrived at the Piccaninnies' camp, Wendy beheld Starkey's cold, rigid body. She began to weep. Deep melancholy and remorse struck Peter at the sight of Starkey's widow. Elu was mourning the loss of her husband and clutching Lizzie to her bosom. Starkey's body was placed on a bed of twigs and branches in the centre of the open field — large stones surrounded it. Some of the men added additional kindling in preparation for the ceremonial pyre.

Father Christmas thought it was unusual because a funeral pyre was incredibly rare in most Native American cultures. Traditionally, the body was left for a two to four day mourning period prior to burial. He supposed it was either for the purification of evil or perhaps Peter's mind had just confused Native American Indian customs with Hindu Indian customs.

Typically, the preparation of the body was solely the responsibility of the family, but since all Starkey had was his wife Elu (and the fact he had saved the entire tribe), this became a communal event.

His body had been mourned throughout the night, and now it was time for the High Priest to begin the ceremony. He blessed the body and asked the gods of the four winds and the spirits of their ancestors to admit Starkey's soul to the Happy Hunting Ground.

"What are they doing?" Michael asked.

"For them," Father Christmas explained, "death is the transference of the spirit. It appears that they must cleanse the body with fire before he can return with their ancestors."

Peter watched the High Priest light the torch.

"Isn't there anything you can do?" Peter asked, feeling the full measure of his guilt coursing through him. "Like with Nana."

Nana *whined* in agreement.

"I don't think so," Father Christmas replied. "I think he's too far gone."

"I would gladly trade my life for his," Peter declared.

Wendy gripped Father Christmas' forearm gently and gazed into his eyes. "Can you at least try?"

As Father Christmas looked into Wendy's soft, baleful eyes, he smiled. "I suppose it can never hurt to try."

Father Christmas was doubtful. He was mostly forbidden to meddle in the affairs of mortals in any lasting or significant ways. He was able to work some magic on Nana because —aside from the magic of Neverland and the sacrifices of the children — she was a dog, and she had given up her life to save Peter. Technically, her death was already the result of his meddling, so — to the powers that be — it was more of righting a wrong that he had been responsible for.

He supposed he could argue the same for Starkey, but the hand of fate was so fickle and mysterious that he couldn't be sure how it all worked. Besides, Starkey was human and had been dead for many hours — and shrapnel was a lot messier than a simple poison dart. But Wendy was right; he should at least try!

Father Christmas rose and approached the tribe. He addressed them in their own tongue, requesting permission to attempt a healing ordinance in the hopes of rectifying his own failings.

They agreed, and the children and all the members of the tribe closed their eyes tight and held hands, gathering around Starkey's body in a circle. Elu hugged her daughter tight and watched on in confusion.

Father Christmas withdrew the magical timepiece from his magic bag once more. He closed his eyes and whispered a silent prayer for the magic to work one last time — praying for Starkey to get one last chance.

"Now gather round," Father Christmas beckoned. He began to wind the clock once more. "As I have mentioned before, the measure of time is a precious gift that we give to one another. It is especially important this time of year to remember that the best gift we can give is of ourselves. Starkey knew this, and he gave everything for us."

The hands of the clock rotated backwards as the carousel rotated around the hourglass faster and faster!

"Now it's time," Father Christmas continued. "We give of ourselves."

The temporal sparks of light glowed and popped within the sands in the hourglass once more. The key's metal butterfly headpiece began to wobble fluidly, flapping and fluttering its wings. The grains of sand rose to the top of the glass.

With the whole tribe donating their time, the shrapnel resurfaced from the punctured wounds in Starkey's body and expelled themselves from Starkey's flesh. The wounds began to heal. Starkey's lungs began to reinflate, and his skin and joints began to limber up.

Elu almost cried seeing her husband's finger twitch. His eyes began to flutter, and finally, he gasped for air!

"Starkey?" Elu called.

Starkey sat up and coughed.

"Starkey!" Elu cried, running to him. Tears of joy flowed down her cheeks.

Starkey stretched out his arms and embraced his wife and daughter.

The tribe celebrated and praised Father Christmas. Wendy's heart was overcome with joy while watching the emotional family reunion. She couldn't ask for a better Christmas wish. As she observed the happiness on the Lost Boys' and her brothers' faces, she noticed someone was missing.

"Peter?" Wendy called.

The disheartened and ashamed Peter Pan had slipped off alone. Wendy found him sitting on a log in the snowbank, looking forlorn.

"It was all my fault," Peter cried as Wendy approached. "I am a bad person."

"No," Wendy replied. "You were tricked. You aren't bad, you're just naive and . . ." She thought for a moment. "I know you don't remember this, but you used to have a fairy named Tinker Bell who loved you with all of her heart. She got jealous of me and tried to trick the Lost Boys into killing me. You had explained that fairies were neither good nor bad. Because they are so tiny, they can only experience one emotion at any given instance. They are either all good or all bad. In a way, I think you're more like a fairy than a boy."

"What happened to Tinker Bell?"

"Well, I ended up forgiving her, and you did too. She even saved your life when Captain Hook tried to poison you, but you brought her back with the power of belief. She was courageous, and despite the occasional naughty moment, she was loyal and true to you."

Peter sighed. "But unfortunately, I don't remember her at all." He thought a minute. "Is there any way for me to be a truly good boy without having to grow up?"

"I don't know."

Father Christmas had been listening to them and approached.

"You know what," Father Christmas said, startling them, "you made a mistake. Now, I know my opinion matters to you, even if you don't like to admit it. But I think what matters more is what you think of yourself. You are a true leader, and there is a lot of good in you. Wendy is right. Just like the pixies, perhaps you're not altogether good or altogether bad. Maybe, from an emotional standpoint, you're too small to register more than one emotion at a time. I know that you want to be good. I know that, in your own way, you're striving to be good. And perhaps that's enough."

Father Christmas flashed Peter a warm smile and wiped Peter's tears with his sleeve.

"You think so?" Peter asked.

"I know so," Father Christmas said with a wink. "Barnaby told me about the Watching-Pools. Sadly, you will eventually forget these experiences on a conscious level; however, the lessons you've learned will stay. Who knows, maybe these experiences will help you grow in time. But for now, use what you've learned for the remainder of this Christmas. And I promise I will never forget you or the people of Neverland."

Peter looked up at Father Christmas with tears in his eyes and gave him a big hug.

"Oh, and remember," Father Christmas added, "just like all children, it's important to choose your friends wisely. When you're with Wendy, you're a good boy. But when you're with people like Captain Hook . . . well . . . I think you see the pattern. Try to keep the good people in your life, even if they seem boring."

They turned and observed Starkey being embraced by his people and the joy in his family's faces.

"They seem so happy." Peter smiled.

"Thanks to you," Father Christmas informed. "It's a good feeling, isn't it?"

"What is?"

"Helping others," Father Christmas replied. "Making someone else happy."

"You're such a good-hearted man," Peter declared. "You must get lots of presents."

"Well, most children leave out a little snack for me."

"I was talking about other things." Peter clarified. "Hasn't anyone given you anything other than a small plate of nibbles?"

Father Christmas looked into Peter's eyes. "Actually, no. I can't say that they have."

"Never?"

"Nope."

"Why? Are you naughty too?"

Father Christmas laughed heartily. "Goodness, no."

Peter found Father Christmas' laughter infectious.

"Why do you do it then?" Peter asked.

"Why do parents enjoy Christmas morning?" Father Christmas queried. "We don't need anything, really. We love making children happy. We love seeing wonder and delight on the faces of the people we love."

"Who do you love?"

"Everybody!" Father Christmas exclaimed. "Every man, woman, and child on god's green earth."

"Even Captain Hook?"

Father Christmas gave him a firm nod. "Even Captain Hook." He sighed. "Of course, he sure tried my patience more than I'm used to. And honestly, I am sad to see what became of him. He always had such great potential. Who knows, maybe he'll use this experience to be a little wiser in the future."

"What about me?" Peter asked nervously.

"I love you too," Father Christmas beamed, placing his hand on the boy's shoulder.

Peter smiled.

"Believe it or not," Father Christmas confessed, "I think I was even more heartbroken to see you on the Naughty List than you were. But it doesn't have to be all bad."

"It doesn't?"

"Look at me! I know I will never get joy from receiving any gifts, but I don't need things to be happy. I create my own happiness by making other people happy. Remember, there are many ways to find happiness, and I think helping others is the best. And you don't need to be perfect. You're all perfect, just the way you are. And as long as you always try your best, you're always a winner."

Peter was silent for a moment, then glanced down at his belt. He unsheathed his sword. "You know, in many ways, this is my most treasured possession." With both hands, he offered it up to Father Christmas. "I want to give it to you."

Father Christmas placed his hand on his heart, deeply touched by the gesture, then shook his head. "That's so sweet! But I wouldn't dream of taking your sword."

"Please," Peter pleaded. "It's Christmas, and I've never given a present to anyone before. And I was thinking that you do so much for everybody that you deserve a present too. Please, let me give you a present."

Father Christmas peered into Peter's soft, innocent eyes and could feel the humble sweetness coming from within. Father Christmas knew that sometimes the best present you can give a person is simply to let them experience the joy of *giving* something to you. He was touched and moved by the gesture — he had always been impressed by children's warm, tender hearts. Slowly, he extended his arms and accepted the gift. He looked at it, feeling emotional.

"Happy Christmas," Peter said.

Father Christmas looked up. "Thank you. It's the nicest thing anyone has ever given me." He had a joyful tear in his eye. "Happy Christmas, Peter!"

Father Christmas hugged Peter, and Peter wept in his arms — he finally understood the true joy of Christmas.

The group said their final good-byes to the people of Neverland. Wendy had offered to give the new Lost Boys a home with the Darlings, but they declined. It was obvious they weren't ready to leave Neverland yet. For them, it was comforting enough to know that Wendy's window would always be open to them when they were.

Father Christmas took Wendy and the others home. Peter regained his strength and fully healed before they reached England.

The window to the nursery was open, just as it had been four years ago. John and Michael flew in and were greeted by the former Lost Boys as Peter helped Nana safely inside.

All the ruckus alerted George and Mary Darling to their children's return. They rushed to the nursery excitedly.

Wendy stayed behind with Father Christmas, watching the family embrace each other, including Peter.

"Thank you," Wendy said with a smile.

"For what?" Father Christmas asked.

"For getting everyone home safely," Wendy replied. "For Starkey and Nana. For helping Peter have a good Christmas."

Father Christmas shrugged. "It's what I do."

"I think Peter has changed," Wendy declared.

"So it would seem."

"Will it last?"

"Who knows?" Father Christmas replied with a shrug. "He did come to terms with his mother. There's no telling how that'll affect him in the long run."

The two watched the children in the nursery, and Father Christmas sighed.

"What is it?" Wendy asked.

"You know something? I've been doing this for a very long time, and this has been the most wonderful Christmas I've ever had. So, I should thank you." He smiled, but there was a certain sadness to it. "It's too bad none of you will remember it."

Wendy looked shocked. "We won't?"

"I know you won't forget Peter or Neverland the way your brothers will. But yes . . . even *you* will forget this."

"When?"

"Before next Christmas."

Wendy's lip began to quiver. "Why?"

"It's the way my magic works." Father Christmas frowned. "I wish I could change that, but I have no control over it. But soon, the memory will seem like a dream."

"Is there anything I can do?"

"Just make the most of the time you have and know that I will be watching over you."

Wendy reached over and gave him a big hug.

From within the window of the nursery, Wendy heard her mother call.

"Well, I think I got to go," Wendy declared.

"Well, you better get to it." Father Christmas winked. "And Wendy, Happy Christmas."

"Happy Christmas," Wendy replied.

She flew to her family, and when she looked back, Father Christmas was gone.

CHAPTER THIRTY-TWO

Peter's First Christmas

"When did you get in?" Mr. Crustison asked.

The Darlings had told the Crustisons that the children had gone to Peter's orphanage far away to help bring joy to other poor motherless children. They didn't hear the children when they arrived — just a sudden revelry from the nursery as if they had never left.

"Just now, grandpa," Wendy acknowledged, giving her grandparents a big hug.

"How was your trip?" Mrs. Crustison asked.

Peter and Michael were so excited to share the exploits of their latest adventure that they completely forgot that they were supposed to be at an orphanage. The Darlings held their breath to see the Crustison's reaction to such an outlandish summation.

After a moment of silence, the Crustisons exchanged a glance and burst into laughter.

"What's so funny, grandma?" Michael asked.

Mrs. Crustison's eyes beamed with the joy of old memories. "You just reminded us of your mother when she was a little girl. Mary used to tell all sorts of wild stories. I suppose it's fitting that the orphanage is called Neverland."

The Darlings breathed a sigh of relief.

"Yes," Mary mused, "why don't you tell us the whole thing from the beginning?"

The kids told the group all about their adventures. The former Lost Boys were enthralled, and the Crustisons were impressed by the kids' vivid imaginations.

"By Jove!" Mr. Crustison replied. "You mean to say that John and Michael pulled Father Christmas' sleigh? And Wendy helped rob the Tower of London?"

"Goodness no, Grandfather," Wendy corrected. "I was kidnapped. I had nothing to do with the crown jewels. That was Peter."

The Crustisons laughed.

"Some children tell stories of spotting Father Christmas," Mrs. Crustison smirked. "But only our grandchildren pretend to have epic adventures with him."

The group shared a laugh. George and Mary, on the other hand, knew better. They didn't exactly believe in Father Christmas to begin with, but something told them that this tale was more than just a story. Nana looked so much younger and more spritely than they had ever seen her — and Nana didn't tell tall tales. The bit about Captain Hook trying to force Wendy to marry him deeply disturbed George and Mary, but everything had worked out.

Even though Peter's time with the Darlings was officially up, he was invited to stay with them the rest of the week to experience his first real Christmas with them. Peter loved spending the week pretending to be just an average boy. There was nothing fantastic or adventurous about their time, but it had a magic of its own.

They went sledding in the hills outside of town. They strolled in the park and spotted a smitten Smee, who was enjoying a romantic carriage ride with Millie, the barmaid. They took Peter to their church and watched local children put on the Nativity. Now, you might think this would be painfully average for a boy like Peter Pan, but for him, it was extra special. There is nothing quite like the magic and warmth of having a loving family to spend time with.

On Christmas Eve, they sang songs, played games, and left out the traditional glass of sherry and a small piece of mince pie for Father Christmas. Of course, this year was extra special for them. The children were so excited that they couldn't get to sleep. They were determined to see Father Christmas, but alas, Father Christmas came and went without detection. Somehow, he had managed to deliver the gifts after they had fallen asleep.

Wendy and Peter wondered if Father Christmas had used any *Sandman Powder* on them. Of course, they knew that they would never know for sure.

On Christmas morning, the children were up bright and early and sprang to their parents' bedroom, eager to wake them up so they could go downstairs and see all the incredible toys. The parents and grandparents made a drowsy descent down the staircase to the Christmas Tree.

The children got everything they asked for and then some. There was even a package left out for Nana.

"Hey, Nana," Michael called. "This one's for you!"

Nana came over, and Michael helped her open it. There was a fancy new collar with a diamond star inside. The inscription read:

THE CHRISTMAS STAR
May it light your way,
like a well-guided sleigh.

Nana *woofed* in excitement and licked Michael on the cheek as he put it on her. Once the collar was on, she sat up properly and *barked*, asking how it looked.

Mary held up a hand mirror so Nana could see for herself.

"It looks beautiful, Nana!" Wendy cried.

Nana *barked* again joyously and spun in a circle from the excitement.

Father Christmas and the Darlings didn't forget Peter either. Peter received all sorts of marvellous presents that morning, but none better than the feeling of being part of a family — even if it was for a little while.

The family assumed all the gifts had been open, so they gathered in the dining room. Peter decided to linger for a bit. He stood there alone, silently savouring the decorated tree and the warm feeling in his heart.

Thank you, god, he whispered in his heart. *Thank you for letting me have this.*

"Peter," Wendy called, coming back for him, "breakfast is ready."

Peter nodded. "I'll be right . . ."

Suddenly, he noticed something hidden in the back of the tree.

"What's that?" Peter asked.

Wendy turned, watching Peter retrieve a little box from behind the tree. There was an envelope on top, so he handed it to Wendy. When she opened it, she discovered a fancy Christmas card inside. She quietly read the handwritten message:

To: Peter & Wendy
From: Father Christmas.

Well, it looks like Peter made it on the Nice List after all. I've decided to give' you something extra special this year. Open this privately with Wendy and make sure the grown-ups aren't around.

"What does it say?" Peter asked, looking over her shoulder.

"It says to open this one in private," Wendy replied.

They excused themselves from breakfast and slipped outside to the backyard. Peter gently pulled back the ribbon and opened the box. There was a large gold ornament shaped like a closed flower bud. There was another note:

They looked at each other.

"What should we do?" Peter asked.

"I think we're supposed to clap," Wendy replied. "And believe."

They shrugged, closed their eyes, and began clapping.

The gold ornament began to wiggle and glow.

"What's going on?" Peter asked.

"I don't know, but keep clapping."

They clapped longer and harder, and the gold orb glowed even more brightly. Slowly, the golden petals of the flower bud began to open. The gold flower continued to blossom and bloom and in the centre of the flower was a small shimmering light.

There was a *fluttering* hum. Suddenly, it stopped, and the light cleared to reveal a small, beautiful fairy. Wendy recognised her immediately.

"Tinker Bell?" Wendy called.

The fairy spoke in a light, airy *tinkling* noise that Peter discovered he understood perfectly well.

"That's a yes," Peter replied. "Is it really you, Tink?"

Tinker Bell *tinkled* a reply that Wendy understood perfectly: "You silly ass."

Peter gave Wendy a surprised glance.

"You'll have to excuse her," Wendy replied with a knowing giggle. "She is a very common fairy."

Tinker Bell gave Wendy a disapproving stare.

Wendy smiled. "Common, but still one of a kind."

Tink smiled, flew up, and kissed Peter on the cheek. She whizzed around their heads before resting on Peter's shoulder.

"How is this possible?" Peter asked.

"I don't know," Wendy replied. "But fairies aren't like you and me. They're made up of belief and magic. That seems like something Father Christmas knows a lot about."

Wendy read the last part of the card:

As I mentioned before, sometimes a good boy needs someone loyal at his side who will tell him when he's being a brat. And Wendy, keep the ornament. You deserve some keepsake of this adventure, even if you forget it. Never forget to be true to your heart and never lose your childlike wonder.

As they read the last sentence, the letter and box disappeared.

* * *

The Darlings once more offered to adopt Peter and let him stay. For the first time, Peter honestly contemplated it. He imagined himself growing up with Wendy and the Darlings but ultimately declined. Peter had made a choice and drew strength from it. He hadn't been abandoned, and he knew that Wendy's window would never be closed to him.

For once, Peter was at peace. He was living the life he wanted. Wendy suspected that Peter's bad dreams — the ones he hid from everybody, including himself — may stop bothering him.

Wendy had vowed never to forget her magical Christmas, but she did. They all forgot everything. But until the day she died, Wendy always put up the gold-flower ornament on her Christmas Tree and would always feel warm and at peace. She didn't know why it gave her such joy — and she couldn't remember where she had gotten it — but she knew it was special.

Smee went back to his life in England and married Millie, the barmaid. He ended up being the father of two boys and three girls. Starkey also had more children and lived a long, happy life. As for Captain Hook, everyone forgot their time with him and just remembered him being kicked into the jaws of the crocodile at the end of their first adventure. No one talked about him much anymore. However . . .

Years later, long after John had grown into a man and started a family of his own, he was on a business trip in Ireland when he beheld an unusual sight. Near the docks, he saw an older man in black. It was a priest with greying black hair. He thought that the face looked oddly familiar. That's when he noticed that the priest had a hook.

Suddenly, a strong sense of *déjà vu* washed over him. Of course, that was crazy because he had never met anyone with a hook before — much less a priest. He just brushed off the notion and moved on, but the encounter would stay with him for quite some time.

Well, you already know the rest. Wendy grew up, got married, had a daughter named Jane, and every spring-cleaning time, except when he forgets, Peter Pan returns. And as it had been written before, it will go on so long as children are gay, innocent, and heartless.

THE END

About the Author

James Bereece is an author and Multimedia Specialist with many years of experience in film production. But ultimately, he is a storyteller. He had his first story published nationally in the 6th grade and continued to write and sell his works.

In his teens, his attention shifted to film, where he worked professionally in all aspects of the industry, utilizing his storytelling in a new medium. After winning awards for the films he made during his apprenticeship program, his focus shifted. Eventually, he created his own production company Tizwix Flix Entertainment, producing videos for local businesses as well as film and television.

With Stories To Die For Publishing, he has published some picture books for children. He is most known for writing the young adult book series, Stories To Die For, which is a homage to Goosebumps and Scary Stories to Tell in the Dark.

He currently resides in Utah, where he enjoys playing games and watching movies with friends and family.

James Bereece

www.ingramcontent.com/pod-product-compliance
Lightning Source LLC
Chambersburg PA
CBHW071217300726

48975CB00002B/264